CRITICS PRA
BESTSELLING

THE ACCIDE

"With its sharp, witty writing and unique characters, Angie Fox's contemporary paranormal debut is fabulously fun."

—*Chicago Tribune*

"This rollicking paranormal comedy will appeal to fans of Dakota Cassidy, MaryJanice Davidson, and Tate Hallaway."

—*Booklist*

"A new talent just hit the urban fantasy genre, and she has a genuine gift for creating dangerously hilarious drama. Fox has created her own unique flavor of the supernatural, and it's a weird one!"

—*RT Book Reviews*

"Fox's rollicking, paranormal romance is absolutely full of laugh-out-loud humor, heart-pumping action and uniquely quirky characters."

—Romance Junkies

"*The Accidental Demon Slayer* was an unexpected frolic filled with smart-mouthed geriatric witches, a talking terrier, and a drop-dead sexy griffin. I read this book in a day; it was hard to put down. Pick it up for yourself and see."

—Night Owl Romance

"In the uberpopular genre of paranormal romance, just about everything has been done before, yet *The Accidental Demon Slayer* keeps it fresh and unique, carving out a place for itself."

—CK2S Kwips and Kritiques

THE DANGEROUS BOOK FOR DEMON SLAYERS

"Fox is back and serving up a second helping of high-octane mania. The world according to new demon slayer Lizzie Brown is full of major potholes and irritating biker witches, and the gaps in this heroine's demon-slaying education are both hilarious and dangerous. The phrase Sin City never rang truer than it does in this supernatural ruckus!"

—*RT Book Reviews*

"*The Dangerous Book for Demon Slayers* has an entertaining story line with paranormal action and adventure at every turn. Fans of *The Accidental Demon Slayer* won't want to miss Lizzie's latest escapade."

—Darque Reviews

"Fox will snare you with humor, crazy but lovable characters and more than a dash of excellent dialogue. In a dictionary somewhere, Lizzie and Gertie are featured under the definition of 'fun.' Enjoy!"

—Fresh Fiction

"A humorous adventure."

—Romance Reviews Today

"*The Dangerous Book for Demon Slayers* is a sharp, witty, refreshing paranormal romance that is out of this world!"

—Manic Reader

"Filled with humor, fans will enjoy Angie Fox's lighthearted frolic."

—*Midwest Book Review*

"This book is a pleasure to read. It is fun, humorous, and reminiscent of Charlaine Harris or Kim Harrison's books."

—*Sacramento Book Review*

DIRE PREDICTIONS

I knocked on the door to Dimitri's room. He opened it wearing a pair of green plaid boxers and nothing else. The man was temptation in the flesh. Too bad we didn't have time for that right now. I placed the book in his hands. "Take a look at this."

I ignored the way he undressed me with his eyes. Instead, I scooted past my personal Greek god and flopped down on his bed. He cocked a brow and sat down next to me, book in hand. He frowned as he read the passage predicting my downfall.

"Chopped in half," I said, in case he hadn't read fast enough.

He ran a finger over the page, contemplating it like an academic. "Split in two," he murmured, focused on the book in front of him.

Oh please. He was far too calm about this. "What's the difference? This is the second death prediction in forty-eight hours."

He leaned close enough to kiss, his chocolate brown eyes fixed on mine. "You are in control."

Had he read the passage? "No, I'm not." I hadn't been in control since my grandma showed up on my doorstep with jelly-jar magic and a demon on her tail.

His fingers tightened on my arms. "You decide your own destiny, Lizzie. Don't let anyone take that away from you."

Oh, so I was supposed to sit around, ignoring the warnings, pretending I was in charge. Not happening. I was a demon slayer. I shook off his grip and crossed my hands over my chest. He'd better feel like a rotten jerk when I turned up dead in a forest clearing.

Other *Love Spell* books by Angie Fox:

THE DANGEROUS BOOK FOR DEMON SLAYERS
THE ACCIDENTAL DEMON SLAYER

ANGIE FOX

A Tale of Two DEMON SLAYERS

LOVE SPELL NEW YORK CITY

To my husband, Jim, who has never doubted my dreams, no matter how crazy they might be.

LOVE SPELL®

February 2010

Published by

Dorchester Publishing Co., Inc.
200 Madison Avenue
New York, NY 10016

ISBN 10: 0-505-52827-4
ISBN 13: 978-0-505-52827-8
E-ISBN: 978-1-4285-0809-5

Printed in the United States of America.

10 9 8 7 6 5 4 3 2 1

ACKNOWLEDGMENTS

First off, I have to say how grateful I am for the wild, crazy, downright fun readers of these books. To Alanna DeBona and Ruth Thompson, who heard me mention my love of Australian biscuits and sent a few boxes.

To Shawntelle Madison for her Web geniusness. Is that a word? Doesn't matter. We'll claim creative license.

To Leah Hultenschmidt, the most awesome editor in the world, who lets me use words like geniusness.

To Jessica Faust, whose only weakness seems to be chocolate and lots of it. I'm with you, missy.

To my awesome friend and critique buddy, Jess Granger, who read the final chapters of this manuscript during a cross-country move.

To Kristie Forester and Noelle Winkle for final reads and of course to Brad Jones and his biker dogs, Harley Boy and Cletus. I'll never forget that first ride.

A Tale of Two Demon Slayers

Chapter One

After all my years of organizing field trips, fire drills and potty breaks for my three-year-olds at Happy Hands Preschool, you'd think I could get two geriatric biker witches through the Las Vegas airport in under an hour. But sometimes the things that look simple on the outside aren't. I've learned that lesson the hard way.

"Don't you even dream about casting a spell on that man," I said to my grandma, who had paused next to a heavyset guy sneaking a cigarette in the nonsmoking area outside the Fly Away Bar and Grill. Her black "Harley's Angels" T-shirt stood in stark contrast to his pinstripe business suit and red power tie.

Grandma tossed a lock of long gray hair over her shoulder as she rooted through her black leather bag. "He won't even know what hit him," she answered in a voice roughened by hard living and an extra-loud rendition of "The Devil Went Down to Georgia" sung in the parking-garage elevator.

I gritted my teeth as a bearded student thwacked my elbow with his taped-together backpack. In all fairness, he was busy avoiding a woman lugging a rolling suitcase that tipped over every three seconds. Was it sad that I envied them? At least they were moving.

Normally I'm a fast walker, an organized person and certainly not the type to be late for my flight. I glanced down the immense glass and silver terminal as six more people joined the already overloaded airport-security line.

Ant Eater, Grandma's second in command, flexed her shoulders and stretched out her neck. "I hope the stuffed suit's not a lawyer." She adjusted her silver-spiked riding gloves. "He might sue you if I kick his ass."

"Nobody is kicking anybody's—" I searched for the right word. "Tuffet."

Seven years with preschoolers had made it nearly impossible for me to curse.

"Okay, now I'm really late. Time to go." I took Grandma by the purse and was about to grab Ant Eater by the silver-stud belt. Then I thought the better of it. Ant Eater took orders about as well as Genghis Kahn tap-danced.

She caught my hesitation and grinned at me, her gold tooth glinting in the late-afternoon sunlight.

Grandma shook off my hold, moved in behind the smoking man, and with the stealth of someone well-practiced at placing "Kick Me" signs, she sprinkled what looked to be sawdust over his back and shoulders. Poor guy was going to think he had dandruff—or that he'd stood too close to a wood chipper.

The man gasped, the lit cigarette teetering on his lip. Meanwhile Grandma uttered something under her breath that sounded strikingly like a Gregorian chant. Fingers shaking, he dropped the cigarette on the floor and ground it out under his heel.

"Once rude. Always rude," Ant Eater huffed.

The man turned to Grandma, eyes unfocused like he was waking up from a dream. "I don't smoke. Do I?"

"Not anymore." Grandma slapped him on the back.

Amazing. And here I thought she was going to Itch-spell him, maybe hit him with a Frozen Underwear bomb. "Is that new?" Never mind what it meant to mess with the man's free will. Or what would happen if GlaxoSmith-Kline ever got wind of it.

"Mixed it up yesterday," she said, with more than a hint of pride.

We'd talk about it later. But at the moment . . .

"I need to go," I said, ducking into the crowd behind what looked to be an entire soccer team heading for Terminal C. "You can see me off at the security line, or you can see me off here. Doesn't matter."

I started walking, witches be darned. I had a sexy shape-shifting griffin to meet. Frankly, it was the only way you could get me on a plane. I wasn't crazy about flying. It was bad enough Dimitri's business had kept him from escorting me to the airport. I mean, isn't that how a romantic trip to Greece is supposed to start?

Besides, Grandma and the gang should have been packing. They only had three days to drive out to New York if they wanted to catch their seniors' cruise to the Mediterranean. It was the easiest way to bring Harleys along. Plus, those witches loved buffets.

Now that I *finally* had a ticket and I almost had a griffin, I wasn't going to let a couple of pokey witches make me miss my flight.

I quickened my pace and took an inventory of the crowd in front of me: several kids in jeans that were either too tight or gangster baggy, an athletic coach who always seemed to find the break in the crowd. I squinted. I'd bet my big toe he was part fairy, but I doubted even he was aware of it. A couple of businesspeople . . . Nothing out of the ordinary, at least from a supernatural perspective.

A nice, normal day. It almost felt strange. It was like I was waiting for something to go wrong.

The two witches clanked behind me. Between their silver accessories and the spells they carried in glass jars, they could hardly move without something banging together.

"Lizzie Brown." Grandma drew a labored breath, but I wasn't buying it. This woman would smoke me in a footrace for a shot of Southern Comfort. "You're as jumpy as a jackrabbit."

"Can't help it. I'm too close," I said, dodging a family of four. Close to a dream vacation, without demons, imps, hellions or anything else that went bump in the night. A blessedly normal trip. Did I even remember what normal felt like anymore? I couldn't wait to find out.

"Hold up," Grandma rumbled next to me, keeping pace.

I ignored her.

They were supposed to make this easy. They were supposed to drop me off at the outside baggage check. Instead, they had to find parking for their Harleys, hit every wrong button on the parking-lot elevator and insult the check-in clerk. Of course American Airlines didn't offer upgrades for demon slayers, even if I had saved Las Vegas and pretty much the entire West Coast from Armageddon. As it stood, I was lucky those two didn't get me downgraded to crazy.

I dug a finger under the strap of my sundress, which had fallen down with the weight of my carry-on, and said a quick prayer of thanks for my ultracomfy Adidas Supernova Cushion cross-trainers.

"You're not late," Ant Eater growled off my left shoulder. "You're two and a half hours early."

Yeah, well that was late in my book. I always liked to arrive for international flights at least three hours prior to takeoff. Next time, I'd add a half hour for each witch who decided to see me off.

"Well, you can take one more minute." Grandma cut in front of me and attempted to detour us toward a metal bench with thin gray cushions. "This is important. Vital," she said, her blue eyes boring into mine.

"No. It can't be." I could practically hear my departure gate calling for me. "Why can't it wait?"

"Loosen your bra straps, okay?" Grandma said, as she led me over to the bench. "I helped save you from a she-demon, you can give me a minute on an airport bench."

"One minute," I said, knowing I was doomed.

Grandma took my hands, her silver rings hard against my skin and her palms rough from riding her bike. "Our situation has changed. I felt it on the way over here, Lizzie. I think you're ready."

The only thing I was ready for was an in-flight cocktail. While Grandma and the rest of the Red Skull biker witches took their magic very seriously, they also had a way of practicing the kind of loosey-goosey lifestyle that gave me hives.

"Ready for what?" I asked, hefting my shoulder strap again. The Port-A-Pooch pet carrier was the best on the market. I'd researched it. But the darned thing wasn't light. Neither was its cargo.

Grandma nodded and Ant Eater reached inside her

black fringed bag. Out came a small wooden chest, about half the size of a shoe box.

Oh help me, Rhonda.

Thick iron bands supported the bottom and wrapped around the lid. Studs drilled into the bands. The tips of them pointed out like switch stars, the main weapon of demon slayers like me. I traced a finger over the wood itself—old and furrowed with carving marks, as if the box had been sculpted from solid wood.

"This was your mother's," Grandma said, her fingers tracing a switch star. "After your mom left us, I promised your Aunt Serefina that if we found you, if you had powers, I'd give this to you when I thought you were ready." She placed the box into my hands like it was a piece of fine china. "I think you can handle it now."

"Oh." The box was lighter than I'd expected. Smoother. I found the bench and sat with the box in my lap.

I tried to tune out the noise of the airport and take this in, be appreciative. For all I knew, this could be a watershed moment—one I'd look back on for the rest of my life. I wanted to recognize the importance of my demon slayer heritage. Instead, my mind kept wandering back to the words Grandma had used. *I think you can handle it now.*

Handle what? Everything I'd handled since Grandma found me two months ago, right before I'd morphed into the Demon Slayer of Dalea, had been much more of an adventure than I'd ever asked for—or wanted.

As uncomfortable as it was, if I was truly honest with myself, the only thing I had a mind to handle was the sexy shape-shifting griffin meeting me at my departure gate.

I studied the protective runes carved into the bottom of the box. "What makes you think I'm ready now?"

Grandma took a seat next to me. "I'm not sure you are," she admitted. "Let's see if you can open it."

Oh lovely, and just what I needed—a test.

The box didn't have a keyhole or a groove indicating where the lid started. In fact, I didn't see any openings at all. "Should we really try to open this here?" In a crowded airport? "Do we know what's inside? I'm going to have enough trouble getting my switch stars through security."

My hand went to my demon slayer utility belt and the five switch stars it held. The stars were flat and round, about the shape of small dinner plates. Razor-sharp blades curled around the edges. The TSA wouldn't like them, but I had to have them on me at all times.

Grandma sighed. "I told you, we put a spell on your switch stars so nobody can see them. Otherwise, you'd have been arrested by now."

Ant Eater nodded, her gray curls bobbing slightly as she looked down at me. "You should have let us take care of your jumbo bottle of shampoo too. I don't know why you insisted on stuffing everything into a one-quart Baggie."

"Rules are rules." A fact Grandma and the gang would have done well to remember. Besides, I was worried enough about getting my switch stars through the metal detector. I didn't need things to fall apart if something went wrong with my Pantene Pro-V.

As for the box? "Please say it's not something live."

A nose snorted from my carry-on. "I heard that."

Ever since I came into my demon slaying powers, my

Jack Russell terrier could speak—real words. I was still getting used to it.

Pirate wriggled an ear, then a nose, and finally his entire top half out of the green Port-A-Pooch. He blinked sleepily. Today, I'd followed my checklist for preparing an animal for flight, which had meant lots of exercise to wear him out and hopefully get him to snooze through a good portion of the trip. It had worked, until now.

"You sounded worried," he said. "But you don't need to worry, because I am on the job." Pirate squirmed the rest of the way out of the carrier and shook off, his tags clinking. "Some days, I think I'm part German shepherd." He sniffed at the box, his little body quivering. He was mostly white, with a dollop of brown on his back that wound up his neck and over one eye.

He gave a full-body sneeze. "No animals," he announced. "In fact, it don't have any smell at all. That's too bad."

I turned the box over in my hands.

Pirate licked at it. "It's pretty."

Sure. Pretty like Pandora's box. My mom hadn't exactly been the best influence on me. And she'd proven that I couldn't trust her. "We'll check it with the luggage and I'll open it in Greece."

"Why?" Grandma asked. "I want to see what's in it."

"You don't know?" I didn't like that one bit.

Maybe it was a good idea to open it with Grandma and Ant Eater here, in case whatever was in there decided to attack.

I tugged at the teardrop emerald around my neck, given to me by Dimitri. It held an endless source of protective magic, which was good, because otherwise it would have been used up a week after he'd given it to me.

I glanced at Ant Eater. "You still have those stun spells?"

She patted her black fringe purse. And I had my switch stars.

No telling what my mom had left behind in this box. She'd shirked her duty, passed along her demon slayer powers to me before dumping me off on my adoptive family in Atlanta. I didn't relish the idea of any more surprises from Mom.

Grandma placed a sandpapery hand on my arm. "Open it, Lizzie. It's part of your destiny."

Destiny my foot. Since when was I going to get to choose my own life? I'd been forced to go up against a mad scientist demon and then a sex-on-the-brain Las Vegas succubus, and right when I was about to take off on a dream trip to Greece with my hot boyfriend, Grandma wanted me to open a box full of trouble.

"If I open this now, I could get arrested, miss my flight, let a creature loose on the airport . . ."

Grandma nodded, admitting the possibility. "Or you could gain a powerful tool that you need right now."

"I don't need anything right now except sun, sand and a shot or two of ouzo."

"So you say."

"So I know."

"Then why are you still holding the box?"

Why indeed?

Heaven help me. The worst part was I knew how to open the box without a latch or a lock. I touched each of the fingers on my right hand to each of the five switch-star adornments on the box. They warmed under my fingers and my stomach filled with dread.

I wasn't kidding Grandma about the "getting arrested" part. My short time in the magical world had taught me that unexpected things could—and always did—happen to me.

"Hold on to your britches." I pulled away the iron bars around the box.

The wood made a low, crackling sound. Grandma let out a whistle as a hairline fracture worked its way across the side of the chest.

Pirate's collar jingled as he danced in place. "Ooh . . . smoky!"

A thin stream of vapor flowed from the narrow slit, giving way to delicate rings.

Fingers stiff with anticipation, I lifted the lid.

Lavender velvet cushioned the inside of the box. Three loops made of the same material lined the bottom, supporting—nothing.

"It's empty," I said, surprised, confused and—I'll admit it—a bit relieved.

"No it's not," Grandma said, huskily. "Touch it."

"Touch what?" I brushed my fingers over the velvet insides of the box. Down lower, close to the empty holders.

"Touch it."

I did. My breath caught in my throat as my fingers scraped a smooth, invisible bar.

"What is it?" I asked, gathering the courage to touch it again. It wasn't any longer than my hand. Round, from what I could gather. It felt like glass, only slicker.

"Is it hot?" Grandma asked.

"No."

"Cold?"

"No. It doesn't feel like anything."

"Or smell like anything," Pirate said.

Grandma whistled. "I think it's a training bar. Your mom used to use one with her instructors. Your Aunt Serefina too. Only theirs I could see. Usually."

"But I don't have any instructors." I didn't even have Aunt Serefina. She'd died trying to save the coven. "I just have you." Sure, Grandma did what she could, but she seemed as much in awe of this thing as I was.

"Yeah, well that's about to change too," she said, unable to keep a smile out of her voice.

I flicked my eyes up to find her looking at me like it was my birthday. "Now?" I'd been asking for this kind of training for weeks, and she picks now.

"Of course. You had—what? Two days off in Vegas while we planned this trip." She said it as if she couldn't imagine what I'd been doing.

"I was recovering from an almost-Armageddon."

"With your hot, sexy griffin."

"We slept most of the time!"

"Oh come on, Lizzie—you're a demon slayer. What'd you think it would be? Sunshine and cupcakes?"

"No. But I could use a week off." Or even one more day.

"Time off is for pussies. I wrangled up a kick-butt instructor for you. Better than the entire team your mom had. Formal training begins in Greece."

Dimitri would love that. "And this is for training?"

"Maybe." She looked inside the box. "I don't know. I didn't plan this part. But there's a way you can find out."

I didn't want to know.

"I saw your mom do it. Serefina too. Hold it. Wrap your hand around it and it'll tell you what you need to do next."

Sure, why not take advice from an invisible bar that had once belonged to my crazy mother?

Problem was, it played to my weakness. I love to know exactly what's going on.

"So this will tell me what I need to do in terms of training?"

Grandma rubbed at the phoenix tattoo on her arm. "For you, probably yes. For your mother, it foretold the attack on our coven." She dropped her hands. "It predicted her sister's death, but hell, it also predicted mine. You don't see me going anywhere, do you? Nobody can tell exactly what is going to happen. Free will is always in play."

Yeah, except for the smoker she'd spelled.

I ran a finger along the bar and felt nothing.

"Try it," Grandma said. "For me. I want to be here when you use it for the first time."

Oh geez. I rubbed Pirate on the head and let out a breath I didn't even know I was holding.

"Okay." I might as well figure out what I had to do next. There would be brainstorming to do, lists to write. Dimitri had a laptop, which meant I could even type my lists. This was sounding better all the time.

I eased the bar out of the velvet loops and paused for a split second before wrapping one hand around it.

Grandma's breath brushed my shoulder. "Clear your mind."

I did. At that moment, I let go of everything and focused all my energy on the smooth glass in my hand. It felt solid, comforting. Warmth flooded my palm and crept up my arm. My breathing quickened as a door opened in my mind. I gasped.

"What is it?" Grandma asked.

"Wait," I said, catching glimpses of a hazy picture. I squeezed my eyes shut and reached for an image just beyond my grasp. I gripped the bar tighter. It was like I was an inch away from opening another door.

"What is it?" Grandma held my arm.

I madc it. The door fell open and I saw Dimitri. He knelt among the ruins of a great stone building in the middle of a forest. Sweat coated his broad back and glinted off his olive skin. He turned to me, his hands covered in blood. I sucked in a breath. This wasn't real.

"Lizzie!" he called, his face twisted in anguish.

Please don't let it be real.

My heart raced and I fought the urge to go to him.

This isn't real.

And then I saw myself lying on the ground, my chest ripped open and my head twisted at an impossible angle.

"Enough!" I smashed the bar onto the floor and heard it shatter.

Grandma yawped. "Damn it, Lizzie!"

I didn't care. My eyes flew open. I braced my hands against the airport bench and forced myself to take deep, even breaths. I was back.

Grandma's worried eyes met mine. "Whatever you saw, you don't have to do it, Lizzie. You hear me? You don't have to do it."

"I know," I said. I didn't want to die. I didn't want Dimitri to have to watch, or find me later, or whatever had happened. I had no idea what I'd just seen. I'd never used an object like the bar before. For all I knew, the thing was cursed, damaged, on the fritz.

"What'd you see?" Ant Eater crouched in front of me.

"I don't want to talk about it." It was a twisted vision. It didn't mean anything.

Besides, no good could come of Grandma and Ant Eater analyzing a prophecy of my death. Grandma had said herself it wasn't always right.

Still, I couldn't get the horrible image out of my mind. Being a demon slayer was dangerous work. I knew that. And yes, people had tried to kill me before—but I'd never had to see, in high-definition detail, exactly what could happen.

This bar had predicted the death of the demon slayer before me. Now it was supposed to tell me what the near future held for me.

Mouth dry, I stared straight ahead, willing myself to focus on the travelers rushing past.

"Stop." I told myself. I was at the airport. I ran my hands up my arms, over my unbroken chest. I was fine. Dimitri was handling paperwork instead of my blood and guts. He would be meeting me at the gate soon. "Stop it." Think of something else.

At least the bar was gone, reduced to a million invisible little pieces.

"Um, Lizzie?" Ant Eater stood and began backing away slowly, her motorcycle boots treading light, as a chorus of tiny shards began crackling all at once. It sounded like an ice storm on a tin roof.

"What's it doing?" Grandma demanded.

"How should I know?" I stood, one hand on my switch stars.

"Hold up," Grandma cautioned. "You draw a star and every TSA agent, police officer and security guard is going to be on you like a chicken on a June bug."

Pirate growled. "I'd attack it, but I don't see it. Now that ain't right." He paced back and forth next to me. "I thought you said we were going to take a vacation from all of this hoodoo."

My thoughts exactly.

We all watched the off-white floor as if we'd suddenly be able to see my family's supernatural gift, one of the many that hadn't quite worked out for me.

"Well," Grandma said, "you couldn't have opened the box if you weren't ready."

"Naturally," I replied, wondering how the heck I was supposed to handle this one.

We never could tell if the bar managed to find all its pieces or how it fit itself back together. But I felt it as it rolled up to me and rested against my right foot.

Chapter Two

Pirate aimed a harsh bark in the general direction of the training bar. "That's one crazy game of fetch you got going on."

"You can't just leave it here, Lizzie," Ant Eater said.

I dug my hands into my hips. "I know that," I said, wishing I could.

That magical aberration had shown me a vision of the man I loved kneeling over my broken body, and now I had to cart it along on my trip as if I actually planned to take it out of the box again. I rooted around in my purse for a tissue and picked the thing up like it was a roach.

"I still say you were ready," Grandma said, eyeing Ant Eater.

Like I was ever ready for half the things that happened lately. I placed the box on the chair behind me and eased the training bar back into the velvet loops. Then I wound an extra tissue around it, as if it were a miniature mummy. Pirate braced his front paws up on the seat next to me and watched.

"Keep your enemies close . . ." I began.

Pirate growled low in his throat, ". . . and your bat-crazy supernatural bar in plain sight."

"Aw, come here." Grandma wrapped me in a giant hug. "You just do what you do best—take care of yourself, accept the universe."

"Okay. Thanks." The hug felt nice, but I had to get away before she started giving me a lecture on the Three Truths of the demon slayer: Look to the Outside, Accept the Universe, Sacrifice Yourself. And one I wanted to add—Keep Closed Boxes Closed.

I shook Ant Eater's hand and, ignoring the box on the chair behind me, reached down to open Pirate's pet carrier. "You ready, buddy?"

Pirate drew his ears back. "Are you kidding? I'll turn that box into kindling. You want it in five pieces or twenty million? You know, I can count now."

"I meant, are you ready to go?" We still had a plane to catch.

His ears drooped back. "No attacking?"

"Not right now," I said, "although I'm sure you'd do a fine job of it."

"Oh yeah, I could take that bar. I could eat that bar with a side of crackly wood box. That box might even taste good. Like the doorjambs back home."

"I told you, no chewing on doors."

"Oh I know." Pirate made a lap around the doggie carrier, his eyes on the box. "It's just hard to stick to a diet *all* the time. Speaking of eating . . ." His tags jingled as he shifted his focus to the Burger King a few stores down. "I hear the Double Whopper is quite meaty and cheesy."

Instead he got my last Schnicker-poodle and a trip through the security line.

The TSA officer, her jaw as tight as her sleeked-back bun, didn't bat an eye at my switch stars or the ancient box I carried. Instead, she set her sights on a tube of Bengay that I'd forgotten in my purse.

Yes, the pungent cream made me smell like one of the

biker witches, but my back had been killing me ever since I pulled it doing a few celebratory gymnastics with Dimitri. It had been worth every twinge. And caress. My body warmed just thinking about it.

The TSA agent cleared her throat. "You must forfeit the item if it does not fit into your one-quart Baggie."

Which I knew it wouldn't, because I'd bought the set of plastic bottles with the Baggie, and everything fit perfectly. And yes, that made me very happy in an incredibly dorky way.

"Let's lose it," I said, watching her toss the Bengay into the trash. At least I had my switch stars.

With the medicine safely in the garbage and my weapons intact, Pirate and I made it to the departure gate with barely two hours to spare. I let out a sigh of relief and plopped us down in the chair with the least gum on the side.

The sun was beginning to set outside the terminal, and Pirate gave a wide yawn. I pulled him out of the carrier and snuggled him close. Dimitri liked to fly internationally at night. That way, he could start the day in a new place.

An airport cart beeped past us, its yellow light flashing. A few travelers looked up. Most didn't.

Pirate curled up in the crook of my arm and fell instantly asleep, as only dogs can. I hoped I could sleep after what I'd seen.

Shake it off.

The creatures—not to mention demons—I'd met over the last two months had probably wanted to do much worse to me. I just hadn't been able to see it in 3-D color before. I settled back into the chair. No sense borrowing trouble from an invisible bar. I'd take each day as it came.

It was easier said than done.

Dimitri—in his usual daring fashion—arrived less than an hour before takeoff.

I turned too fast and almost woke up Pirate. I eased the little guy into his carrier, and before I knew it, Dimitri's solid weight pressed against my back.

Mmm . . . he smelled like rich amber and pure man. I ran my fingers lightly over his olive skin. "Missed you," I said, thankful for once that his griffin nature let him move a hair quicker than other men.

"Good," he rumbled against my back. The sound of his voice, the crisp Greek accent, made me glad to see him all over again.

I smiled up at him. He grinned back, his angled features softening. He wore a crisp, blue shirt cut to fit his broad shoulders, and black dress pants. Everything about him was polished, except for the way his thick, ebony hair curled around his collar.

A ribbon of pleasure trailed down my spine when his eyes swept over me. I'd waited thirty years for a man to look at me like that.

His hand lingered on my shoulders. "Your back still hurting you?" he asked, with a trace of guilt.

"I told you, it was worth it." I'd never made love on the back of a Harley before. We hadn't planned on that, but things tended to get out of hand with Dimitri.

Of course, I loved every minute of it.

I rubbed my spine, releasing a waft of Bengay. Dimitri noticed it too. He tried to hide it, but his nose wrinkled slightly at the pungent odor.

"It has to get better," I said. "TSA took my drugs."

"Praise be to national security." He handed me a Diet Coke and pulled a Hershey bar from his pack, my two feel-good foods. Did I say the man was a keeper?

I unwrapped the chocolate and bit into it, savoring the creamy texture. I've never been crazy about flying, but somehow being here with this man made it all worthwhile.

"My sisters can't wait to meet you, Lizzie," he said, smoothing a lock of hair behind my ear.

Pirate let out a grunt that turned into a loud doggie snore. Dimitri couldn't stop grinning, although I didn't know whether it was due to Pirate or the anticipation of going home at last. "Diana has already unearthed pictures of my more awkward years, and Dyonne is most eager to tell you the story of my first shift into my griffin form."

"When was that?" I asked.

"Not long enough ago for them to forget," he said wistfully.

Dimitri stole the corner of my Hershey bar and slid it into his mouth. "The first shift happens during puberty," he said, "and—like everything else at that time—it can be awkward."

Was my big sexy griffin blushing?

I cocked an eyebrow. "Do tell."

"Suffice it to say, a few parts didn't make the transition."

I wrapped my arms around his waist and pressed myself to him. "Seems all there now."

"I wouldn't blame you if you want to double-check," he said, his voice rough against my cheek.

"Let's get to Greece first." I gave him an extra little rub, just to tease.

Dimitri booked us first-class seats, which thrilled me to my toes because I'd always flown coach, and usually with a super-saver ticket, which meant I was in the last boarding group. The bin space, blankets and pretty much everything else were usually gone by the time I got to my seat. No more.

I even asked for double snack mix.

"They're not serving food yet," Dimitri said against my ear as he fastened his seat belt.

"I know," I said, adjusting the window shade. I couldn't see much besides the lights of the airport, but it was still a window seat. And I was happy. "I figured they'd want to know early." I eyed Pirate's doggie carrier underneath the seat in front of me.

"He's doing pretty well for his first flight," Dimitri said.

"Yeah, well we haven't taken off yet." And Dimitri hadn't witnessed Pirate's first ride on a motorcycle. Suffice it to say, Pirate didn't always take well to new modes of transportation.

But Pirate was the least of our worries. "Take a look at this," I said, retrieving the box from under the seat in front of him. I showed him the bar and leaned in close to tell him what I'd seen.

He nodded thoughtfully. Worry clouded his eyes. "We'll take it under advisement," he said simply.

Whatever response I'd expected, that wasn't it.

"You sound like a lawyer," I said, hurt he wasn't taking my imagined death more seriously.

Dimitri kissed me on the head, his warm breath lingering on my forehead. "What do you want me to say? That I'm scared every day something is going to happen to you?"

I pulled back, surprised to find him as tense as I felt. "Yes. No. I don't know." I burrowed against him again.

He squeezed my hand. "Look at me, Lizzie." His sharp features were almost too sincere. "I'll protect you. I promise."

My modern woman sensibilities wanted to protest. I could take care of myself. I was a demon slayer. Besides, I think that on some level, every one of us needs to believe we can hold our own against the monsters in life—especially the ones we were put on this earth to conquer.

Still, I loved Dimitri for wanting to swoop in and rescue me. I ran my fingers down his strong jaw. "Thank you."

Of course, now that I had him warm and fuzzy, I had to figure out a way to tell him I'd not only complicated his homecoming with visions of my own death, but now I was adding biker witches and demon slayer training. In the end, I figured the direct approach was best.

"Grandma is coming," I said, running my fingers down his arm. "She wants to start my training on Santorini as soon as she arrives." I'd give us less than a week alone. Tops.

"She told me," he said with a slight edge to his voice. Dimitri and Grandma hadn't always seen eye to eye. "In light of the circumstances, I can't think of a better way to spend our time together." A slight wariness entered his voice. "Did she mention what I was doing when she interrupted me?"

"Surprisingly, no." Grandma wasn't the best at keeping secrets.

He seemed relieved. "Okay, well then it's best I explain when we have some time in private."

Wait a second. "So it would be okay to tell me if Grandma already spilled part of it? What did she catch you doing?"

He fiddled with the airflow knob above us. "I'll explain later."

"Lovely. Can I at least have a hint?" All I knew was that it was important enough to keep him from going to the airport with me.

He made sure his tray table was in the upright and locked position. "Everything has checked out so far."

"Famous last words." I hated when he tried to take care of things for me. And I had a feeling that whatever this was, I wanted to know. "So are you going to tell me or . . . oh!" I gasped and gripped his arm. "There's a creature on the plane," I hissed. "There!"

I pointed to a small, brown, scaled *thing* scrambling in circles on the cockpit door. It was a lizard with immense pointed ears and a tail as long as my arm. Its feet were like a monkey's, complete with tufts of brown hair at the wrists and—holy cow—the creature turned to stare at me, its weathered face breaking into a crooked sneer that showed off a set of jagged teeth.

I gripped the seat in front of me and craned my body up for a better look as I reached for a switch star.

Dimitri stilled my hand. "Hold it, Lizzie. It's only a gremlin."

"What, like that *Twilight Zone* episode? 'Nightmare at Twenty Thousand Feet'?" We hadn't even made it off the runway.

"You do realize you have a flair for the dramatic," Dimitri said, keeping his eyes on me while the creature wiggled its eyebrows at us.

I looked around the cabin. The other passengers were still settling in, some of them grazing the monster as they passed. It gave them slimy kisses and reached into their pockets.

Dimitri leaned closer. "Gremlins like to cause trouble, especially with electrical systems, but they're not going to bring a modern plane down. They sneak onboard all the time. And believe me, you want them here rather than on the ground switching around your luggage tags."

The stewardess brushed right past the creature as it stood on the cockpit doorknob and began what I could only describe as a most obscene dance.

"She's not going to do anything?"

"That's right," Dimitri said, as if he understood what I couldn't possibly comprehend. "You haven't flown since you gained your powers."

"I've been busy," I snapped.

"She can't see him," Dimitri said. "No one can. Well, unless they have magical tendencies. Even so, one would have to be looking for problems." He made sure to emphasize that last part.

"Well excuse me." Yes, I was a demon slayer, and so far, it had brought me nothing but trouble. Now with this added death threat, I'd be crazy not to keep an eye out. As much as I would have liked to make this a private vacation for just me and Dimitri, I was glad Grandma would be there to begin my training. Maybe then I'd know more of what to expect.

The creature popped its head out of the galley. It ripped open a bag of snack mix and began chomping it loudly, with its mouth open.

"Of all the nerve." That was probably my snack mix.

"Don't interact with it too much," Dimitri cautioned, "or it might follow us."

"Onto our connecting flight?"

"They like cars too, although not as much as planes. It's basically anything mechanical."

Lovely. The last thing I needed was a gremlin on my Harley.

I yanked my gaze off the creature. Instead of giving in to the urge to take one more look, I took a small notebook from my purse and focused on a new entry in what I was hoping would become a guidebook for demon slayers. So far, I had way more chapters than I'd ever planned.

> *To be added to* The Dangerous Book for Demon Slayers, *Volume Two, subsection C: Magical creatures, benign.*
>
> *What the gremlin lacks in aggression, it makes up in its unflagging desire to sabotage and disrupt. Teeth are long and jagged, although the one creature I've witnessed seems to prefer biting into Gardetto's Original Recipe snack mix as opposed to anything else. His striking blue eyes and*

I braced myself as the plane sped down the runway and took off with a lurch.

> *the obvious intelligence behind its stare make this creature*

"Ohhhh . . . Lizzie," I heard from the bag at my feet.

"It's okay, baby dog," I said, wishing I could do more.

The bag suddenly became very bumpy. "You said flying. Right. Okay. Well, I don't like this kind of flying. Did you feel that? It's like a rattle. Oh, and now a jiggle. I don't think the bolts are tight on this airplane, and ooh biscuits . . ."

"Think of it like a Harley," I said, resisting the urge to unzip him. We didn't need a dog loose on the plane, even if FAA regulations didn't strictly forbid it.

"I can't, Lizzie. I just can't. It's not natural," Pirate protested, as I reached down into the bag and found a wet snout.

The plane jolted and Pirate retreated to the far end of his bag, muttering under his breath. I was going to owe him a trip to Burger King for this one.

Dimitri touched my shoulder. "Lizzie."

I leaned back into my seat. "It breaks my heart to do this to him," I said, eyeing the bag. He was better off in it. I knew he was. Still it would make me feel better to hold him.

"Lizzie," Dimitri said. "I need to tell you something while it's loud in here."

He looked as intense as I've ever seen him. "You know what you were asking before? About my business? Well, the situation didn't unfold as I'd hoped. I'm sorry I have to explain it so quickly, but—"

We both cringed as we hit an air pocket and the plane dropped sharply.

"When I needed to find a demon slayer—you," he corrected. "When I needed to find you, I used old griffin magic. I don't have time to explain it all now, but basically, I traced a thread of your power and I used it to find the rest of you."

I tried to digest that. "Wait. Before I was even a true slayer?" Dimitri had been the first one to find me.

"Yes," he said.

My stomach twinged. I knew he was powerful, but it still humbled me every time.

"It's a form of protective magic that I used for my own purposes. And I'm sorry."

Oh no. "What do you have to be sorry about?" I asked, not sure I wanted to hear the answer.

He looked guilty. "When protective magic is used to expose instead of to guard, it makes the subject particularly vulnerable."

"You mean me. It makes me vulnerable."

"Yes," he admitted. "I was desperate," he said quickly. "I needed to find you."

Wonderful it had worked out for him. But what about me?

"And now?" I asked.

"Someone else could use it too," he said. "I've kept the thread well protected, hidden in something we griffins call a light box. It never leaves my study. Only someone tried to break in last night. Diana drove the creature off."

"Creature?" As if we hadn't run into enough creatures. "What kind?" I demanded. "Is the magic safe?"

He ran a frustrated hand through his hair. "I don't know. Diana didn't get a good look. And she hasn't been able to inspect my office. My wards are too strong for her."

"Great. Nice work."

"I made inquiries today. All day. There were a few who knew I was using the thread to find you."

"Like Grandma?"

"No. I never told her. Although she suspected when JR blew into town."

"What? So now you're calling in the werewolves?" Sure, JR was Dimitri's friend, but his pack had also tried to kill me. If I was somehow exposed, I'd rather keep it to ourselves.

"Lizzie, it's not like that."

"Well, what is it like?"

"I'm trying to explain," he insisted. "We don't have much more time."

He was right. The plane had started to level out.

Dimitri noticed it too. "I only told trusted allies. JR. Max."

"Max?" Dimitri despised Max.

"We used the thread to help track you down when you went missing in Las Vegas. Besides, as a hunter, he's sensitive to your energies. I needed the help. Now, do you want to hear how it went?"

"Of course." And I would have appreciated knowing before now.

"From what I found today, I don't think you're compromised. Yet."

"Gee, thanks."

He ignored my sarcasm. "We'll know for sure once we get to my home. I'll take you to my study, show you the light box, and then you can watch me destroy it."

"You didn't have any right to create it in the first place."

"I know," he said softly. "Do you want apologies or information?"

"Both are overdue."

"We couldn't do anything about it before now. It

would have only fed into your fears. You were feeling weak already."

"Thanks for reminding me." Here I was, worried about visions of danger, when he had my rear end out there for the world to see.

Then I asked him the worst question of all. "So what happens if somebody did steal it?"

Dimitri swallowed hard. "The possibilities for destruction are limitless."

Chapter Three

I spent the rest of the flight lavishing attention on Pirate and ignoring Dimitri. Once the plane leveled off, we couldn't discuss the risk Dimitri had taken with me. We didn't know who could be listening. And I certainly didn't feel like talking to him about anything else.

Pirate nudged my wrist with his cold nose. "Lizzie. Did you hear me, Lizzie? I said B-five."

I tried to shake off my dark thoughts and focus on the travel-size game of Battleship on the tray table in front of us. A weak overhead light shone down on our game, while the rest of first class slumbered in the pockets of black that was night on board an airplane.

Inhaling, I flicked my eyes to the expectant Jack Russell terrier making swirls on the window with his stubby tail.

"Hit," I said, trying not to smile. One must not grin when losing the battle.

"Ha!" He danced in place. "I knew it. I knew you liked to play 'em high. You've been playing 'em high all night."

"Now that you've got most of my ships—" I began.

"Again," he added with no small amount of glee.

I threw one hand up in a mock gesture of surrender and placed a round red peg into my largest battleship. "We should really be getting some sleep."

"Oh no. No way I'm sleeping when I'm winning. Besides, I'm not going to shut one eye with that weaselly looking thingamabob ready to jump us."

I followed Pirate's narrowing eyes past the sleeping Dimitri to the gremlin, legs splayed and snoring on the seat across the aisle. "I think he's out."

Pirate twitched his ears like he did when he was thinking hard. "He could be faking. A watchdog can never be too careful."

Times like this, I wished I could borrow some of Pirate's energy. "I could have sworn I wore you out before the flight."

"Um-hum," Pirate said. "Good for you I can power-nap." He studied the flip-up game board in front of him. "B-six."

"Hit."

I let Pirate obliterate the rest of my fleet before I leaned my seat back and closed my eyes, satisfied. Pirate had adapted rather well to air travel. My job, at least in that department, was done.

As far as the rest of it?

There was nothing I could do at the moment about my mother's invisible bar or the supernatural risk Dimitri had taken—or for that matter, my sunken battleships. *Tomorrow.* I needed to be fresh for tomorrow.

It took me a while to fall asleep, and I doubted Pirate closed his eyes at all. From time to time, I'd wake and listen to him sniffing at the stale cabin air and feel him quiver as he watched the gremlin.

We landed in Athens and then boarded a puddle jumper bound for the island of Santorini. The Aegean Sea swirled like a rich blue cloud below us. White waves crested over the surface and streaked out from under the ferries and pleasure boats crisscrossing the Cyclades islands. All told, there were more than two hundred spots of land dotting the Aegean.

As we passed over the lush green islands, I tried to guess which might be inhabited, and if there were homes, what kind of people lived in the middle of a small ocean. Most of all, I wanted to be down there, under the hot sun. I wanted to dip my fingers into the churning waters. I wanted, for once, to be free.

I brushed my fingertips against the cold glass of the window and glanced back at Dimitri. We'd moved on to the polite stage, which was worse than being mad.

The issue of the stolen magic hung in the air between us and would until we had the privacy to talk it out. Even then, things wouldn't be completely resolved until we reached his study to learn once and for all if we had a problem on our hands.

Pirate had curled up in his Port-A-Pooch once he was convinced the gremlin was no longer a threat—at least not to us. Shortly after we began our descent, the thing had given an explosive fart before it began squeezing into the overhead bins. I could hear it as it moved its way down the plane, shifting luggage.

I ignored the banging and focused on the beauty outside my window. The islands looked so peaceful from twenty thousand feet.

Maybe my life would finally make sense here in Greece.

Things could be simple if I let them. First, we'd make sure the magic Dimitri used to find me was safe and then destroyed. Then I'd put away my mother's box. Grandma would be here soon enough with an instructor who understood that sort of thing. At long last I'd have the time and the guidance to learn about my new powers. In the meantime, I could relax.

After the pilot turned off the "fasten seat belt" sign and bid us good-bye, Dimitri took the bag with my sleeping dog and wrapped his other hand in mine. I adjusted my sunglasses as we made our way down the staircase of the plane and onto the tarmac below.

"I feel like a visiting dignitary," I told him jokingly, giving a presidential wave for effect.

He squeezed my hand. "You are," he said, ushering me toward a pair of brunettes inside the glass terminal. They wore matching coral necklaces and expressions of excitement.

They sprung upon us in a flurry of hugs, cheek kisses and olive blossoms.

"For your hair." A willowy sister with an upturned nose and a yellow sundress slipped a spray of tiny white flowers behind my ear. I inhaled the scent of unfolding buds and freshly cut grass. She admired her handiwork before throwing her arms around me. "Oh I am so glad to finally meet you!"

"That's Diana," Dimitri said with obvious pleasure as he gripped his other sister and held her tight. He squeezed his eyes shut and I stopped to enjoy the moment vicariously.

When Dimitri left Greece, he didn't know whether he'd see his sisters again. Now he was home.

I hugged Diana and marvelled at the fact that this was

the woman who'd ridden a monstrous horse named Zeus through a raging thunderstorm and straight into the family dining room.

"Diana." Her square-jawed sister laughed, her bronze-coin earrings jingling. "Give Lizzie some air."

Diana giggled and launched herself at Dimitri.

"I'm Dyonne," said the sister in the bronze-coin earrings and khaki shorts. She offered me a hand and then dragged me into another hug, my neck pressed against her chunky necklace. "Oh who cares? You're family now, right?"

I wasn't so sure but found myself grinning anyway. Who could be polite and detached around these two?

According to Dimitri, they'd always been a little wild. I didn't blame them a bit. They'd lived their lives under a demon's curse, knowing they'd fall into a coma when they reached the age of twenty-eight, and die twenty-eight days later. Dimitri and I had saved them.

Diana broke away from Dimitri, admiration and a few unshed tears shining in her eyes. "Our rescuer, in the flesh. You're officially forgiven for using my Han Solo lunch box for target practice."

Dimitri's mouth quirked into a sideways grin. "You said you'd forgive me if I rescued Princess Leia from the carob tree."

"Bah." Dyonne took a playful swipe that Dimitri deftly avoided. "You only did it because Princess Leia was wearing a slave-girl bikini."

Dyonne turned to me, her short-cropped hair falling in layers around her eyes. "Good thing for us, our brother's taste has improved." She winked.

"I don't know about that," I said, feeling the color creep up my cheeks.

"I'm sorry," she touched my arm. "I didn't mean to embarrass you." Her face glowed with pleasure. "I'm just so glad to have you both here. You don't know how long we've waited to have him back, to be a nice, normal family, you know?"

I nodded. I did know. I was still looking for that.

"A dog!" Diana lifted a yawning Pirate out of his carrier and ruffled him thoroughly.

"Aw, that's nice." Pirate soaked up every pet. "Oh hold it. That tickles."

Dimitri pulled Dyonne aside, but I heard each word he said. "Are there any new developments regarding the item in my study?"

Dyonne sobered at once. "Not that I can tell. I ran a few tests. So far, they look good. But you're the only one who'll know for sure." She caught my eye and I detected a flash of worry, or perhaps guilt, before she broke away.

"The car's waiting around front," she said to everyone. "We'll grab your luggage and head out. Christolo made your favorite, Dimitri. Pastitsio, with a cucumber and feta salad."

Dimitri's eyes lit up. He took my hand and picked up the pace. "Once you've had Christolo's cooking, you'll never want to leave." He squeezed my hand.

"Ohh . . ." Pirate licked his chops. "I could go for some noodles right about now."

I'd tell him later about the twenty-pound bag of Healthy Lite dog chow I'd shipped with our luggage.

On the way to and from baggage claim, the sisters informed me that my handsome Greek lover was allergic to broccoli, defended the entire family from a werewolf attack at age sixteen and had a habit of going out in rainstorms to rescue worms from the sidewalks. I also discovered the magic Dimitri used to find me could be very, very dangerous in the wrong hands.

"It's okay. Dimitri can fix it," Dyonne said, as if she was trying to convince herself too.

Dimitri slipped his arm around me as we sat in the backseat of his sister's battered old Mercedes. I didn't have to be strong all the time, did I? At least that's what I told myself as I relaxed into the nook of his shoulder.

We passed olive groves and vineyards growing in endless rows along the side of the road, their flat green leaves turned up toward the sun. Meanwhile Diana pointed out landmarks, as Dyonne, with her Mona Lisa smile, focused on the road. This had to be the most naturally bright and beautiful place I'd ever seen. The radiant blue sky went on for miles. The air itself smelled sweet. No wonder Dimitri had been so anxious to return.

In addition to the rustic splendor, he had a family on Santorini, a home. I understood more than anyone the value of a place to call your own, probably because I didn't have one.

I'd spent my time in Atlanta trying to fit in, be normal. And then I'd lived my first month as a demon slayer trying to do things the way others said they had to be done. I wanted to learn. There was nothing wrong with that. But at the same time, I wondered if I'd finally turned a corner. I wanted to live on my own terms. I wanted to decide for myself who I needed to be. And as I took stock of

Pirate with his head out the window, I realized my true home might not be anything like I'd imagined.

Diana held her arm out to the breeze as we passed olive farms and small stone houses that looked as if they'd been there as long as the island.

Dimitri took my hand and I eased closer into his embrace. "Diana, why don't you tell Lizzie what you saw in my study?"

Diana shot me an anxious look in the rearview mirror before she said, "Dyonne and I were returning from the stable when we saw green glowing slime pouring from the windows."

Dyonne nodded, her hands on the wheel of the ancient white Mercedes. "Dimitri's private little joke, since he'd green-slime Diana and me whenever we'd try to snoop through his record collection."

Dimitri shook his head at the memory. "You two never did learn." He sobered. "Just because someone attempted to break in doesn't mean they succeeded. At any rate, I hope they used more magic, rather than less. The lock on that door is good, but no match for an expert thief."

"Less magic?" I pondered the thought. If we didn't have a magical creature on our tail, I didn't know what it could be.

Dimitri tipped my chin up. He looked at me intently. "I've kept the magic well protected. You know that, don't you?"

"Sure," I said, not convincing anybody.

His jaw flexed, even though he tried not to look affected. "Our big problem—the one I tried to address before we left—is that someone learned the magic existed. I wanted to know who. Since we didn't have time to complete a thorough investigation, I'll be just as glad to destroy it."

He should have done it before now. Of course, we'd been busy saving Las Vegas from a demon invasion.

"You shouldn't have created it in the first place," I said.

He watched the narrow two-lane road ahead. "I know." He didn't say what we were both thinking—if he hadn't, he never would have found me. And if he hadn't found me, his sisters would be dead.

Through the rearview mirror, I could see Dyonne chewing at her lip. Great. I'd made her feel guilty about something she couldn't control. "Don't get me wrong," I said. "I'm glad he did everything he could, it's just—"

"Don't worry about it," Dyonne said. "Believe me, I'd be ticked too. Thank goodness the study is warded"—she eyed Dimitri through the mirror—"very well, to keep things out."

"Exactly." Diana braced an arm on the seat and twisted around. "He doesn't even get ants on the windowsill. Sure, somebody might have tripped the slime, but that doesn't mean they were able to make it past the door. Dyonne and I couldn't even slip inside to see what was going on. We could only take pictures of the tracks in the slime outside the door."

"Tracks?" I asked. "What kind of tracks?"

Dimitri looked guilty. "It's difficult to say."

Diana pulled an envelope out of her purse and handed me a stack of photos shot from various places in a long hallway. All showed a large wooden door from different angles, and around it, a moat of slime.

"The goop doesn't hold shapes well." Diana steadied herself as Dyonne steered us around a sharp curve. "It gives off a sharp electric charge. I don't know how anybody could have gotten past it."

"I do," Dyonne muttered. "It had to be someone with more ability than you or I. That's not hard."

I winced. The sisters hadn't exactly been given the opportunity to practice offensive magic. From what Dimitri had explained, thcy'd spent their entire lives trying, hoping, failing to defend themselves from the curse that would kill them.

The wind whipped through the open windows of the car as we passed the remains of an old fort. The weathered stones rose high on two sides, collapsing into a kaleidoscope of flowering brush. Vivid pinks, yellows and purples gave the sun-bleached ruins an enticing air. It was as if colors burned more intensely in this part of the world.

"It's going to be okay, Lizzie," Diana said. "We wouldn't let anything happen to you. Not after you saved us. And thank you. I know I told you on the phone after I woke up. Still . . ." She paused, as if the two words weren't enough. "Thank you."

"I was glad to do it," I said. And I was. Diana and Dyonne deserved to have their lives back, to be happy for once. They'd lived in the shadow of death for so long.

Even though I wouldn't be riding any horses up the grand staircase of their house, I didn't blame Dyonne and Diana for enjoying every minute they'd been given.

In a lot of ways, I envied them. I hadn't enjoyed life enough lately. Granted, I'd been busy saving the sisters, and then tied up preventing Armageddon on the Las Vegas

Strip. But now . . . maybe now I could finally stop and smell the olive blossoms. Or at least have a minute to think.

Before I could ponder too long, Dimitri jerked upright. My head tumbled off his shoulder and I had to brace myself against the seat to keep from sliding backward.

"What is it?" I asked, drawing a sharp breath as I spotted the sprawling white villa.

"Step on it," Dimitri ordered as Dyonne hit the gas and made a hard left into the long, cypress-lined drive.

Batlike creatures streaked across the sky, arching at sharp angles. They dove, disappearing behind the trees, only to swoop back again. My demon slayer senses kicked into high gear. The winged monsters practically radiated evil. No doubt they were primed to attack.

They stalked the smooth white walls of the villa. The house was classic Greek, with hot-pink flowering bougainvillea bushes and blue shuttered windows. It was an immense structure flanked by a lone tower rising off the right side. Green sludge bled from the spire like it was an open wound.

I gripped the seat in front of me, unable to take my eyes off the oozing window and the largest of the things hovering inches beyond it. "That's your study, isn't it?"

One look at Dimitri's grim expression told me I was right.

"They smell like imps," Pirate said, jumping into my lap.

"No," I said, fighting the dread, while at the same time recognizing the leathery bodies, the bent frames, imagining the sharp, razorlike teeth. "Imps don't fly."

"Yeah, and you also said dogs don't talk." He wheezed a wet doggie sniffle against my leg.

That seemed to be the theme of my life lately.

We'd run into imps before and found them blood-thirsty and twisted beyond all redemption. And what the imps represented made my stomach plummet. Imps served as minions of the devil. They were spawned from demons, which meant whoever had spread the word about my exposed magic had intimate knowledge of who could hurt me the worst.

My emerald necklace hummed as the bronze chain unclasped itself and snaked down my neck. Even though I knew Dimitri's gift did nothing but protect, I still stiffened as it wound its way around my right shoulder, the metal stretching and moulding to form a hard bronze epaulet with a teardrop emerald gleaming at the center.

Into battle we go.

Chapter Four

I should have been terrified, and I was. But I also felt cheated.

Was it so terrible to want a nice, normal vacation with my boyfriend? Just once? Didn't I deserve a magical getaway without eight different brands of demonic creatures?

I mean, here we were racing straight for a traditional Greek villa. It stood postcard perfect at the edge of a black volcanic rock cliff overlooking the impossibly blue Aegean Sea. Emerald green hills rose on the other side. And other than the leathery black creatures soaring above the cliffs, it looked pretty darned nice.

Could I even enjoy the towering beauty of the cypress-lined drive? Look for more than a moment at the fountain in the middle of a small lake? No. I had to fight minions of the devil.

Fate couldn't resist one last dig. I jumped back as Dimitri's crisp blue shirt landed on the floor in front of me.

I turned and saw him removing his white undershirt as well. "What are you doing?" I asked, mild annoyance giving way to a sudden preoccupation with the broadness of his chest. Once he removed his tailored clothes, everything about him seemed larger and more potent.

"Shifting," he said, his hair spiking at odd angles. Dimitri hated to ruin his clothes with an unplanned shift.

Okay, I could see his point. If the imps attacked from the air, he could be a more effective fighter in griffin form.

The car jumped a pothole and I tumbled against Dimitri, bracing my hand on the most perfect abs this side of the Mediterranean.

"Any change in the imps?" he asked, depositing me on the seat next to him. A lock of black hair fell over his forehead as he reached for his belt buckle.

"No. But they seem to be circling in a pattern." They weren't attacking. Yet. "You going to take off your pants too?" Just my luck I wouldn't be able to enjoy that either.

Dimitri braced one hand in front of me and caught himself on the seat back a second before Dyonne slammed on the brakes.

"No time," he said. Dimitri had his car door open before she'd even come to a full stop. "You ready, Lizzie?

"Oh yeah." I was right behind him, slamming the door on Pirate before he could protest. I unhitched a switch star, ready for the onslaught. Holy moley, I craved it.

It disturbed me as much as it fascinated me.

Don't think, just act. I dug my fingers, hard and white, into the handles of the switch star.

Dimitri planted himself next to me, unwilling, it seemed, to shift with battle so close. I didn't see any weapons on him but certainly wasn't foolish enough to think he didn't have his defenses in place. His breathing was hard and focused. As I watched, his skin took on a fine sheen, almost like a glow.

It felt good to be fighting next to him as an equal. For so long, he'd tried to protect me. At first, I was grateful for the support. But after I'd learned more about what I could do, it was downright insulting. I may not have known everything about the magical world, but I could hold my own.

The imps circled above us, holding to the same formation I'd detected earlier. "Why aren't they attacking?" They had to have seen us.

One by one, they dove for the window. Each time, they'd bounce off with an audible *zing*, like big leathery insects on a bug zapper. Only these things didn't die. They'd circle and dive again. And again.

The protective charm Dimitri had cast over his office didn't show signs of breaking. Then again, what did I know about magic windows?

"Maybe they don't want a full-out battle," he said, thinking, his eyes widening when something clicked into place. "Maybe they just want you."

Holy Hades.

They didn't need to attack me outright. They'd be able to hurt me bad if they managed to get to the magic Dimitri had used to trace me. I had no idea how to defend myself against an internal assault.

"Come on!" Dimitri gripped my arm, heading for the house.

"Wait." I opened the car door and Pirate fell out.

He popped right back up and scrambled against my bare leg. "I'm fine! Nothing to see here."

"Now," Dimitri ordered.

"Come on," I said, grabbing Pirate around the middle.

He squirmed against me. "I can take an imp."

I propped Pirate under one arm and my mom's wooden box under the other. It wasn't the most effective fighting pose, I'll give you that, but I wasn't about to let either fall into the wrong hands. As to what I'd do when it came time to fry a few imps . . . well, I'd figure it out.

I hated to admit it, but most of the success I'd had as a demon slayer had been when I let go and let my instincts guide me.

"This way," Dimitri called as he ran for the front door of the house.

I about tripped up the slate stone porch as Dyonne and Diane started to shift right in front of me. Claws erupted out of their hands and feet, and thick lion's fur raced up their arms. Red, purple and blue feathers cascaded down their backs and formed wings as bones snapped and their bodies expanded. "We'll head around the—" Dyonne's intense voice ended in a snarl.

Even though I knew in theory that these two women could morph into griffins—with the bodies of lions and the heads and wings of an eagle—it still shocked me to watch their bodies grow to the size of two monster trucks. Diana took off on a set of massive wings, with Dyonne right behind her.

"Lizzie!" Pirate leapt out of my grasp and followed Dimitri inside the house. "I smell them, Lizzie!"

I was right behind them, through the bright blue door and into an arched entryway. To the right, a set of white stone steps seemed to grow out of the house itself. Dimitri gripped the iron banister as he took them three at a time. Pirate raced out front. I followed a step behind. Higher and higher. My Supernova cross-trainers slapped against the hard white stone. I hated imps.

I could see them in my mind's eye—with their weasel-like faces and bodies of thick, hastily constructed people.

Purple eyes glowed from under dark, furry brows, and dark hair clung to their twisted torsos.

One screeched on the floor above as glass shattered.

No!

We dashed around the corner and down an arched hallway, up a small flight of stairs and down another hall toward a pool of slime at the far end. Dimitri slopped straight through it, reaching back for me. I missed his outstretched hand and got the shock of my life. Fire shot straight up my legs and zapped me up the spine and down to my fingertips.

"Mother fuddrucker!" I twisted sideways and knocked Pirate backward and out of the line of fire, but not before I heard his yip of pain.

"Lizzie!" Dimitri grasped my arm and the shock waves stopped as quickly as they'd begun.

I twisted around. "Baby dog!"

Pirate's fur stood on end and he walked in hazy circles on the gray slate tile. "Buttons always talked about his electric fence and I said, 'Oh I can handle an electric fence,' but if that's an electric fence . . ."

I pulled Dimitri through the muck, my entire body throbbing from the original impact. "Pirate, are you okay?" He didn't look so good.

He blinked twice, one ear straight up, the other curling under. "Urkle." He tried to shake off, but it turned out as more of a neck and shoulder wiggle. "Why don't I guard the rear?"

"Yes," I said. "Do it." We didn't want him anywhere near the imps. Last time, he'd gotten cut up pretty bad, although I had to admit, he'd held his own.

"Lizzie." Dimitri ran a hand along my back, maintaining contact—which seemed to be a pretty good idea, since I had muck on my shoes. "Pirate's clean. We need to go. Now."

We waded back through the slime to the thick wooden door of Dimitri's study. I could hear the imps' heavy, wet breathing on the other side.

"Touch me at the waist," Dimitri said. "Don't let go until you have absolutely no contact with the slime."

No kidding.

He turned the key in the antique lock.

I gripped the hard muscles above his dress pants as he pressed his thumb to a point right above eye level and pushed. The door groaned open and I gasped at what had become of his office. Burn marks singed the floors, stone sculptures lay crushed and broken, papers scattered everywhere.

A blackened imp hurled itself against the red slate floor to the left of Dimitri's antique wood desk. The floor echoed and plumes of smoke rose each time he threw himself down.

I pushed my way around Dimitri. "What the—?"

"They've found the safe."

A gray-streaked imp hissed from its perch on the windowsill.

"Get down!" Dimitri smashed me onto the cold hard floor, his body falling on top of me as a monster on the windowsill flung a leathery arrow at us.

I winced as it clattered against the wall behind us and fell to the floor.

"Get up. We need to separate. They're hurling curses." Dimitri dragged us sideways as another arrow whizzed past.

We rolled to the left as I dug my slimy tennis shoes off without untying them. Then, for lack of options, I tossed one at the window imp. It smacked him right in the forehead, the goo zapping him backward out the window.

"Ha!" I pushed away from Dimitri, aiming a switch star at the imp currently making a big char hole in the floor. The bronze on my shoulder made it harder to throw. Still, I cleaved the imp in half, the two sides of its hairy black body sizzling as three more imps poured in the window.

Dyonne caught a claw on the outside ledge, tearing part of it off as she snapped her eagle's beak through the window. But her head was too wide and the imps too fast.

One of the imps from the window leapt onto Dimitri's antique desk, and the wood disintegrated on the spot.

"Holy Hades!" My stomach flip-flopped, shocked, as the imp fell into a pile of ash.

Dimitri's eyes widened. "Kill it!"

His forehead glistened with sweat as he worked some kind of incantation over the broken window.

Right. I leveled a switch star at the thing's head, slicing it open, as the other two from the window leapt into the study. I caught one of them as it took cover behind a potted ficus tree in the corner. The imp fell forward and the tree wilted and turned to dust before my eyes. Another one landed on the oriental carpet by a massive fireplace. The carpet curled and blackened.

Sweet Mary. Everything they touched aged and died.

"Lizzie!" Dimitri yelled as the last imp hurled a curse directly at me. I dodged as it struck my bronze-clad shoulder, bouncing off.

I gasped, panic shooting through me. But the bronze had protected me. Thank God.

The imp launched itself straight for my head. I grabbed a switch star and stepped backward to throw, when an electric shock radiated through my body. A momentary panic seized me. I'd stepped on a gooey tennis shoe. I flung the switch star hard. It zinged sideways as I fell, the imp crashing straight for me.

"Lizzie!"

I forced every bit of focus I had on the switch star hurtling back to me. It sliced straight through the imp as I rolled sideways, scrambling to avoid the body.

"Jesus!" Dimitri tackled me, crushing me against the hard floor with his weight. "Lizzie." He yanked me upward, inspecting me before hauling my body against his.

I shoved against him. "What are you doing? Where are the imps?"

"Outside." His chest heaved against me and it felt, well, nice. "For now. I sealed the window to keep out anything demonic."

He pulled away, his face a maze of worry, "Lizzie, I thought I'd lost you."

Before I could tell him that would be hard to do, he wrapped me in a crushing kiss. He was all heat, fire and tongue. I kissed him back, hard. Either one of us could have been dust on the floor, like the plant or the desk. By the sheer grace of the heavens, we'd survived.

I could not lose this man, this life. Not yet. He was solid and strong against me. Ribbons of pleasure wound through me. I felt his relief and his love and, yum, him against my leg.

He groaned, or it might have been me, as we luxuriated in being alive and whole. Way too soon, Dimitri pulled away, looking as dazed as I felt.

I ran a finger along his jaw. "Mmm . . . That was almost worth getting zapped."

Dimitri frowned. "No, it wasn't."

"Oh yeah? Let's make sure."

I tipped my lips to his and delighted in his swift and utterly complete surrender. I'm not sure how long we kissed. I didn't care. He was my port in the storm.

A small boulder crashed through the open window, bringing us back to reality.

I stiffened, ready for attack, and saw Diana, in human form, perched on the windowsill. Oh my goodness. It was at least a fifty-foot drop.

"Don't worry about us," she said, shaking out her mass of dark hair, easing a leg inside the window as Dimitri murmured an incantation to allow her to pass. "We were happy to drive off the rest of the devil's spawn while you two made out."

"Where's Dyonne?" Dimitri asked, evidently used to this kind of behavior.

"She's going the long way—around the house, up the stairs." Diana shivered as if she found the whole thing a complete bother. "Dyonne also has to stop by her room on the way up." Diana winked. "She lost her dress."

"How did you manage to keep yours?" I asked.

Dimitri always shifted back naked. Not that I was complaining.

Diana lifted the skirt of her yellow sundress and showed me a loop under the hem. "I tie it to my tail before I finish shifting."

"It's dangerous," Dimitri added, making it clear they'd had this discussion before.

Diana rolled her eyes. "Pshaw. I haven't done it in any

griffin battles. Let the imps try to grab it"—she wiggled her rear—"or my tail."

Speaking of such, "How did you touch those things? They turned everything in here to dust."

"Griffins have Skye magic," Diana said. "Cursed imps can hurt us, even kill us. But they can't . . . well . . ." She waved a hand over the ashes on the floor.

Dimitri wrapped a protective arm around me. "Cursed imps can only disintegrate things that owe their existence to the earth—the carpet, my plant, my desk." He cringed slightly. It had been a nice desk.

"And people like me," I said.

Dimitri nodded. "For all your powers, it's still a matter of dust to dust."

I'd remember that.

"Are we safer in the house?" I asked. Aside from a burn hole in the floor, the imps hadn't been able to damage it.

"Perhaps," Dimitri said, his fingers playing along my arm. "The house has been soaked in generations of protective magic. Still"—he leaned forward and treated me to a lingering kiss on the forehead—"let's not test the theory, okay?"

That was more than fine by me.

"What I can't figure out is why they were going for the floor safe," Dimitri said, moving away from me.

He brushed his foot across the remains of his desk and over one of the slate tiles. "I keep our family histories in here, but nothing else of consequence."

"And the light box?" I asked.

Dimitri led us to the massive stone fireplace behind what had been his desk. It was white like the walls, blackened inside from generations of fires. He said a few hushed words over a carved griffin head at the apex of the mantel, and it opened with an eerie creak.

We crowded around him to see as he pulled out a drawer the size of a cereal box. He peeled away layers of gossamer cloth to reveal a thin glass lantern with bronze fittings. A wisp of light danced inside like a flame.

My stomach tingled. "Is that my magic?"

Dimitri stood silent for a moment. "No." He cast his eyes down, hesitant to say what came next. "From the color of this flame, it seems as if your magic has been missing for quite a while."

I stepped back, shock washing over me. "Gone?" I'd prepared myself for the possibility, but it still felt like a punch to the gut. "And what do you mean it's been missing for a while? I've only known you for two months."

Wouldn't I have sensed it if I'd been compromised? I had to believe I'd have had an inkling. If something was working against me, I'd have felt weaker, I'd have felt exposed—I'd have felt *something.*

Dimitri looked as horrified as I felt. "From the blue of the flame, I'd say it's been two weeks. About the time you were hanging out with *Max* in Vegas." He couldn't let it go.

"Oh, so Max broke in here and did this?" Dimitri had blamed a lot of things on the half-human, half-demon Max, but this was stretching it even for him.

"No," he said with a forced calm. "I'm merely giving you a timeline. Whoever—or *what*ever—has taken this thread of your magic hasn't used it yet. Or you'd know it."

Diana's fingers shook as she brought them to her mouth.

I was both relieved and disturbed. "Why would they

take part of my magic and not use it?" It didn't make sense. "Are you sure I'd feel it?"

"Yes," Dimitri said, with more conviction than I would have liked.

"Lizzie?" Pirate called from the hallway. "Ohhh biscuits," he said, his voice wavering. "You have to see this."

"Whatever it is, don't sniff it, don't lick it and don't eat it." I threw open the door and barely avoided running right into Dimitri's killer slime.

Son of a sailor.

"Pirate?" I fought to keep my voice even. "Don't move."

Chapter Five

Dimitri and I stood dumbfounded as Pirate hovered on the other side of the door. My dog drifted a foot above the slime, doggie-paddling in midair.

"Pirate?" My jaw slackened. "What did you do?"

"Nothing, Lizzie. I didn't do a thing, I swear. I was sniffing the hallway, minding my own business, and bam!"

"Bam?" I stared at his furry paws churning in the air. "You're going to have to be more specific than that."

Pirate gave me the startled, wide-eyed innocent doggie look he'd perfected after years of sneaking Pup-per-roni Bites out of my purse. "I hit a cold spot and it was like hopping in the bathtub at the Posh Pooch. Only not so smelly." He did a doggie version of the breaststroke. "I'll bet I look fierce."

Concerning was more like it. "Dimitri?" I hoped he'd have some explanations. And fast.

"This isn't my magic," he said, watching Pirate doggie-paddle into the room. "Diana?"

"Not Skye magic."

I reached down to touch the air under Pirate's paws. "It's cold."

Pirate's tail hadn't quit. "I know. It surprised me too, but you get used to it after a while."

I crossed my arms over my chest. "It doesn't feel demonic." At least not like anything I'd ever seen.

Pirate's tail stopped wagging. It was a valid concern. If Dimitri and his sisters hadn't created it—and I certainly couldn't fly—it stood to reason that someone else had left it behind.

"Come on, Pirate." I reached down for him. "Time to get out of the pool." While I was glad the power hadn't come from the imps, I still didn't want Pirate playing around with unknown entities. He must have seen the look on my face, because he started paddling harder—in the other direction.

"Hey." I lifted Pirate off his invisible airstream.

"Aw, Lizzie." He scrambled against my arms. "Where's your sense of adventure?"

"Stick close to me," I said, "and don't go near those arrows over there." Exactly how did one go about cleaning up curses?

Dimitri left and came back with an industrial broom. He used it to sweep away the toxic remains of the imps, as well as the char marks on a section of red slate.

"Do you have an extra broom?" I asked. I was used to cleaning up messes in preschool. Granted, imp parts were worse than baking-soda volcanoes and half-digested hotdogs, but I wasn't going to complain.

"I don't have anything else soaked in enough protective magic," Dimitri said, ignoring the fact that a quite a few of his broom bristles had, indeed, turned to ash. "If you can handle the curses, I'll get the rest of it."

"Deal."

Dimitri began piling the imps in the fireplace while I went looking for curses.

I found both of the arrows near the back wall. They were rough-hewn and brown, made from a material

I didn't recognize. It could have been wood, except for the small moving particles inside. The points of the arrows had dug chunks out of the plaster wall, meaning they were sharp, or powerful—probably both.

"Stand back, baby dog," I said, wondering if it would be safe to switch-star these things with other people in the room.

But Pirate wasn't listening. He'd found Diana. Since she couldn't clean, she'd plopped right back down on the windowsill and given Pirate a nice lap. He lolled his head off the side of her leg and arched his back as she scratched his belly and cooed sweet nothings into his ear. Some guys had all the luck.

I stowed my mom's magical box on the fireplace mantel before returning to the arrows on the floor. I didn't have much experience with demonic curses. If I tried to blow them up with a switch star, would they scatter cursed bits like a land mine? Would they rear up and attack? It didn't look like they were alive, but then again, things had a way of popping up and surprising me.

"Dimitri, I'm going to have to fire on this," I said, unhitching a switch star, hoping I was right.

"Okay, Lizzie. Give me a second." He tossed the last imp into the fireplace. "Hell and damnation." He patted himself down. "My matches were in the desk." We both looked to where the desk had been. Only a few scattered ashes remained.

"Diana?" he asked.

The breeze from the window blew wisps of hair about her face as she stroked Pirate's belly. "I quit smoking. Dyonne too."

"Good," he said, and then as an aside to me, "I've been after them for years."

"Subtle as a sledgehammer," Diana added. "But truly, why go to the trouble of quitting if we were going to be dead by age twenty-eight? It's not as if we had to worry about our lungs, or even frown lines, for that matter." She tucked a lock of hair behind her ear as Pirate bucked and squirmed at the interruption. "Anyway, we're alive and we quit," she said, as if daring Dimitri to push it.

He didn't.

"Do you need to burn the imps right now?" I asked. Dead was dead, when it came to imps. "I'd rather get rid of the curses."

Dimitri used the broom to push a path through the slime outside his office. Then the three non–demon slayers took shelter behind the spelled door while I pulled out a switch star and—I'll admit it—said a little prayer.

I hit the first curse with a switch star and it exploded with a screech worse than fingernails on a blackboard. I winced and heard Pirate howl. An acidic dust settled on my face and arms. I held my breath and blinked as my eyes watered. I could feel particles of it behind my eyelids, like hot sand. I used the inside of my shirt to wipe some of it away. My mouth tasted metallic. Still, I wasn't writhing on the floor, so I took it as a good sign.

The thing had dented my switch star, however. I held my finger in front of the spinning blades in order to stop them. With some effort, I managed to bend the metal back into place. One blade remained a bit rumpled, but . . . well, I was about to damage it yet again. I threw the star at the second curse. That one wasn't as bad, probably because I was expecting the shriek and the stink.

A breeze from the open window took some of it away as my friends ventured back into the room.

"Makes me wonder what they'd have done if they hit me," I commented to no one in particular.

"Most of them fling you to hell," Dimitri said. "Hence the expression."

God, they tasted awful. "Excuse me?" I asked, sweeping up the remains of the curse.

"Go to hell."

"Right." I deposited the particles in the fireplace. We were going to have one big evil bonfire before we were through.

"Now that we've got that handled . . ." Dimitri popped open a floor panel to reveal a black metal door with a combination lock.

The rest of us gathered around, eager.

Dimitri glanced up and cleared his throat. "If you don't mind. If someone is going to bewitch and torture this combination out of anyone, I'd prefer it to be me."

Diana nudged me as she crossed her arms, and we turned our backs. "Gallant, as always."

Dimitri dialed the longest combination in history, then pulled the vault open. Inside lay an envelope, a homemade book made of orange construction paper and something small wrapped in blue cloth. He carried the objects to a clean spot in front of the fireplace and we gathered around.

He shifted his weight from side to side and for the first time seemed uncomfortable. "I don't see what anyone, besides me, would want with any of this."

I touched the old orange book. A green string bound together several pages and on the cover, written in a child's hand, it said, *Dimitri's book about Dimitri*. Two smiling creatures flew in the clouds below the title. From my experience with preschool drawings, I knew they could be anything from bears to ice cream cones, but I had a feeling these were griffins.

"Mom made that with me shortly before she died," Dimitri said.

Diana took the book and studied it.

"This," he said, pulling a folded parchment from the envelope, "is a copy of our family tree. There are others in the house. But this one was illustrated by my father, for me. It was a tradition in our clan."

Diana looked up from the picture book. "I still say we should hang it."

"I know," he said, automatically. "I remember the day we drew it together. His leaves were green, as they're supposed to be. I made mine yellow for fall."

Diana snorted. "You just had to be different."

"Yeah, I did." He folded up the paper quickly, as if the memories were still too fresh.

"And what's that?" I asked, resisting the urge to pull open the blue cloth and see what it hid.

"It's important to me," he said, lifting it gently, "but nothing of interest to a demon."

The mention of the word *demon* jarred me out of the moment. I pushed it down. *Focus.* I had a fresh perspective on this. Maybe I could see something the rest of them didn't.

Dimitri unwrapped the package to reveal a jagged

aquamarine stone. It fit easily in his palm and radiated a quiet beauty. One could feel calm and harmonious simply looking at it.

"This is a piece of our mother's Skye stone," he said. "It's the only part that she didn't—" He stopped, unwilling to go on. "I'll tell you later." He cleared his throat. "My sisters work with their own larger stones, the ones that contain the most energy." He touched a reverent finger to the very center of his mother's stone, and it glowed in recognition. "This fragment is of sentimental value only."

"Are you sure?" I asked.

He tried to smile. "Yes. Diana and Dyonne have the real power over our ancestral home and lands. If you don't believe me, just ask them. My sisters will be more than glad to tell you how the lines of ancestral magic run through the women in our line."

"It's true," Diana said, touching him on the shoulder. "Big Brother here may have the strength to protect, but we're the ones most closely tied to our home. It's the way it's always been."

I nodded, realizing how it had been even more tragic, then, when the women in his clan had no hope of living to an old age. They died young, knowing their clan would wither and fade. I'd seen how Dimitri's tree narrowed rather than widened at the top.

He gave the stone to Diana and it practically pulsed in her hand. "Diana is regaining more of her powers every day."

"More like refinding." She stroked the stone and it glowed even brighter. "We'd been so focused on the curse, we hadn't spent much time exploring what else we could do."

Now they'd be free to live.

Too bad I was still trapped. I'd never be free until we could find who had taken that part of me. "So if we assume the imps weren't after anything in your safe, and my magic has already been stolen, why did they break in today?"

Dimitri tugged a hand across his forehead. "I don't know."

"Did you use that Skye stone to track me?" I asked. "Maybe they need it to use what they stole."

"Impossible," Dimitri said. "The stone is merely a conductor. We use them to capture words and emotions—the things we put out into the universe."

Diana broke in. "In English, what he means is that our magic isn't about focus objects, but rather, how they're used."

Now I was officially confused. "Let's bring it down a notch."

Dimitri took my hands. "I employed protective magic to track you." He smoothed a wisp of hair away from my face. "I wanted to watch over you and learn whether you could be the person to save my sisters. I used my mother's stone to channel my energy, but it was only a tool, not the source of anything. Dark powers wouldn't use a Skye stone."

"Oh yes?" I asked. From my experience, dark powers would use anything that would suit them.

"A dark-magic practitioner or any creature with a strong enough tie to the evil arts would use their own conductor." He grew somber. "Lizzie, it's important that we retrieve the protective thread. Whoever stole it could use the connection to harm you or manipulate you in other ways."

My stomach sank. "How so?"

"They'll try to direct you, to guide your feelings."

"I can fight back," I said, hoping I was right.

"It's more than that," he said. "They'll use it to rob you of yourself, to dilute your free will."

Jesus, Mary, Joseph and the mule. Now what the heck was I supposed to do about that?

"At least it hasn't happened yet," Diana said, trying—and failing—to sound optimistic.

We were in trouble.

My magic was gone. We didn't know where to find it. And the big question still hovered over our heads: when would whoever had it use it?

Dimitri thought for a moment. "Perhaps Amara can help." He glanced at Diana. "Is she here?"

"Not right now," Diana said, "but later, yes."

"Amara?" I asked.

"You'll meet her tonight," Diana said.

"Be on guard," Dimitri added, only half-kidding. "It'll be an experience."

Dimitri returned everything to the floor safe and secured it once again. While he cleaned up the slime and re-spelled the office, I gathered up my mom's wooden box and let Diana show me my room. Pirate followed a few feet behind, sniffing at the corners of the hallway.

I knew what he was doing.

"Pirate, I don't want you floating again."

"Aw, but Lizzie—If it was demonic you'd know about it and I always wanted to be able to jump really, really high and this is kind of like that and I don't see why—"

"Pirate." For all my powers, I wasn't particularly crazy about magic, especially the kind I couldn't control.

He mumbled to himself the rest of the way, something about the unfairness of being a dog.

Diana led us from Dimitri's study to the second floor of the building. The white hallways left plenty of room for all three of us to walk side by side if we'd wished. That is, if Pirate hadn't been ten feet ahead with his nose to the ground. At least he was where I could see him.

"Amara and her brother are staying in these two bedrooms," Diana said as we came to the rooms closest to the stairway.

"Oh," I said, pausing outside a yellow painted door, unable to think of anything else to say that wouldn't be downright rude.

Diana guessed. "I think Dimitri assumed they'd be gone by the time you two returned," she said, touching a conspiratorial hand to my arm. "I don't blame them for wanting to stay. They come from the Dominos clan, which is very large—and loud."

Dimitri had mentioned the Dominos clan. He'd pledged himself to them when his clan all but died out. He'd also asked for their help when we were in Las Vegas. That was before things had gone south so quickly.

"So they've been here for a while?" I asked.

Diana nodded. "Amara and Talos came to help Dyonne and me during what we thought would be our final days. They protected us, cheered us with gifts." She touched her necklace. "They kept us company." She paused. "They would have been there to witness our final minutes. Griffins cannot die alone, or"—her gaze dropped to her toes—"well, it's just bad. Anyhow, they promised to stay with us." Her fingers skimmed the yellow door. "They've been here ever since, almost like family. You'll meet them tonight."

"Do you think we should check on them?" I asked, hand raised to knock. No telling what could have happened if they'd run into a stray imp or three.

Diana shook her head. "We already did. Christolo, our cook, was the only one home during the attack. Dyonne found him hiding in the pantry. She really should have put some clothes on first." She started down the hallway once more. "Amara and Talos went out for the day."

"Oh," I said, moving on. "What a lucky day to be out." Not that I wanted to accuse her friends of anything, but it did seem strange for them to disappear right before an attack.

"They might have figured we'd be busy picking you up. Or"—she turned back to me—"they could have sensed something coming. Amara is psychic."

"For real?" I'd never met a psychic, except for the one at the Georgia State Fair. And even at the age of eight, I had a feeling that Mystical Marge had a tarot card or two up her sleeve.

"I'll bet that's why Dimitri thinks she could help you."

I hoped that wasn't our only plan. I liked to count on things I could see—my switch stars, a nice antidemonic spell, perhaps a few healing crystals from my utility belt. Sure, I'd stop to watch the occasional History Channel special on Nostradamus or the 2012 predictions, but if I was going to bet my missing magic on something, it had better be something I could use.

The doubt must have shone on my face, because she quickly added, "Amara predicted that Dyonne and I could be the ones to survive the curse on our family." She paused outside another painted door. "Thanks to you, it happened."

Interesting. Perhaps I'd talk to Amara about the vision I'd had at the airport.

Diana opened the door to a cozy room with a plumped-up canopy bed that reminded me of "The Princess and the Pea." The bed was covered in a white and green vine pattern, with a half dozen pillows and a Greek cross hanging on the wall behind it. The room had a large, rounded window overlooking the gorgeous green hills behind the house.

"This is for me?" I asked.

"Officially, yes," Diana said, with a bit of humor. "And just so you know, Dimitri is across the hall."

How convenient, although it was a bit of a shame that comfy bed would probably go to waste.

"Oh, and if it makes you feel any safer," she said, easing open the wardrobe in the corner of the room, "this bottom drawer has a solid lock. The key is on the dresser."

"Thanks."

As I turned the key, I couldn't help thinking that for a house as open and welcoming as this one tried to be, it sure had a lot of places to keep secrets.

Chapter Six

I showered in the small bathroom off my room and changed into a pink flowered sundress and sandals. Despite the brightness of my surroundings, I couldn't keep my own dark thoughts from surfacing.

Someone had stolen a part of me.

A few months ago, I would have thought it was impossible. Of course that was before I came into my powers and learned more than I ever wanted to know about demons, imps and things that go bump in the night—and in all hours of the day as well.

I eased onto the bed and tried to remember my yoga breathing. Our teacher had talked about centering ourselves, finding that quiet place. It was harder than it sounded, sitting still, letting your mind roam free.

Even when my biggest worry involved keeping Pirate away from Mrs. Cristople's tabby cat, I usually ended up composing to-do lists in my head while my classmates communed with the universe.

This time, I really tried. I closed my eyes and looked inward, focusing on my soul, my strength, my power.

My complete lack of control over the thread that was stolen from me.

I didn't even like it when my keys weren't on the third hook of my kitchen organizer at home. Now I kept a new set in my front right pocket. All the time.

I slipped a hand into the pocket of my sundress. Sure enough, I had the SpongeBob keychain one of my preschoolers had given me. I just didn't have a vital part of my being. I clenched my fingers around the keys, wincing as the metal dug into my skin.

Eerily enough, I didn't feel any different. How could someone have snatched such an important piece of me without me even missing it?

I still hadn't managed any major revelations by the time Dimitri came to escort me to dinner. His loose-fitting cream shirt accentuated his wide build and olive skin. And as I was about to compliment him on his legs—Dimitri hardly ever wore shorts—he pulled me in for a kiss that warmed me from head to toe.

His lips brushed mine once, twice. "You ready, Lizzie?"

"Always," I said, taking his hand.

Despite everything that had happened, Dimitri seemed more relaxed here. I couldn't even put my finger on exactly what it was. We certainly hadn't enjoyed a typical homecoming. It was more like landing in Oz.

Perhaps Dorothy had something there when she said there's no place like home.

We made our way down to the first floor of the house, passing through the main entryway, with its amber walls and gorgeous tile floors. I hadn't noticed them before, and with good reason. This time, I paused to admire the pair of mosaic griffins, standing proud, their powerful lion's tails wound together as they flew over olive groves and vineyards.

"It's beautiful," I told him, running a toe over a sky blue section.

He squeezed my hand. "My grandfather had it commissioned for my grandmother as an anniversary gift. I forget which one. See here." He led me toward the back hallway where the sky gave way to the heavens, and in the center, to Dimitri's family crest. "See the long pointed rays coming down from the sun? They represent the four elements."

"Earth, ocean, fire and air." I didn't get an A in Greek mythology for nothing.

"The other rays represent the twelve griffin clans. The sun of Vergina is the symbol of all griffins and is incorporated onto the markings of each clan. On my family's crest, it's situated in the clouds. We are the Helios, which means we are of the light and sky."

I studied the gold and blue crest. "Isn't that true of most griffins?"

"The most well-known, maybe," he said, giving in to a moment of pride. "But other clans draw power from earth or fire.

"Or water."

"Yes. The Dominos clan is of the sea."

"That's the clan who took you in."

"Our fathers were friends. I asked for their protection and received it when my sisters were about to succumb to the curse."

He fixed his gaze on the Helios crest, the symbol of his family, his home, everything he'd tried so hard to defend. "We need the Dominos now as well. There aren't enough of us left. Of course, in return, I'm pledged to aid them in any way they need."

I didn't like the sound of that. "Hopefully, it won't be anytime soon."

"It won't." He stood directly in front of me, his expression earnest. "This time, I promise, Lizzie. I'll do everything in my power to make sure the next few weeks are just about us."

He ran his thumb along my lower lip, and I was about to reach up and kiss him when Pirate dashed in from the side hall. His claws clattered across the floor as he rounded a potted fig tree, slid five feet and ran straight into my left leg.

"Have you seen a cat? Medium build? Beady eyes? Smart mouth?"

"I think Dimitri would have warned us if you had to worry about a cat," I said, reaching for my dog as he danced out of my grip.

Pirate tended to have an active imagination. Pair it with his ability to see ghosts, and well . . . Who knew what he'd been chasing?

Dimitri scanned the corners of the entryway. "Actually, one of our guests . . . has a cat," he said, with a reluctance that worried me. "I'm not sure if she brought it with her. Frankly, I thought she'd be gone by the time we arrived."

Pirate circled twice before sitting. "Ornery gal?" he asked, his tail thwomping the floor, "Likes to talk tough?"

"Are we talking about the cat or the guest?" I asked.

"We'll find out soon enough," Dimitri said. "Come with me."

We walked through the back hallway and into a dining room the size of the entire first floor of my condo back home. Arched ceilings and doorways gave it a majestic feel. A sturdy, highly glossed table stood in the middle of the room.

The honey gold wood shone in the evening sunlight

and maintained the aura of polished elegance, despite the take-out bags littering the far end.

"Christolo extends his apologies," Dimitri said. "While he held up admirably during the events of this afternoon, our dinner did not fare as well."

A long-faced Greek man unloaded the food.

Next to him, a beautiful olive-skinned woman watched us enter the room. She wore a white pleated dress that was both stylish and traditional at the same time, like a modern version of the old goddesses.

My griffin paused in the doorway, and I didn't think it had anything to do with the Papagalos Restaurant bags or the smell of braised lamb shanks and rosemary.

The woman wore a wry expression as she lifted her wineglass to us in a silent toast before touching it to her lips.

Dimitri stiffened. "Amara."

The tension between them was palpable, and I didn't miss the way she tilted her head, exposing her long neck as she eased her wavy black hair from her shoulders. "Hello, Dimitri." Her crisp Greek accent gave her words a heady feel. "I've been looking forward to seeing you."

She strolled toward us like a model on a catwalk, glass in hand. "You must be Lizzie," she said, offering her hand.

I took it, ignoring the way she pursed her lips.

"See?" she said, turning to the man who unloaded the bags. "I can shake hands like an American. Heaven knows she can't greet us like a griffin."

I forced myself to smile. "Want me to greet you like a demon slayer?" She was just asking for a switch star up the rear.

"Charming as usual, Amara," Dimitri said tightly.

"Lizzie, I'd also like you to meet Amara's brother, Talos."

Talos gave a quick nod, his eyes coolly assessing me.

"They've been helping my sisters with their recovery," Dimitri explained. "Speaking of those two—"

"We stopped down to the cellar for an extra bottle of wine," Dyonne said, breezing past us and plunking a bottle of red Mavrotragano onto the table.

At least the food was good. Dyonne had ordered lamb shanks with orzo pasta and all of the fixings.

I dug a fork through a wedge of fried haloumi cheese, wondering how long Amara would be staying and trying my darndest not to look at her. It was tough, considering Dimitri had positioned himself at the head of the table, I sat to his right and Amara had inserted herself to his left. Diana and Dyonne lined up on the other side of me, and Talos took the same position on the other side of the table, like opposing armies.

"You going to stab her with a fork?" Diana whispered in my ear.

"What?" I looked down and discovered I'd basically drawn, quartered and gutted my cheese.

Amara, for her part, launched into yet another story of one of the baths she and Dimitri had taken together as children. "We're both royal griffins, you see," she said, pursing her glossed lips, "so it made sense for our parents to bring us together."

Dimitri looked as disturbed as I felt. And how did she keep her lip gloss on during a meal?

I started in on a new piece of cheese as Dimitri wiped his mouth with his napkin. "Amara, I don't think we need to hear any more about the past. It's been over for a long time," he said, looking at me while talking to her.

Lovely. It was as if both of them were talking to me and I had no idea what to say back.

Amara winked at me as if I were in on the joke. "Of course past is past." She stabbed a grape with her fork. "I mean, yes they wanted us to get married. But nothing was final. We were not officially engaged until two years ago. When we both agreed to it."

I flicked the cheese straight into Talos's lap.

Dimitri was engaged?

Shock rocketed through me. Dimitri—my Dimitri—had been engaged to *her*?

I schooled my expression, unwilling to let Amara get the best of me. It was what she wanted, and darned if I'd give her the satisfaction. At least nobody but Talos seemed to have noticed my flying haloumi. He looked as embarrassed as I felt as he wrapped it in his napkin and scooted it down the table.

I realized I was bending my fork, dropped it on the table and reached for my wineglass.

Dimitri, his ears red and his mouth grim, looked primed and ready to do a little fork origami of his own. "It was long ago, Amara. Hardly worth discussing now."

Talos cleared his throat. "Not that long."

"Two years," Diana insisted.

"You were both very ill." Amara lobbed a patronizing smile at Diana. "We couldn't begin to think of our own happiness. It wasn't the right time."

"Or the right situation," Dimitri fumed.

"He means person," Dyonne volunteered.

"Dyonne," Dimitri warned.

"I'm just saying," she said, elbowing Diana, who knocked into me.

"Oh, how dare you?" Amara asked in mock offense. "And after I hear your little demon slayer needs my help."

The table grew silent. I was tempted, so tempted to tell her I didn't need her, that I'd never accept help from someone like her. But I didn't.

No matter how much she taunted me or smirked. Despite the insinuations or the attitude, I'm a demon slayer and sometimes my life wasn't pretty. In fact, it could be downright disturbing. I didn't have the luxury to pick and choose who came to my aid. She could plant a stripper pole in the middle of the table and start gyrating and I still wouldn't back down and refuse the help I needed.

I would choose to take the high road when it came to griffins like Amara. Better yet, I could hope the low road would lead her straight over a cliff.

I ignored the way she leaned over the table so that her boobs practically fell out of her dress. "I understand you're psychic," I said to her.

She treated me to a smirk. "I've been known to sense things from time to time."

Okay. I'd play. "You knew to get out of the house before the imps came calling today."

Her eyes held mine. "Sometimes, I can see things coming. Today smelled like sulfur and demons."

Dyonne huffed. "A warning would have been nice."

"It could have been anything," she said with the shrug of a well-sculpted shoulder, going back to her meal. "Migrating harpies or a lost manticore. One of the furies might have gotten out again. ASPCC usually has a handle on it."

Diana nudged me. "The All-Species for the Prevention of Cruelty to Creatures."

"Gotcha," I said, but it was time to cut to the chase. "Can you help us retrieve the contents of Dimitri's light box?" I asked. "You're aware the magic he used to trace me has been stolen."

She raised her chin. "I was told." She glanced at Dimitri. "And, yes, I will see what I can do."

"But will you really help?" Dyonne interjected.

"Yes," Dimitri answered, "she will. Because Amara knows that if my magic falls into the wrong hands, it will hurt me too." He leveled a warning glance that none of us missed.

Amara flushed. "While I can't say I approve of your . . . choice of lifestyle, I am bound by the pact our families made to protect each other. And, besides," she said, the guile lifting from her face, "I'd never let anything happen to you, Dimitri. You have to know that."

Dimitri studied her and we all watched as something passed between them. "I know, Mara."

A dull thud formed in the center of my back.

Mara? So now it was Mara?

She gave a small smile. "Then let me begin right away." She lowered her fork. No wonder the woman was skinny. She hadn't eaten more than two grapes.

"It will take a few minutes to prepare," Amara said as she slid away from the table. "You finish your dinners." She eased behind Dimitri, her hand barely grazing his shoulder. "I'll meet you in the gardens in half an hour. And Lizzie," she said, curling a perfectly manicured finger in my direction, "I need you to come with me."

Chapter Seven

She led me out the back door of the house and onto a large patio covered by a redwood pergola. Yellow and white roses scented the air and tangled over the latticed timbers. Cotton panels billowed in the cooling evening breeze. In the distance, past the gardens, I could see vineyards stretching up the base of a large hill.

It was like stepping out onto a page of *Better Homes & Gardens*, the kind of spread that looked amazing, but still you wondered if anybody really lived like that.

Amara turned to me, lips pursed, and ruined the image. "Before we go any farther, I want to get one thing straight."

I braced myself. "Shoot."

"I'm not doing this for you."

I studied her for a second, the crease in her forehead, the spit in her eye. "I figured that part out." I didn't need her affection, just her talent.

Too bad for Amara, she couldn't come to Dimitri's rescue without helping me too. It was clear from the way her face twisted how much she despised the situation. The wind blew her wavy black hair around her shoulders, yanking at a single silver feather she'd attached behind her ear with a beaded clip.

"Come on," I said, noticing the shadows growing long over the garden. "It's getting late." I didn't relish the idea of being outside in the dark with only the ice queen for company. The quicker we had our part done, the sooner the others could join us.

I made it down the steps and halfway to the garden before I realized she wasn't following. I stopped and turned. "Amara?"

She stood at the top of the steps, the edges of her mouth turned up into a hard smile. "Dimitri and I were promised at birth."

Oh geez Louise. "You might want to tell him that."

"I understand he's been sidetracked. It takes an amazing man to do what he did for his sisters." Her voice grew husky with pride. "And to succeed! To break a centuries-old curse."

If she started crying, I was going to shove that feather up her nose. I knew exactly what Dimitri had done. "I was there."

She looked at me like I was some kind of puppy that had followed Dimitri home. "Now he's with you because of some kind of displaced loyalty." She braced her hand on a porch support, thick with climbing vines. "You don't belong here, Lizzie. Look at this place," she said, plucking a yellow rose petal and rubbing it with her fingers. "This is his home. My home. Dimitri and I are of the same people. Surely you can see that."

Maybe, if I were as delusional as Amara.

"Oh come on," I said. The wind blew my hair into my eyes. I pulled it away and tucked it behind my ears. "Aren't there any other nice griffins for you to date?" I asked, taking two steps back toward the porch. "You're cute. You come from a good . . . clan," I said, revising the rah-rah speech I'd given my single friends over the years. "It's time for you to move on."

She practically snarled. "You may have helped him get those pain-in-the-ass sisters back"—she closed the distance between us, her chin quivering—"but now you've outlived your usefulness."

"Pain in the ass?" Interesting. They didn't look like bosom buddies in there, but I hadn't realized the venom ran so deep. I wondered if Dyonne and Diana knew.

Amara towered a step above, looming like a spectre of Valentines past. "Dimitri doesn't owe you his life, and I won't have him giving up his pure-blood future on a whim."

Ah, so she hadn't sensed the change in him, that I'd given him part of my demon slayer essence to save his life. We still didn't know all of the ramifications from that particular move.

She leaned closer, her eyes cold. I felt her breath on my cheek, like she expected me to back away. Little did she know, I was used to hanging out with biker witches named Ant Eater and Crazy Frieda.

I sighed. If we hadn't needed Amara, I'd have told her where to go. But since we didn't have time to be standing around debating . . .

"Can we just do what we came out here to do?"

She stared at me, her face smooth, beautiful and uncomfortably close. I blinked, waiting. "Every minute you stand here is another minute you get to spend with me."

That did it. She lifted her chin. "Fine. Follow me."

Peonies and night-blossoming jasmine lined the wide garden path. We passed small ponds with big, fat fish.

Up to our right, I could see a life-size statue of a naked man, turned to display an amazing backside. His bronze muscles stretched tight as he opened his arms to the sky. On top of his head, a stained-glass crown of orange and red caught the setting sun.

"That's Helios," Amara said, as if she knew where my eyes had gone. "Ancient god of the sun." She paused and bowed her head slightly, giving the statue more respect than she'd shown me, Diana and Dyonne combined. Helios was the namesake of Dimitri's clan, not hers.

I gave the statue another look. "Nice butt." Although my own Helios man had a better one.

"Helios married a minor water goddess," Amara said, with a superior toss of her hair.

She had to get that in there.

I'd have admired her persistence if it didn't make me want to tip her into a nearby pond.

When is she leaving again?

Biting my lip, I fought back a whole string of Southern comebacks. I was raised better. Besides, I had bigger things to worry about—like the part of me that had gone missing.

I plucked a fat leaf off the next bush we passed. It snapped thick and sticky under my fingers as I shredded it. Of course, the sooner we could get on with the ceremony and hustle Amara out of here, the better.

"Are we almost there?" I asked, my sandals crunching on the rock path.

Amara hummed, clearly in her own little world.

After a few more minutes of walking, she said, "Dimitri's late father gifted me with my own meditation area in the main gazebo," Amara said. "In time, I'd like to have it expanded and perhaps even have it enclosed. It would make a wonderful three-season room."

I ignored her. And for a second, I almost felt sorry for her. It would be horrible to plan your life around somebody who didn't feel the same.

We made our way past the last of the rosebushes and into a clearing where four paths converged around a gorgeous stone pavilion. It reminded me of a small, round version of a Greek temple. A series of white stone steps led to entrances on four sides. And at each point, sky blue pillars supported a high, domed ceiling.

"It's beautiful," I said.

She nodded, opening a small outlet cover at the base and flipping switches until tiny white lights illuminated the structure inside and out. It gave it an otherworldly glow that made the growing dusk seem even darker. I straightened and looked out at the growing shadows of the garden. The insects seemed louder, the air heavier.

"Come." Amara smoothed her dress and ascended the stairs as if they were altar steps.

The painted frescoes on the inside resembled a clear blue sky, with streaks of sun darting from the blaze of heat in the center. It was as if the Helios clan watched over this very spot. As we neared the top of the stairs, I saw painted waves cresting over the polished stone floor.

"It's a potent place for me," Amara said.

"Is it magical?" I asked.

"Only to me. As you know, memories hold power."

She leaned back against a pillar and closed her eyes. "This is where Dimitri kissed me for the first time."

I couldn't help it. I had to look away. I willed my stomach to unclench as I took the last few stairs with my eyes on my feet. My joints stiffened, but I kept going. I didn't even want to imagine those two together. In fact, she needed to pack up and leave as soon as this ceremony was over.

"So what exactly are we going to do here?" I asked, making my way away from her and the pillar. A large stone table looked as though it was permanently affixed at the midpoint of the circle. Stone dolphins frolicked at the base.

She opened her eyes slowly. "I'm going to perform a ceremony that will link me to both you and Dimitri."

Apprehension snaked through my body. "Linked? How so?"

She seemed lost in thought. "Think of it as a psychic tie. When I'm tuned into both you and Dimitri, I'll be able to sense exactly what he took from you."

Amazing. Creepy, yet—I had to admit—exactly what we needed.

I ran my hand along the cool stone of the table. This woman could sense a part of me I couldn't even feel. She may not have had couth, but she had talent. And if Dimitri trusted her, I had no choice but to do the same.

Amara leaned against the pillar and stared out into the garden. "His magic will feel like him," she said, with a little too much relish for my taste. "I'll know it instantly. Once I get a handle on his protective magic—and the part of you it holds—we can trace the individual who has stolen it."

"Kind of like following psychic bread crumbs," I said.

She gave me a withering look. "You Americans are so crass."

"But am I right?"

"Yes, that's an accurate enough way of describing what you can't hope to understand."

I leaned against the table, arms crossed. "I'm going to be so glad when you're gone."

"Likewise," she said. "Now if you will be seated." Amara moved to a small armoire on the far end and unlocked it. "We'll prepare."

The coolness of the stone bench seeped through me as Amara placed several objects on the table. A small painted urn, an assortment of shells and—

"A bronze knife?"

"You are familiar with griffin magic?" she asked. "Wait. Don't answer that."

She filled seven crystal bowls with clear water and arranged them in a circle. Smirking, she placed an eighth bowl in front of me. This one was metal and banged up a bit. Next to it, she placed the longest, sharpest pair of scissors I'd ever seen. And for the crowning glory? A razor.

"You'll have to use soap," she said, turning back to her supply closet. "I don't keep shaving cream out here."

Dread swelled in my stomach. "Exactly what am I shaving?"

She turned to me, positively radiant. "Why, your head of course."

I about tipped over sideways. "Oh no."

"And your arms and your legs if you have any stubble," she said, wrinkling her nose as if I were some kind of scraggly thing. "I need you completely hair free."

I didn't get it. "How does *hair* get in the way of magic?"

Granted, I'd only seen magic through the eyes of Grandma and the Red Skull witches. They were hairy. They also did a lot of strange things with ingredients I didn't want to keep in my backyard, much less in a spell cabinet. But the Red Skulls had one big thing going for them—deep down, I knew without a doubt they cared about me. Amara would just as soon throw me under a bus.

"I'm not doing it," I told her. Not without a lot more explanation.

Her eyes widened. "We have to do it. For Dimitri."

There had been one other time where I'd refused to do something during a magical ceremony. That had come back to bite me. Hard. But that was a long time ago, at least in terms of my demon slayer training. Things had changed. I'd changed. I was no longer on the outside of the magical world, looking in. I'd been to hell and back. Twice. I'd honed my skills and my natural feelings, and right now my instincts were telling me *no.*

"I knew it," she said. "I knew you didn't really love him!" I saw the fear in her eyes but something else I couldn't quite put my finger on.

It put me right into teacher mode. Eight years of dealing with preschoolers will teach you a thing or two about when somebody is fudging.

And how to flip it right back on them.

I dug into the pocket of my sundress and pulled out my cell phone.

"Who are you calling?" she demanded.

"The Red Skulls," I said calmly, hoping Amara didn't know my phone was not international. Heck, after the long flight here, I doubted it was even charged. "My grandmother is a powerful witch. I'd like to get a second opinion."

Amara pursed her lips as I dialed.

"Of course, if you're lying," I added, doing my best to act unconcerned, "I know a couple of sisters who wouldn't mind holding you down while I shaved *your* head."

Okay, that was pushing it, but I had a hunch Diana and Dyonne would back me up.

Amara seemed to feel the same way. "Fine," she hissed. "No shaving." Color dotted her cheeks. "I need a snippet of your hair and your name on a piece of paper."

"Sounds reasonable," I said, flipping my phone closed. I needed a trim anyway.

"Do it now," she said, shoving the scissors at me. "It needs to soak for at least a half hour."

I drew my black hair over my shoulder, noting some split ends. It's not like I'd had time for a proper trim since I became a demon slayer. Saving the world had come first.

When I'd snipped away at least some of my split ends, I sprinkled them into each of the seven bowls.

Amara followed me, plunking royal blue stones into each dish. I could feel her watching me. When we were finished, she handed me a crystal fountain pen.

"He needs me," she said, almost under her breath.

I eyed her as I scratched out my name on a section of thick parchment. "Look, as much as I'd like to debate with you about my relationship, the fact of the matter is that I love Dimitri and he loves me." I handed her the paper.

She began shaking her head slowly, but I forged on. "I can understand your not wanting to be around us, and that's fine. I'm glad you stayed and I'm very glad you can help us with the missing magic. After that, you're going to have to let go."

"I'm not helping you, Lizzie," she said slowly, folding the parchment into teeny tiny pieces. "You are a side effect. I'm helping Dimitri. I love Dimitri. As misguided as he is, I wouldn't be able to bear it if something happened to him—especially because of you." She pinched the paper tight. "Retrieving the magic he used to find you will be the last step in his mission to save his annoying sisters. I'm honored to have a part in this final chapter," she said, eyes blazing. "Years from now, he's going to love me for it."

I didn't bother responding. It wouldn't matter to her, and besides, I could see Dimitri walking out of the darkness of the garden.

Amara smoothed her dress. "Please," she said, motioning to the table.

I sat facing Amara, and Dimitri slid onto the seat next to me, his thigh coming to rest against mine. "Where are your sisters?" I asked. Or for that matter, Amara's brother.

"They're back at the house," he said. "Unlike your family's magic, which seems to thrive on chaos, our clan works best when we focus our energies."

I nodded. It made sense. Yet as I looked out into the blackness of the gardens, I couldn't help feeling a little exposed.

When my hair had soaked in the bowls and Amara had sung a lilting melody in Greek, we were finally ready.

"Quiet now." She stood opposite us and held her hands over the table. "I call to my spirit guides. To Maia. To Aethra. I call to those who can see the yet unseen." A soft wind scattered her hair about her face as she closed her eyes, transfixed. The water in the bowls began to bubble softly.

Dimitri took my hand under the table. His warm, steady grip reassured me. Everything would be all right. It had to be.

"I call to you to trace what is untraceable." Her eyes flicked open. "Dimitri, I need you over here, please."

Dimitri untangled his hand from mine. I immediately felt the chill as he rose and went to her, his white shirt blowing against his muscular chest from a wind I certainly couldn't detect on my side of the table. Amara planted her hands on his chest and sucked in a breath of pleasure.

It had better be the magic talking.

"It isn't enough," she murmured, fingers splayed, leaning into him. "I need skin-to-skin contact." She slid her hands to the top of his shirt and flicked open the top button, then the one below that, and the one below that. She bared his chest like a starving woman after crumbs. Dimitri pushed her hands away and finished unbuttoning himself.

He shrugged out of the shirt and tossed it onto the floor.

"Perfect," Amara murmured, moving in, close enough to kiss, drawing her fingers across his wide shoulder.

"Can't you just hold his hand?" I muttered under my breath, realizing I wouldn't like that very much either.

A muscle in his jaw twitched. "This doesn't mean anything," Dimitri said, his voice hard.

But that's where he was wrong. It meant a lot to Amara. How much, he had no idea.

The water in the bowls bubbled harder.

Her pink tongue touched the corner of her lips as she drew her hands down his dark, muscled chest. "I can feel it," she said, her voice husky. She raked her hands slowly back up. For a moment, I thought she was going to thumb one of his nipples.

I could see she was aroused. I braced my palms on the cold bench, ready to stand, when Amara blew out a slow breath and retreated. The bubbles in the bowls slowed, the strands of my hair churning in lazy circles. Dimitri glanced around him, as if he too sensed it was over.

Amara took Dimitri's hands in hers. "I have good news," she said. "I felt your magic and it is alive and strong and"—color crept up her chest and neck—"intoxicating."

"Where did it lead?" Dimitri asked, breaking the contact.

Hurt flashed across her features before she composed herself once again. "That's the part I don't understand," she said, shaking her head. "It's right here, on your estate."

Dimitri looked as surprised as I felt. "Impossible. Why would anybody steal it and keep it here?"

Amara seemed mildly offended. "I don't know, but I'm certain it's here," she insisted. "It's not in the house, but it's definitely on the grounds. I can't tell you exactly where. I'm a psychic, not a diviner. But I can tell you whoever—or whatever—is holding it feels twisted and dark." She touched him on the arm, worship in her eyes. "I'm so worried about you, sweetheart."

"Okay," I said, rising from the table. "That's enough." I was a good little demon slayer while she played her games, but if we were done with the ceremony, she was done taking liberties.

Surprisingly, she broke contact with Dimitri, a wide smile on her face.

"Let's clean up and get back," he said, shrugging into

his shirt. "If we do have enemies on the grounds, we need to come up with a game plan."

We let Amara handle the bowls. I tried not to trip her while I returned her scissors—and her razor. Dimitri studied the bronze knife. "What was this for?"

Amara hesitated. "If touching didn't work," she said, running her fingers through the air as if she were stroking a lover, "I might have had to cut you."

Naturally, she'd opted for the touching first. I shook my head as I stowed her scissors in their case. Of course touching was better. I had to stop letting her bother me.

Amara joined me, practically thrumming with excitement as she wiped out the bowls with a chamois cloth.

"You're certainly happy," I said.

She turned to me, her eyes bright. "I saw something else."

I tried not to cringe. "What?"

"I'm not leaving. You are."

Chapter Eight

"Emergency meeting," Dimitri announced as we poured into the dining room for the second time that night—the Dominos clan on one side of the long wood table, Dimitri's sisters and I on the other.

Dimitri stood over Amara, his entire body tense. "Are you positive it hasn't left the grounds?"

Amara clenched her small hands into fists on the table across from me, her attention riveted on Dimitri. "I know it doesn't make any sense, but that's what I saw," she said. "I am *not* wrong. The threat to Miss Brown, along with the magic you used to hold it, is still *here*"—her voice cracked—"somewhere."

Why was I more scared than comforted? Despite the coolness of the night, I could feel myself sweat. I couldn't imagine why the thieves hadn't fled to the mainland—or heck, another dimension—unless they needed to be close to me in order to do something terrible. I squashed down a wave of panic.

I took a deep breath and stood. I needed to move, to think. "There has to be another way to find it."

Dyonne glanced at the psychic. "She's done everything she can."

"I know that," I said, thinking, walking just to walk.

I did have to give Amara credit for refusing to do another rub-all-over-Dimitri ritual. I'd actually been the one to offer. If she'd thought she could see more, I'd have been all for it.

But Dimitri's ex had turned me down flat, too frightened for him to even consider what she could get away with.

Amara knotted her hands together on the table in front of her. "There is a terrible threat tied to both of you," she said, her eyes darting from Dimitri to me. "I don't know why your enemies would stay here on the grounds of the villa unless they are forced to do so." She turned to Dimitri. "Are you sure you didn't tie your magic to this place?"

Dimitri plowed a hand through his coal black hair, leaving a wave of tousled locks in its wake. "I didn't need to tie it anywhere. I only needed it to find Lizzie."

His eyes locked with mine and I saw the desperation, the worry, as well as his unspoken apology.

"What about you, Dyonne?" Talos folded his long fingers in front of him. Amara's brother had been so quiet, I'd almost forgotten he was there. Talos seemed reserved, determined, yet the type of person who thought things through, who didn't talk unless it was important.

Worry pricked at me. I could tell from the dread written across his features that Talos was about to bring up something I didn't want to hear.

He swallowed. The tension traveled down his long neck as he gathered his thoughts. "The day after Diana and Dyonne woke up from the curse," he said, choosing each word carefully as he remembered, "after we gave thanks in the garden—"

Dyonne hitched a brow. "After Diana tricked you into climbing the pomegranate tree?"

"Yes," he answered, a blush tinting his cheeks. "Afterward you called to your Skye magic. You thanked the heavens for your safe delivery from evil, and together you made blessings over the house."

"We set up a protective barrier to protect the family from any more demonic surprises," Dyonne said slowly, remembering.

I stopped next to Diana. This could change everything.

Talos lifted a slim finger. "If nothing can get in, maybe nothing can get out either."

Diana clapped a hand over my arm. "By Helios himself, that could be it. We sealed the house. Of course we were thinking of threats from the outside."

Talos held up a palm like a professor making a point. "Now to play devil's advocate, I must point out that the thieves were able to get in."

"And the imps," I said, loath to point it out.

Diana shook her head, unfazed. "But," she said, "what if our spell worked better at keeping things *in* than keeping them out? Everybody knows we're not up to full strength. Talos is helping, but a month ago, we were completely powerless. It's not like everything comes back right away."

Dimitri had stopped pacing. His eyes narrowed, considering it.

"We don't know for sure," I said, not wanting to celebrate too early. Granted, it helped to know our enemies might be trapped. Sort of. It was certainly better than knowing they were waiting to ambush us. But it didn't mean the spell would hold forever—or that they wouldn't discover a way around it. They'd sure figured out how to bypass the security in Dimitri's office.

"So let's find them," I said. "Would we recognize Dimitri's magic if we saw it?"

Amara stood. "I would."

"I would as well," Dimitri said, coming up behind her. "Come," he said, touching her shoulder. "Mara and I will search the grounds."

Mara. I squashed down a thread of jealousy. Now wasn't the time.

"I'm coming with you," I said. "I may be able to lead you to it." My demon slayer instincts had guided me to threats in the past. Of course, those had included poisonous snakes, rabid bats and telemarketers. Still, I was willing to stumble on a hostile badger or a swarm of hornets in order to root out our new enemy.

Amara squinched her nose. "We'd actually be able to cover a lot more ground without you. Unless you've learned to fly in the last five minutes."

"Lizzie can ride with me," Dimitri said, unbuttoning his shirt.

Talos rose from the table. "While you do that, I will work with Diana and Dyonne to concentrate their Skye magic." His eyes widened as Amara slipped her dress from one shoulder.

Oh no. She was *not* going to get naked right here, although no doubt she'd enjoy it.

"You three, go," Diana said. "We can try to get a better hold on things." She winced, apologetic.

She had nothing to be sorry for. It was a wonder she'd woken up at all last month. Nobody expected her to have her powers fully charged. Besides, from the sound of it, she and Dyonne had bought us valuable time.

Dimitri took my hand and we headed for the back porch.

Outside, I spotted Pirate by the rose garden, chasing fireflies.

"Time to head in, little guy," I said. Just in case.

"But I'm busy!" my dog protested. "See that one?" He leapt up, missing the lightning bug by a foot. "And that one? Can't let this one get away."

Dimitri tried a new tactic. "Pirate, I think Christolo needs you in the kitchen. You can help him start a bacon breakfast casserole for tomorrow."

Pirate spun so fast he almost ran smack into a climbing rosebush. "I am on it," he said, dashing past us. "It will be the best breakfast ever."

Sure. Since yesterday's breakfast.

Dimitri winked as he moved past me and down into the garden.

How I loved that man.

Amara nearly tripped over Pirate as she left the house. "Watch it!" she said to my dog, her eyes on Dimitri.

The bodice of her dress pooled at her waist. Her scrap of a white lace bra highlighted more than it hid. I was glad Dimitri hadn't bothered to look back at her. Maybe he already knew what he'd see.

While Amara staged a one-woman show behind us, Dimitri stalked out into the garden. He drew his white shirt off and tossed it over a hedge, his wide back beautiful in the moonlight. While I would have preferred to see his khaki shorts go next, I was thankful he didn't make a move to take them off in front of Miss Exhibitionist.

The shorts ripped at the seams as he shifted in them. His muscles stretched and grew. Brightly colored wings unfolded from his back—red, blue, purple and green, his feathers tipped in gold. It was an immense reminder of the power he held. And as thick lion's fur sprouted along his back and legs, I couldn't help being amazed all over again that I shared a life with the extraordinary man in front of me.

Dimitri bent his massive lion's body low to the ground and I climbed onto his back. He'd allowed me to ride before, but it still gave me a thrill. I loved the feel of his massive back underneath me. His fur was smooth and warm, like a cat's. His back was much too wide to straddle, so I rode with my legs over his shoulders and my fingers twined in the thick fur at his neck.

Amara padded in circles in front of us. Her lion's body shone almost white in the side-porch light, with a silver beak and massive silver and blue wings. She bent her head and called to Dimitri. Her voice sounded like an eagle's screech.

He returned her call, pawing at the ground. I wrapped my fingers around him extra tight. "All set," I said, bracing for takeoff. Griffins were like Ferraris. They could go from zero to two hundred in about five seconds flat.

And to imagine, I used to get woozy on the back of a Harley.

My teeth clacked together as Dimitri bolted skyward. The wind buffeted my face and body, and I tried not to think of the stomach I'd left back on the ground.

When we leveled out, I gave him a quick caress on the neck and readjusted my grip. His massive wings beat in a steady rhythm, sending a gust of air against my calves on each downward stroke.

A full moon shone its watery light on the darkened landscape below. Shadowed trees rose up over uneven ground. Waves pounded the edge of the black cliffs as all kinds of night creatures called out to the heavens.

Lights glowed from the house below as Dimitri and Amara made a wide arc over the front drive and back toward the darkened gardens. I frowned. If there had been something back there, I'd probably have sensed it while I was on the ground. We were limited in what we could see with our eyes—not that it would make much of a difference. Whoever had stolen from us wasn't going to be sitting out in the open.

We'd have to rely on my demon slayer instinct to run toward danger, then count on Amara's psychic abilities once we arrived.

Dimitri's massive wings stroked the night sky with a heavy, rhythmic *whoosh, whoosh.* We flew past the garden, over the hills to the north. I strained my senses, trying to detect anything unusual, anything strong enough to indicate evil.

At the edge of the hillside, where the cliffs dropped into the ocean, I felt a tug and an intense desire to see where it led. This could be it.

I squeezed my knees into the curve of Dimitri's shoulders and pointed toward an outcropping of rocks at the top of the cliffs overlooking the sea.

Amara saw and nodded, leading us straight down.

Dimitri and I dove after her. The wind streaked against my face, and my stomach lurched. Whoa Nelly.

Maybe I wasn't so used to this.

That's the thing you don't notice about birds until you actually fly like one. They dip and weave in the sky and look so graceful doing it. When you're along for the ride, it's a whole different story.

I closed my eyes and said a silent prayer of thanks that it had been a few hours since we'd eaten dinner.

The pull of the rocks grew stronger. Something was down there. I could see the threat like a dot of light in my mind, along with the overwhelming urge to leap off Dimitri's back and belly flop straight for it.

"There," I yelled over the beating of wings, pointing toward a shadowy outcropping of volcanic rock that resembled a claw. It was large, at least five feet across and jagged at the edges. A few scraggly weeds clung to the top before giving way to a precarious drop straight down the sea cliff.

I held my breath and tried not to fidget as Dimitri drew closer. Oh yes. My demon slayer senses clanged in my head. Ever since I'd come into my powers, I was insanely attracted to anything that could chop me in half or send me falling to my death.

This place was perfect.

I wanted to unwind my legs from Dimitri's back and cling to the black rock cliff. Instead I forced myself to take it slow. I reached out and touched the sharp, pockmarked volcanic rock. Power simmered under my fingertips, and I groaned at the pleasure of it. It felt so good and so wrong at the same time.

I licked my lips. "This is it." I could feel the danger lurking underneath the stone.

But how would that piece of me—or our enemies—have found a way inside?

I pushed harder. Whatever lurked there wanted to come out. I could feel it. All I had to do was move a mountain.

The rock bit into my skin.

Dimitri nudged his head underneath my hand. "No," I told him. "Please." I didn't know what could happen to me, much less him. If my powers had led us here, I hoped I could handle what we found. Besides, a griffin might be able to survive a fall to the rocks below. I wouldn't bet on a demon slayer.

Blood trickled down my hand and over my wrist. The stone jiggled and I realized I was only trying to move part of a cliff. The rocks had caved in on something. I focused all my energy on the stone under my hand, willing it to give. It was close. "Almost"—I cringed—"there!"

The rock gave way, plummeting into the ocean below. Inside, a strange piece of marble lay in a tangle of woven straw. The rock itself was pitted, roundish and yellow as an Easter egg.

"Dimitri?" I didn't want to invite trouble, but something had led us to this artifact.

He nodded his mammoth head as I eased my fingers around the rock. When it didn't burn, I slipped it, along with most of the grassy covering, into the pocket of my demon slayer utility belt. Perhaps he could tell me more, once he'd shifted back. At any rate, I wasn't going to risk our find plummeting off the cliff into the ocean.

We continued our sweep of the grounds, flying low

along the cliffs and then out over the shallow waters of the ocean. It would have been hard to detect a boat if they didn't shine their lights, but like I said, we didn't need our eyes as much as our senses. We circled above the house again, then past the lawn and over dark forest beyond. I could feel tinges of danger. Still, I couldn't locate the source.

It was everywhere.

Chapter Nine

You'd think the hardest part of riding a griffin would be launching from zero to three hundred feet in a split second, or holding on during a dive. Nope. It's actually the first few minutes after dismount, when your legs are jelly and your entire body feels like you just stepped off a roller coaster.

It was in this slightly woozy state that I leaned against the wall in Dimitri's foyer and eased the yellow stone out of my utility belt. In the light, it looked like a rough piece of marble. I couldn't even explain what had led us to the collapsed rock face or why I'd felt the need to excavate it.

Dyonne had greeted us at the door. Now she stared at the stone with as much confusion as me.

"It didn't belong there," I told her, although that didn't really explain why I'd decided to keep it.

"It will be trouble for you," Amara said, the corners of her mouth turning upward.

Oh please. "Will you finish getting dressed?" She still hadn't zipped up the side of her dress or found her bra.

Dimitri had gone straight to his quarters for a new pair of shorts. If she thought she could hold out until he returned, she was nuts.

"Let's just get to work in the morning," said Dyonne, as she ushered us toward the stairs. "I don't know if it was the imp attack or the fact that the Skye magic is a bit more than we can handle right now, but"—she shook her head—"I don't know what I'm doing anymore."

I gave her a squeeze on the arm, hoping to reassure her when I didn't quite have the words. I knew what it was like to have something special inside that you didn't quite know how to use. She'd get through it, and so would I.

"You know what?" I said, pausing as a thought grabbed me. "I'll be up in a minute."

They ascended the staircase while I stopped by the library directly off the main foyer. As nice as it was to fly at nausea-inducing speeds over Dimitri's home, I intended to learn something about the history of the place as well. Knowledge is power, and besides, I've always loved research.

Amber wall sconces bathed the library in warm pools of light. Built-in bookcases crowded the circular room, stretching at least two stories high around arched windows. A family crest and a stone memorial were set into the wall, dedicating this as the library of Nikkos Kallinikos, circa 1789.

The room smelled like old books and plaster. I set to work on the shelves to the right of the door, starting at the lowest shelf and working my way up. Then I moved to the bottom of the next shelf and worked my way up. At first, my wobbly legs protested. Soon, I was too wrapped up in the books to notice.

I found comfort in the systematic search. More than that, I didn't want to miss anything important. Most of the books on the first set of shelves had to do with the history of the Greek city-states and early Mycenaean culture. Then middle history, modern history, flora and fauna. I used my pointer finger to skim the thick volumes.

While in another life I could have happily spent a month in here, tonight I had a purpose. I found two black leather history books on a low shelf near the center of the room. One focused strictly on the Kallinikos family, the other on the griffin clans themselves. Fifteen more minutes of searching and I had a history of the house, including maps of the estate.

I smiled as I made a quick search of the rest of the books, just to make sure I had the most important volumes. Sure, Nancy Drew might have sleuthed her way into answers about the house and its past. I believed in taking a more direct approach.

It might not be sexy, but I was nothing if not practical. I hefted the thick volumes into the crook of my arm and made my way to the stairs.

Who knew? The next part of my research might be quite stimulating. After all, I fully intended to involve my griffin boyfriend.

I returned to my room to find Pirate running from the door to the dresser and then back again, his nose to the floor. I stacked my research books on the long dresser to the right and clicked open the crystal buckle on my utility belt. "Pirate, what are you—? Hey!" His cold nose brushed my toes.

"She was here. With that cat. See? Cat hair here and cat smell here and cat hair here." He shoved his head under the dresser. "Mmm . . . crumb. I tell you, I don't like that cat one bit."

Pirate was excitable anyway, but this was like Pirate on Starbucks. His entire body quivered.

"Wait," I said to his stubbly little tail. "Who was here?"

"Ohh . . . Lizzie. Amara and that no-good Isabelle,

although I should call her Fang Breath." He yanked his head out from under the dresser. "Don't you worry because I chased them off, watchdog-style."

"Good." Amara had no business coming in here. Whatever she had to say, she could have said downstairs. She sure didn't seem like the type to hold back. Besides, knocking on the door was one thing. Sneaking in was another.

Pirate cocked his head to the side. "Can I bite her next time?"

"No," I said, not really meaning it.

"She gave you a book," Pirate said, hopping on the bed and leaning to sniff a rich blue journal on my nightstand. "She said it was her mama's and that you needed to see what was inside." He let out a wet doggie sniffle over the leather-bound volume. "Personally, I think the entire thing smells like trouble."

As if we hadn't had enough of it lately.

I took the straw-wrapped stone from my utility belt and placed both it and the belt on the nightstand next to the bed. "Ohh." He paraded straight across my lap, his paws digging into my thighs. Pirate, of course, didn't notice. "Pretty!" he said, inspecting my find.

"Right," I replied, rubbing him on the head. "But no sniffing, chewing or licking. I'm not sure what it is yet."

"Aw, now that's no fun." Pirate lost interest almost immediately. He pawed at the thick white bedspread, curling up at my side as I picked up Amara's gift.

"So this was her mother's," I said to myself. Though it would have been hard for Amara's mother to dislike me as much as her daughter did, I was sure I wouldn't be doing cartwheels at whatever the book had to say.

As I opened the front cover, I realized it was a journal. The title page read, *Predictions of Alana.*

Perfect. Mom was psychic too.

Or at least she thought she was.

I slammed the book shut and scooped up Pirate. "Come on. We're going to have a talk with Amara."

"You take Amara. I'll do a growly-dog number on the cat. I might even throw in a snarly bark. That move is not just for the UPS guy!"

"Pirate," I said, storming out into the hall. "Let me do the talking."

"Now that's no fair. You always get to talk."

Amara answered on the first knock. She wore a silky white nightgown and an amused expression.

"Why were you in my room?" I demanded.

She tilted her head. "To lend you my mother's journal, of course. Have you read it?"

"I've been more concerned with you picking my door lock."

She feigned surprise. "I'm good, but I'm not that good. You left your door open," she said. A white Persian cat yowled at her feet. She scooped it up and stroked it, watching me. "Just read the book. I think you'll find it fascinating."

Pirate's entire body vibrated as he growled.

"Oh please," she said to my dog. "It's a scandal we only have one cat around here. We griffins have an affinity for cats. And birds. Although that can prove troublesome."

"Just stay out of my room," I told her.

I should have returned the book as well. But I didn't. Like I said, I'm not one to refuse a tool.

Pirate and I trudged back to our room and plopped down on the bed to take a better look at Amara's "gift." I'd decide for myself whether the journal proved useful.

The edges of each page were lined in gold. A torn piece of parchment marked a place near the end of the book. I opened it and found an illustration of a gorgeous sunset done in watercolor. Below it on the thick, unlined paper was an entry in flowing black script.

There shall be a woman who comes between what should be and what is. She wears the emerald and her name is on the lips of the beloved. She will be lost at the Callidora, the first time in joy, the second time in death. She will be split in two.

Oh lovely. Another death prediction. My fingers went to Dimitri's emerald at my neck as my gaze fell on the armoire with my mother's training bar locked inside. Let's see, I could either be gutted or chopped in half. Choices, choices . . .

Pirate rubbed his muzzle against my hand. "Oh now, Lizzie, don't be sad. We can get you a different book."

I slipped my fingers behind his ears, rubbing until his back leg began to quiver.

Yeah, well I had a better idea.

I knocked on the door to Dimitri's room.

He opened it wearing a pair of green plaid boxers and nothing else.

The man was temptation in the flesh. Too bad we didn't have time for that right now. I placed the book in his hands. "Take a look at this."

I ignored the way he undressed me with his eyes.

Instead, I scooted past my personal Greek god and flopped down on his bed. He cocked an eyebrow and sat down next to me, book in hand.

Dimitri's room was the same size as mine, with slate gray walls and a cherrywood sleigh bed. The furniture was more masculine, but arranged the same. It was tidy and comfortable. Still, it didn't feel like him.

"This isn't your room," I said, almost to myself.

"No," he murmured, slipping his hand into the book and finding the parchment marker. "I moved to be closer to you and my sisters."

Dimitri angled his head. "What am I looking for?" he asked, opening the book.

I blew out a breath I didn't even know I was holding. "Just read the passage."

His face darkened as he opened the volume. "It's a journal," he said dryly, as if he already knew what it was and wasn't quite ready to admit it to me. He leaned over it, feet planted on the floor, a lock of black hair falling over his forehead. I watched him frown as he read the passage predicting my downfall.

"Chopped in half," I said, in case he hadn't read fast enough.

He ran a finger over the page, contemplating it like an academic. "Split in two," he murmured, focused on the book in front of him.

Oh please. He was far too calm about this. "What's the difference? This is the second death prediction in forty-eight hours." And the next time Grandma asked me to open something of my mother's on the way out of town, I was going to drop her mystical bar straight into checked luggage.

He closed the book with one hand and pointed to me with the volume. "I know where you're going, and you need to stop."

He had to be kidding. "Why? I consider this fair warning."

"No," he said, drawing my hands to my sides. Shoot. I'd been gesturing like an Italian grandmother. Dimitri studied me carefully. "You can do something about a warning," he said. "This is merely fearmongering."

"Merely?"

He leaned close enough to kiss, his chocolate brown eyes fixed on mine. "You are in control."

Had he *read* the passage? "No, I'm not."

I hadn't been in control since my grandma showed up on my doorstep with jelly-jar magic and a demon on her tail. "I haven't survived by being stupid. I've had two warnings. Two. The first one I could put down to my mom's crazy magic. The second one I have to start taking seriously."

His fingers tightened on my arms. "You decide your own destiny, Lizzie. Don't let anyone take that away from you."

Oh, so I was supposed to sit around, ignoring the warnings, pretending I was in charge. Not happening. I was a demon slayer. Besides, what part about being chopped in half did the man not understand?

I shook off his grip and crossed my hands over my chest. He'd better feel like a rotten jerk when I turned up dead in a forest clearing.

"Do you have a limestone building on the estate? Preferably in the middle of the woods?" I asked.

He thumbed through the book, not answering. It didn't

matter, anyway. I could be killed anywhere. Dimitri, on the other hand, was as stubborn as they came. From his rock-hard head down to his size-twelve shoes.

"You're not listening to me," I said.

"You think so?" he asked, clearly frustrated. Well, he could join the club. "Tell me, Lizzie. What else did you have to say?"

"That was it." If he didn't get it by now, he never would.

"So I listened," he said, as if that answered it all.

No he hadn't, or he'd have realized I could be in real trouble here. I didn't know what was coming after me, only that it wanted me in pieces. Heck, I'd seen it with my own eyes, thanks to my mother's crazy bar. Now part of me was missing on the grounds, we couldn't find it and I couldn't get the man who was *supposed* to love me to take it seriously.

I felt so alone.

He placed a warm, strong hand on my leg. "Here's what you need to do about this."

Oh fun. Solutions. "Can you just listen and admit I'm in real trouble here?"

"Do you want to know what to do about it or not?"

I so wanted to say *not*. "Lay it on me, Merlin." Not that I was going to like it.

He slid an arm around my waist. "Trust yourself."

I sighed, refusing to lean against him the way I always did. I wasn't going to give him the satisfaction. "You'd better be glad I don't have my switch stars."

His fingers tightened on my hip. "You're not going to let this go, are you?"

I turned to look at him. "How long have you known me?"

Okay, so it had only been a few months. Still, we'd been through a lot.

Dimitri nodded. "Very well." He released me and stood. "I have something to show you," he said, irony tingeing his voice as he reached into his dresser drawer and pulled out a Maglite. "We're going on a field trip."

I won. A grin tickled my lips. "Let me go get my switch stars."

Dimitri grabbed his jeans.

We made our way through the darkened house to the even darker outside. Dimitri flipped on his light as we descended the thick, white steps at the front of the house. The Mediterranean air blew warm against our faces and the waves pounded the rocks below.

"This way," he said, shining his beam onto a white rock path that wound away from the cliffs toward a break in the trees at the other side of the house.

The white stone soon gave way to the island soil, rocky and strewn with bits of shell and pumice stone. High trees rose on either side of us, their lean trunks built to sway in the harsh coastal winds.

We walked for several minutes, listening to the buzzing of insects and the tree branches swaying in the night. Abruptly, the trees ended, and we stood in a large clearing. Woodland rose up on all four sides and the moon shone down on the ruins of what looked to be an old church.

I stopped cold. I'd been here before.

This was the place from my vision.

Broken stones had tumbled until only the portions of the walls remained. Dark pink flowers and weeds grew from the crushed limestone benches, and trees had begun to invade the walls.

I'd seen the horror that would happen here.

The stones themselves seemed to glow with a light of their own.

Right now, it was a wildly beautiful place, arresting in its simplicity. But I knew.

"This is the clearing I saw," I said, my voice hoarse.

Dimitri ran a hand down my back, lingering at the curve of my hip. "I was afraid of that."

My heart began to pound, readying for battle.

"My family has held this land from the very beginning of time," he said, as if he were talking about the Holy Grail.

"You have to be kidding," I said, still trying to believe I was there, on the very spot I'd seen. Granted, I hadn't caught a lot of detail while I watched myself, my chest torn and bloody, but I knew enough to be very, very scared.

"This is our gathering spot." Dimitri walked toward the ruins and I followed. The moonlight slid over his back as he moved among the rocks. "The Helios clan is tied to the sun and sky," he said, "but we are rooted in the earth of our home as well. This is a sacred place."

I took care on the uneven ground. I could feel the power and the magic. It surrounded us. Important things happened here.

Yet if it was so vital, I couldn't help wondering why it had been abandoned.

As if he knew what I was thinking, Dimitri said, "This was once an exquisite temple. This section here," he said, leading me to a section where stones jutted out, fighting the encroachment of a cluster of bushes, "this was the base of a massive tower with a bronze bell that gleamed in the sun."

He stood looking to the sky. Hundreds of stars shone above us. "I wish I could have seen it."

"You never did?"

"Drawings. Pictures from the past," he said, stepping closer, touching the rocks as if they might fall to pieces in his hands. "This building crumbled as my family did. When the curse came all of those years ago, we lost the ability to maintain our magic. This is not merely stone and plaster, but the heart of our family. With the death of my sisters, it would have collapsed to dust." He paused, deep in thought, and then said almost on a whisper, "Now we have a chance."

I kissed him on the arm.

He turned to me, his lips brushing mine. Dimitri was so strong, so determined.

"You're not going to die, Lizzie." He drew his fingers down my cheek. "You're going to prosper. Here. With me."

I wanted to believe that.

"We have a choice," he said, studying me. "We decide." He stood tall, gazing over his family lands. "Do you believe this place can be beautiful again?" he whispered.

"Yes," I said. This man could do anything.

He pulled away slightly, his hands cradling my chin and cheeks. "Why is it so easy for you to believe in me, and not in yourself?"

Heat snaked up my body. I didn't know. I broke away and almost stumbled against a cool slab of stone that seemed to have weathered the ravages placed upon Dimitri's family. "What is this?" It lay close to the ground. No weeds grew around it. It looked to be a small altar, whiter than the rest, with a carving of a sixteen-point sun etched into the front.

Dimitri crouched next to me. "This is a *domato*, which means home. We dedicate our power here."

"So this is the source of your strength?" Here, in the open?

I wasn't overly familiar with magical families, but that seemed strange even to me.

"No." The sober weight of the word hung between us. "This is a place of sacrifice. It is also a place of great love. For generations, each member of my family has come here to receive their own portion of our Skye magic. These rocks around us," he said, standing in the middle of all of them, "these are Skye stones."

I felt myself frown. The jagged gray rocks littering the ground didn't look anything like the beautiful aquamarine stone Dimitri kept locked in his office. The portion of his mother's Skye stone had appeared as flawless as an uncut jewel. It was a wedge of power and possibility. These were just . . . rocks. Dirty ones.

Dimitri chose a stone and hefted it in his hand. "I should say that these will become Skye stones," he said, placing the rock on the altar. "When a female member of my family reaches the age of six, she comes to this place. In the past, generations of our clan would gather and watch as the Argillos would choose a stone." He paused. "Roughly translated, *argillos* is clay, something to be molded and perfected, turned into something more than it is. You understand?"

"Yes." I nodded.

Satisfied, he continued. "The Argillos chooses a plain stone like the ones you see here." He gestured to the ground and I picked up a stone. It was rough and heavy in my hand, an ordinary piece of rock. "At the altar, the Argillos takes this rough ingredient and imbues it with part of who she is." He wrapped his hands in mine, closing them as best as they would fit around the stone. "She infuses it with her love and power and dedication to her family. It is no longer a mere stone, but a beautiful relic of the power inside each one of us."

I opened my hands. "The rock changes too?" Mine sure hadn't.

"It becomes a Skye stone, clear as cut glass. Almost impossible to break. It is strong and whole like the one who creates it."

"But this place, this altar, almost feels alive. If each stone is connected to one person . . ."

"As I said, this is also a place of sacrifice." He stood for a moment in front of the stone slab, his back to me. "When the curse came to my family, each of the women of my line was stricken down by the demon Vald on the twenty-eighth day after their twenty-eighth birthday. The first, Danae, refused to be taken with what little of her power she had left. She feared the demon would use it to grow stronger. So she came here on her twenty-eighth birthday."

Dimitri bent his head, as if in prayer. "Usually, the stones are used as conductors, a way to focus the magic within. But that day, Danae infused her Skye stone with every bit of her remaining magic. Then she embedded it into the rock of this altar." He brushed his fingers over the softly glowing stone. "The others did the same. Generations of women giving back their strength and their love. This is a very powerful place."

"They gave away their magic." I couldn't imagine choosing to face death completely unarmed.

"They did it for the good of their husbands and their children," Dimitri said quietly.

He turned. "This is where things changed for me. It happened on the day my sisters came to place their magic back into the altar. It would have been the end of our clan—of the two women I loved most in this world. I said no." He took two steps toward me, towering over me. "I had been looking for a slayer. I was close. I couldn't let the last remaining members of my family—my own sisters—die. So I used my protective magic to find you." My stomach churned at the thought as he continued. "I drew out a thread of you in order to determine your location. I had to find you," he rumbled. "You must understand that."

I shook my head. "I know you didn't mean to hurt me."

He gave a sharp laugh. "I don't know if that's true. Lizzie, I—" He looked to the sky. "I didn't know you," he said, almost to himself.

Then to me, his eyes blazing green like they did when he'd lost the veil of nice society, he said, "I didn't set out to hurt you."

I believed him, but I knew it wasn't the whole truth.

He stood, his shoulders rigid, and admitted it. "At that point, I would have done anything, sacrificed anyone to save the last of my family."

The crazy thing was, I understood. Dimitri didn't fight for power or glory, he fought for the people he loved most.

That's how it began. The question was, where did it end?

"And what about now?" I asked.

He shook his head. "Never. I can't believe you even have to ask." He took me in his arms, his touch grazing my cheek. "You know I love you. We *will* find those who stole the link to you. I'd do anything and everything to save you, the same way I saved my sisters."

"I don't need you to save me." Help me, yes. But so far, I was the one who had solved problems for myself.

He studied me, running his hands up my arms, my shoulders, my neck. He traced his fingers along the sensitive spot right behind my ear. I felt the warmth of his touch ease through my veins.

"You are strong, Lizzie," he said, drawing me closer, his lips brushing my forehead. "Believe in that," he whispered against my cheek, his lips tracing across my skin in what was almost a kiss. "I do."

He slipped a hand behind my neck and lowered his mouth to mine.

Mmm . . . the man knew how to take his time. He kissed me slowly. Gently. For all my faults and fears, despite my imperfections and the way I tended to turn his life upside down, this man wanted me. He showed me with every taste, every touch.

He took my mouth, my lower lip, my mouth again with a stark desire that drove slivers of pleasure through me.

I closed my eyes and leaned into him, savoring the heat of his chest, running my hands along the hard lines of his back, embracing this man who had stood alone far too long. I could never get over how large he was, how potent. He was rock-hard steel and strength. He tried to hold it in check, but anyone could see the power thrumming underneath. I ran my hands along his waist, down his thighs.

I could feel how much he wanted me.

He loosened my ponytail, tossing the band into the grass as his fingers wove through my hair, sending a shiver from my scalp to my toes. This man knew me so well.

Knew how to love me.

He kissed me and touched me until my pulse pounded and my blood surged through my veins. I kissed him back with everything I had to give, pushing, demanding, willing him to take it all and then some.

With a moan he wrenched himself away. "Here," he murmured, his voice thick with desire.

Dimitri led me away from the ruined temple into the soft grass beyond.

My body ached for him, and that tiny part of me—the wild child, the bad girl, the one who didn't like things all neat and organized and perfect—sighed with pleasure.

I'd always wanted to make love in a field under the stars. And now, here—with this man—it would be perfect.

"Lizzie." He slipped the strap of my pink sundress off my shoulder, kissing my bare collarbone. Then he eased away the second strap.

He looked up at me, eyes glittering with desire.

"Dimitri—" I barely had time to ease away from a stray stone before he was on top of me, over me. The weight of him pressed me into the soft earth.

He fitted himself to me. We rocked together as his mouth devoured mine. I kissed him with abandon, relishing the pleasure of this man, this moment.

But still I wanted more.

I grazed a hand down his body and found the hard length of him.

He leapt, groaning. "Lizzie," he began, his voice low and husky.

"Hmm?" I whispered as he stilled my hand.

He throbbed with excitement. I could feel it as I touched my tongue to the salt on his neck.

"Wait," he gasped.

He was hard and ready, almost to the edge. I could feel it.

"I'm not a patient woman," I whispered in his ear.

I was near panting and he wanted to take it slow.

"I'm trying to make this last," he said, sounding like he was almost in pain.

"Good luck."

He slid his hands up my calves, massaging them, running the rough pads of his fingers over my breasts, down my stomach, sending shots of pleasure though places I didn't even know could feel that good. He worked his hands up the backs of my legs, over my knees, under my dress and higher still.

I dug my fingers into the curve of his back, urging him on as he slid my underwear aside. I heard myself moan as he swept his hands under my hips and entered me.

He dove into me hard, possessing. His power, his presence, was overwhelming. This place, this man, it seemed as though everything I'd done had led me to this moment.

I reveled in him, matched his pace, wound my legs around his hips and pulled him even deeper, until we came together in the ultimate fusion of body and soul.

Afterward, he held me for a long time as we lay in the soft grass and watched the stars.

"I can't believe we did this," I said, tracing the outline of his chest. "Here."

He chuckled. "I can't think of anything more life affirming."

"Mmm . . . you could call it that." I found myself enjoying the quiet camaraderie. "Magical too."

Dimitri kissed me on the head. "This is a place of old power, a site of great importance that we call the Callidora."

My stomach clenched. Heart pounding, I remembered the prophecy.

She will be lost at the Callidora, the first time in joy, the second time in death.

Chapter Ten

Sweet heavens. I bolted upright. "It's coming true already."

Dimitri leaned back on his elbows, a few stray twigs in his hair giving him the wild-man look. "Haven't you listened to anything I said?"

"Of course I did." I was in control of what happened to me. I could choose where to go, how to act. "And then you said 'Callidora.' "

One word and I was back on a collision course with destiny.

I stood, straightening my dress and brushing the dried grass from my arms and legs. I still ached from where he'd entered me.

Dimitri rose as well, not even bothering to cover himself. "Are you going to believe me or something you read in a dead woman's journal?"

Oh, so Alana was dead too. It didn't seem like people lived too long around here.

"I'm going back to the house." I turned to leave, stumbling over a section of buried ruins and more than one ugly rock/future Skye stone. I didn't even bother with the Maglite as I made my way over the uneven ground. I'd be much safer after I left the Callidora.

A small animal skittered into the underbrush as I found the trail. The air was thick with insect calls and the earthy scent of thick trees and scrub. Dimitri joined me, tugging on his jeans as he caught up. He didn't say anything as we walked. Worse, his belt hung open and he'd left his top two buttons undone.

He held the Maglite near his waist. In the reflected glow, I could see his well-muscled stomach and the narrow strip of hair that trailed from his navel all the way down to the promised land.

Some might have thought it was sexy. And it was. Except the whole situation had me on edge. Well, that and the fact that a part of me wanted to button those pants all the way. Leaving anything half-done drove me a little bonkers.

"Talk to me," he said.

I took a deep breath. "Okay, but no more advice about what I should do. I have to work this out my own way."

He nodded. "Of course." I knew what this was costing him, which made me appreciate the company even more.

I wanted to learn more about the threat against me. Perhaps then I could do something about it. I had a feeling I could gain even more from Alana's journal, if I could only pinpoint how else to use it.

"Was Amara's mother powerful?" I asked.

Rocks crunched under my sandals. Dimitri had taken a keen interest in the path ahead of us. His flashlight bobbed over the trail. "From what I've heard," he said, the words coming slow, "Amara's mother had a gift."

"I see." It made sense. These things were often passed down, and Amara had sure known enough to get out of the way of those imps.

"Lizzie," he said, as if he knew where my mind was going. "A threat has no power. Things have been trying to kill us from the first moment I met you. Remember that mercenary water nymph? What about the angry werewolves? The sex-crazed she-demons?"

"Not to mention the hellhounds."

"And yesterday's imps. We could have died many times over and we didn't."

Okay, he had a point. Still, it was as though all of the pieces were coming together. "What if this is the time they get us?"

"What if it's not?" he demanded.

I shook my head, wishing I could explain. My demon slayer senses might not be going off, but there was a palpable danger around us. I couldn't quite picture what was going to happen next. We didn't have enough information. But I knew it was going to be big—and bad for me.

Dimitri, in true male fashion, wanted everything to be black-and-white. If it hadn't been obvious from the way he walked, shoulders back, head raised, I could just as easily have heard it in the way he ground out each and every word. "I don't believe in prophecies," he said. "I believe in free will." He stepped in front of me and I nearly ran straight into him. He stood looking down at me, a thunderstorm of determination. "If I'd listened to prophecies, my sisters would be dead. They were fated to die and I did something about it."

"You don't believe at all." It was more of a statement than a question.

"The danger in any kind of oracle is when we make it our only possibility. It's not. Our fate is in our hands, Lizzie. Not in someone else's." He took me by the chin. "You of all people should know that."

Frankly, I didn't know what to think. Dimitri *had* changed his family's fate. He'd stood up for his sisters when no one else could, and he'd been willing to go to hell and back to do it. I admired his courage. I was darned glad to have him on my side now, but at least he'd had an enemy to fight. He knew he needed a slayer to defeat Vald, and he'd found me. I, on the other hand, didn't know what I was up against or where the danger would come from.

I was about to tell him when a powerful dread hit me. I reached for my switch stars.

It was coming from directly above us. The black sky shimmered with stars.

I screamed as a searing pain tore through me, forcing me to my knees.

"Lizzie!" Dimitri caught me before my face hit the ground. I dug my fingers into his sides as fire burned me from the inside.

Lightning ripped across the sky, and thunder boomed. I held tight to Dimitri, fighting through the pain.

"Theoi!" Dimitri dove sideways with me as lightning struck the ground to our right.

The resounding boom nearly deafened me. I clutched him with everything I had as energy raced down my arms. It hurt to breathe.

"I've got you." Dimitri grated, surrounding me, a rock in the storm. I pressed my cheek against him and gave in to it.

It took everything I had to simply survive.

I don't know how long I held on to him before the horror began to fade. I braced myself against him and pushed my sweat-soaked hair out of my eyes.

"Lizzie?"

I swallowed, trying to find my voice.

"I'm fine," I lied.

Dimitri didn't say anything. He just held me as we watched a pea green vapor leach across the sky. It advanced like an invading army, obliterating everything in its path.

An empty chill bled through me. I couldn't stop shaking.

Dimitri rested his chin on my shoulder. "I'm not going to let anything get you," he said.

I pressed even closer to him. "I think it already has."

We sat that way for heaven knows how long as the sky melted into brownish green sludge. It blocked the stars and the moon, throwing us into an eerie darkness. Worse. Even as I regained some of my strength, I felt something shift inside me.

"They used it," I said, the enormity of it burning in my chest. "They used that piece of me."

Dimitri gripped me tighter. "I know."

I pushed away from him before he could start blaming himself again. We didn't need introspection. We needed action. If only my body would cooperate.

Legs wobbly, I stood and placed a shaking hand on my switch stars.

I had to do *something.*

It was as if I was about to tip over the edge into the abyss and was powerless to stop it. I had to wait, stomach churning, head light. My enemies had struck and there was still no one to fight.

My fingers dug into the switch star at my belt and it took all I had not to fling it into the nearest tree.

Fight me, you miserable cowards. Fight me!

As if in answer to my prayer—or my worst nightmare—my senses zeroed in on the path directly in front of us.

"What is it?" Dimitri asked.

He tried to step in front of me. With more determination than strength, I stood next to him instead.

"Don't know," I whispered, shaking my head. Even when I wasn't trying to recover my strength, my new powers had been somewhat unpredictable in the woods. I tended to home in on angry badgers and bloodthirsty mosquitoes as often as purely evil entities, but this felt like controlled evil.

I took a deep breath, feeling more like myself.

"Let's get it," I said, forcing my legs to work. I didn't like going in weak, but we needed to figure out what had just happened, and our best chance would be to attack when it was fresh.

"What do you see?" Dimitri asked as we took off through the woods.

I couldn't even tell him. But I envisioned it like a dot in my mind. It was malice in the flesh, like nothing I'd ever felt before. And it was off the trail to our right.

"This way," I said, storming through the underbrush. Brush and sticks slashed at my feet and legs.

I could hear Dimitri behind me. He hadn't pulled out the light, and I sure didn't need it. I knew where I was going.

"There!" I pointed to a large evergreen tree to our right, shadowy and almost completely dark.

Dimitri shone the Maglite on the fleeing form of a woman.

"Amara?" I yelled.

"Too short," Dimitri said as we both took off after her.

He was right. Amara stood at least a head taller, and she had long black hair. This dark-haired woman had hers clipped to her shoulders.

Dimitri quickly outpaced me, his light bouncing through the woods and catching the woman. Even as she ran, I felt her rage—like that of a startled beast.

I didn't know what would happen if she turned around. Would she talk? Would she attack?

Would I have to shoot?

She tore through the woods like she was born to it. Dimitri too. His griffin nature made him faster, more agile. I could hold my own thanks to my demon slayer mojo.

But what did she have?

"Lizzie," Dimitri stopped dead. "Do you see her?"

I reached out with my senses, past him, around us.

She was close. "She's—" I nearly screamed when she rushed toward me from the left. I drew a switch star, ready to use it, shocked as anything when she tagged me on the shoulder and ran.

Her touch stopped me cold. I recognized the burning power of it, knew it like a forgotten memento or a memory I couldn't quite place.

And then she was gone.

"I don't feel her anymore," I told Dimitri as he halted at my side.

"What do you mean?" he asked, out of breath.

"She's gone," I said, shocked to the core.

"How is that possible?" he asked.

"I don't know."

Dimitri, bless his heart, didn't ask again. We made a

thorough search of the area and found nothing. When we finally admitted to ourselves that we'd lost her, Dimitri took my hand and led us back to the trail, where we walked in silence.

She couldn't just disappear. No immediate threat had ever dropped off my radar before.

I didn't understand it.

She couldn't go from enraged to benign that quickly. Something had to have happened when she touched me.

Pinpointing that moment of change both comforted me and terrified me.

Whoever that woman was, she'd been using my magic. I knew it in my bones.

I stopped dead. "She's the one who stole that part of me."

Dimitri's features hardened. "We'll find her."

"We'd better." We didn't have a choice.

"Lizzie." Dimitri touched my arm. "Are you sensing anything right now?"

I stopped cold. "No."

"Well, I hear something."

Dimitri tensed for battle. He flicked off the Maglite and reached for the knife at the back of his belt.

The woods rose thick and menacing on both sides of us. There wasn't even anything to duck behind. We stood firm, side by side, welcoming the fight.

I held steady, waiting for my emerald to change, hoping it could give me some indication of what we were about to face. It lay flat against my chest.

A beam of light streaked across the trees in front of us. At least it was human.

I hoped.

The switch star in my hand spun and hummed.

Voices filtered down the path. "Are you going to tell her?" a feminine voice asked.

"No," a male answered. "And you won't either."

We waited with our light off and weapons drawn.

Both flashlights trained on us. At the same time, Dimitri blinded them with his light.

"Hold up!" I yelled.

It was Amara and Talos, squinting against the glare.

My limbs tingled with released tension while my heart pinched with disappointment.

Dimitri lowered his high beam. "What are you two doing out here?"

With the dark-haired thief on the loose. Right after the sky turned green.

Amara slapped a delicate hand to her chest. "Dimitri!" Perspiration dampened her cheeks and hairline, and uncertainty rolled off her in waves. "You scared me to death." She gave a brittle laugh. "We were just checking up on some of the Skye magic your sisters used earlier."

Right.

"You know what that is?" I asked, pointing to the sickeningly green sky.

Talos all but shivered. "Yes, it means someone is working some scary fucking magic against us."

"Would you happen to know who?" Dimitri stepped closer.

Talos shook his head. "No. Isn't that what your demon slayer is supposed to do?"

"While you're doing what?" Sneaking around in the woods. I didn't trust either one of them.

Talos stiffened. "I'm trying to keep this entire place

from crumbling around us. Look, Dimitri. You know your sisters aren't strong right now."

"What's your point?" Dimitri grumbled.

"Talos has been helping them improve," Amara said. "Slowly. But something bad happened tonight while we were out trying to help Lizzie."

Everyone's eyes settled on me.

Talos sighed. "Before tonight, I'd encouraged your sisters to hold back, to let their powers return gradually. Tonight they tried to use the full force of their magic and discovered they're growing weaker instead of stronger."

"Why didn't they come to me with this?" Dimitri demanded.

"They were devastated." Talos ran a hand through his hair. "And quite unreasonable. Why women think they can solve their problems with near hysterics is beyond me."

"We decided to see what we could learn," Amara said, effectively cutting off her brother. "Their magic is indeed weaker than we expected. In fact, we're detecting some irregular pathways in the energy guarding the estate."

That was exactly what we didn't need. "Are you fixing it?" I asked. Those energies were the only thing keeping my stolen magic in this dimension.

Talos winced. "Not exactly. We're of the sea. We can observe Skye magic, but we can't directly influence it."

"We're doing everything we can," Amara said.

But they weren't telling me everything. Eight years of teaching preschool had given me an instinct for the truth. More than that, the clanging in my head hadn't gone away.

"What's in your pocket?" I asked, rubbing at my temples, knowing it wouldn't make a darned bit of difference.

Talos appeared startled. "I don't know what you're talking about." But he'd paused for a fraction of a second too long.

Score one for the demon slayer.

"Show us," Dimitri ordered.

The siblings exchanged glances, and Talos drew out a chunk of Skye stone the size of a billiard ball. It shone in the beam of Dimitri's Maglite with a brilliance and a fire I'd never seen before.

Talos licked his lips. "It's Diana's." He steeled himself under Dimitri's glare. "She doesn't know we have it. Your sisters are going through a crisis of confidence. We promised them we'd do everything in our power to help them."

Dimitri's jaw tightened. "Stealing is helping?"

Talos frowned. "It is not stealing, and yes, we are helping. Tomorrow, we're going to tell them about their failing protective wards. I'd rather not outline the problem without being able to offer a solution, or at least a direction."

His story made sense, but Talos and Amara didn't. I was getting a bad feeling about these two.

"We're not going to work any spells," Amara said, her voice unsteady. She was sweating like she'd run a marathon.

"Why should we believe that?" I asked.

Facts were facts—they'd stolen from the two people they'd sworn to help.

"We can't," Talos stated. "Not with Skye magic. But

this stone is showing us where we need to focus our energies tomorrow." He ran a hand down his narrow chin. "Walk with us."

Okay, I'd bite. Dimitri and I gave each other a quick nod, then accompanied Talos and Amara up the path toward the house. We walked about fifty yards up to a slight bend in the trail. "It's right about here," Talos said, glaring at his open-mouthed sister.

"Go ahead," Dimitri ordered.

I stood to Dimitri's right, a hand on my switch stars, just in case.

Diana's stone glittered with a life of its own as Talos held it at an arm's length in front of him. He took a few steps forward, then one to the side. It took a moment for me to realize he was using it as a homing beacon. It led him to the edge of a group of bushes. As he stood near, the Skye stone began to hum.

Talos raised his eyes to the heavens. "Can you see it?"

My stomach tightened as I looked up at the churning green sky. "It doesn't look any worse than before." It didn't look any better either.

If the power of Dimitri's clan had been compromised . . . I touched my emerald necklace. A gentle current of magic ebbed and flowed, but it was weak.

Next to me, Dimitri murmured, "Ah yes." He crossed his arms over his chest. "A thinning in the protective barrier."

"Where?" I asked.

"The yellow streaks," Dimitri said.

I didn't see any yellow streaks. "Can we fix it?" I asked.

He let his fingers trail down my back, more for comfort than for anything else. "Dyonne and Diana can."

Amara avoided looking at her brother or us as she reached into a side pocket in her dress and pulled out a folded parchment. "I've made a map of the areas most affected." She spread it out over the ground.

Dimitri shone a light on the map, and I was startled to see exactly how far Dimitri's lands reached. His estate was the size of a large college campus. On this map, his home practically hovered on the eastern cliffs. The gardens stretched to the north and west behind it all the way to the vineyards and the hills. And to the south and southwest, we were in the middle of a much bigger forest than I'd imagined. It had seemed easier to manage when I'd been on the back of a griffin.

"We're here?" I asked, pointing to the portion of the trees closest to the house. The woods took up the entire central portion of the map.

"More like here," Dimitri said, pointing to a red *X* halfway between the ruins and the house.

Heavens to Betsy. We were going to pass under two more weak spots before we made it back.

If Amara and Talos were telling the truth.

Dimitri seemed to see the weaknesses, which made their story more plausible. Still, I couldn't get over the feeling they were in this for reasons of their own.

Amara trailed a polished fingertip over the map. "We haven't surveyed much beyond this immediate area. It's most important to neutralize any threats to the Callidora and, of course, the house."

"Yes," Talos said, folding his arms over his long, thin chest. "We don't want to overload Diana and her sister tomorrow."

Oh sure. Because shoring up their ancestral temple

and childhood home would be quite enough. Sometimes, these magical people needed to think before they talked.

Dimitri stood. "I understand what you're doing, but I don't think my sisters will be very appreciative."

Right on. These were the people they'd trusted to protect them, and look what they'd done. At least Talos had the consideration to look guilty.

Dimitri took an extra moment to study the man in front of him. "Are you in love with Diana?" he asked slowly.

The other griffin's mouth parted slightly. "I hardly see what that has to do with the problem at hand."

Dimitri shook his head. "Fine. Don't answer. But here's a word of advice. If you want to gain Diana's affection, don't keep secrets." He took the stone from Talos. "And don't borrow this again."

I didn't see Dimitri again that night. Instead, I stood at the window of my room holding Pirate, watching the green sky churn.

His heart pitter-pattered against my palm. "This is one time in my life where I'm glad I'm color-blind."

"Me too, buddy." I didn't want Pirate exposed to this any more than he had to be. I rubbed him between the ears. "What do you say we grab a book?"

Pirate always liked to snuggle with me while I read before bed. Of course that usually meant whiling away an hour or three with Paula Deen or the Barefoot Contessa. I loved cookbooks, even if I never made anything. Pirate just liked the pictures.

"Settle in, young squire," I said, inviting Pirate to curl

up next to me as I cracked open the books I'd borrowed from the Helios library.

We needed to focus on something I could control—like facts. Maybe I'd even learn something important, like what to do next.

I understood griffins were loyal. I knew they treasured their history. The symbols of the twelve clans were carved into the sun of Vergina itself. Still, I wondered just how much we should trust the Dominos clan.

Dimitri considered them allies. His late father had been close to the patriarch of the Dominos. According to Greek mythology the sea and the sky shared an affinity.

I couldn't help smiling to myself. Amara thought she was talking down to me when she said I was an outsider. Here, it could be an advantage. I had to think it allowed me to see things from a fresh perspective.

The three books weighed a ton as I moved them from the long dresser to the table next to my bed and sank in next to Pirate, who promptly rolled onto his back.

The dog knew what he was doing, because my right hand immediately came into contact with his soft tummy fur.

Absently, I began stroking.

"Oh yeah." He arched into my hand. "That's the ticket."

I opened the volume of family history in my lap and began reading. The villa was older than I thought.

The original building had consisted of the library itself, which had been the study of Sir Nikkos Kallinikos. Eighteenth-century diplomats and statesmen—some of them even human—visited him there.

In the century that followed, Dimitri's great-grandfather

Adelphos built the villa around the library, preferring to have his clan even closer. When the villa was complete, he moved the family and many of their artifacts, including the solid wood banister, from the original house. A pair of antique griffin heads, hand-carved by Nikkos himself, snarled at the ends.

I also learned that Amara had been in the Helios library.

The second book I opened, a large red volume with Greek lettering etched in gold, contained extensive maps of the estate, including one identical to Amara's—minus her work on the strength of the protective shields. I had to give her points for research and accuracy, even if I didn't like the idea of her rifling through Dimitri's things.

Pirate let out a loud doggie yawn. "You know I could go for some popcorn right about now."

"Pirate," I warned, turning the page.

"Crunchy. Slathered in butter, with just enough salt to make you think you've died and gone to heaven."

"Pirate." I'd probably gained five pounds since my dog learned how to talk. He had a habit of talking me into snacks I wouldn't have even considered before.

"I don't think they have popcorn downstairs," I said. Besides, I wasn't about to go snooping in Dimitri's kitchen. His library was quite enough.

But Pirate was on a roll. He pawed the bed next to me. "I'll bet they have crusty bread. Fresh from the oven."

"No."

"Cheetos?"

"No." I reached for the last book.

He tilted his head. "What are you doing, anyway?"

"I'm trying to learn more about the griffin clans," I said, cracking open the worn volume.

"Ahh." He sniffed the pages.

I began reading, very much aware of my doggie watching me.

"You know, you could just ask Dimitri," he said.

"I could." And I had. "I'm looking for the kinds of things he might not think to tell me"—or that he would refuse to tell me so that I didn't worry.

Well, I liked to worry.

It made me feel safer.

"Like look at this," I said, after a few more minutes of reading.

I directed Pirate to a foldout page where some of the family trees intersected. "They know each other. They work with each other. And at first glance, they seem to be one big happy family."

"Well that's nice," he said.

"Is it?" I asked. "Take a look at how the lines cross. A female griffin can marry into another clan, but it's a single crossing-over. And then she seems to be almost absorbed by her new people."

"Well, you know," he said, curling up next to me. "You get busy. You forget to call. It's hard to write. You lose your pen."

Yeah, well I had a feeling it was more than that. "And listen to this." I read some of the entries to Pirate.

Cronos the Conqueror.

Patrikios the Heartless.

"These read like the histories of the Scottish clans."

"Ohh . . . I liked *Braveheart*."

Television and popcorn. I had to get my dog on a better routine.

"What I mean is that while griffins are intensely loyal, they seem to focus that loyalty on their own clans."

"So they're no good at sharing?" Pirate asked.

"Or coming together."

"But those Dominos people are friends, even if they did bring along a cat."

"Oh I know that." And if Amara had her way, she'd be a lot more than friends. "Dimitri seems to trust them. And they did pledge themselves to protect this place."

I looked up clan oaths. They were rare—and binding.

But I didn't know exactly what they'd pledged. Or what kind of loopholes a two-thousand-year-old griffin clan might be able to uncover.

I did know enough to keep my eyes open.

By morning, the oppressive sky had dissipated. Only a few scattered clouds held tinges of pea green sludge. I met Dimitri and his sisters at the breakfast table.

"What are we going to do?" I asked, taking a seat next to Dimitri.

"Train," Diana replied.

She made no mention of the borrowed Skye stone, and after a warning glance from Dimitri, I didn't bring it up either.

Pirate danced in circles around Christolo as the portly Greek served up an amazing-looking bacon breakfast casserole. "Don't look so glum, Lizzie. We have bacon!"

"One small slice," I said, right before Pirate helped himself to a portion the size of his head.

Dimitri hadn't taken his eyes off his sisters. "Be careful."

Diana rolled her eyes. "You see how he talks to me?"

Dimitri's jaw tightened. "If you overdo it, you'll be no good to anyone."

"Yes, yes," Dyonne said with a wave of her fork. "We'll be careful. But we also need to be aggressive. Now is the time." She grew serious. "We saw what happened in the sky last night. And Dimitri told us . . ." Her face fell. "Oh, Lizzie. We will figure this out."

I wasn't tracking. "The green sky had nothing to do with your Skye magic. Whatever was out there last night was pure evil."

"Yes," Diana said. "But if we had full use of our Skye magic, we'd know instantly what's on this estate and what is not."

Hope surged. "So you'd know who—or what—attacked me last night."

I didn't realize how tense I'd been until a little of it eased away. If Dyonne and Diana could actually tell me what was after me—or even what had happened—at least I'd know what I was dealing with. And I wouldn't have to walk outside and wonder if I was about to be attacked at any second.

"Lizzie likes our plan," Diana said to Dimitri.

He didn't seem convinced.

Dyonne nudged me. "He's just worried because he can't watch over us 24-7."

"Talos has agreed to patrol the estate with me," Dimitri said. "After last night, security is even more important."

"I'll help with the Skye magic," I said. "Whatever you need." If they could help lead us to the woman who'd stolen my magic, I'd be crazy not to do everything I could to assist them.

Besides, I was eager to learn more about their Skye magic. It was such a personal form of power, similar to my own abilities. Maybe I could help them harness their energies, or even learn a trick or two myself. The more I understood about what was happening here, the better.

We ate quickly and started off.

Pirate declined to join us.

"I'll just help Christolo finish up here," he said, licking his chops at the leftovers.

Okay, so maybe we'd start back with the Healthy Lite dog chow tomorrow.

The trauma of last night had me wanting to appreciate the little things—like giving Pirate a bit of pleasure, or the sweet kiss I gave Dimitri before we headed out. Because what we had faced—and what we had yet to encounter—scared the bejesus out of me.

I touched a hand to my side, remembering the searing pain of last night. I still felt an aching hollowness inside my chest, as if a small part of me had been ripped away.

"Don't worry Lizzie," Dyonne said, several steps ahead as we cut across the large lawn at the front of the house. "We will grow stronger and we will find that missing part of you. Then you'll be safe. I promise."

"I know," I said, wanting to believe, as we hurried past the tower that housed Dimitri's study.

There was no trace of the imp invaders or the slime they'd unleashed. I had to hand it to Dimitri. Griffins sure could do windows, inside and out.

"One question," I said to the sisters. "When you regain full use of your Skye magic, will you be able to tell us what those creatures were after in Dimitri's study?"

Diana winced, shaking her head. "No. Our magic works

to protect our family and this estate. It doesn't reveal motives behind attacks. However, once we have the house and the grounds fully protected, any cursed imps will be in for a world of hurt."

"Griffin-style," Dyonne added, the twinkle in her eye giving way to sharp pain as she doubled over, clutching at her stomach. "Sorry. Cramp."

Diana rushed to her. "For goodness sake, slow down." She helped Dyonne lean against her and glanced at me. "Our power affects our health," Diana explained, brushing Dyonne's long, spiky hair back and out of her eyes. "When we feel good, the sky is the limit. Literally. When we don't—" Diana struggled to hold on to her sister as Dyonne shook off her grip.

Dyonne's face had gone deathly pale.

"Look, if you're not ready—" I began.

"What? Would you quit?" Dyonne demanded.

Good point.

"Got all I need right here," she said, patting the lump in her pocket. "Let's go."

I kept an eye on Dyonne as we continued across the grass. At the far side of the house, the lawn gave way to a rocky warning track about five feet wide. On the other side, sheer black cliffs dropped down into the dark blue waters of the Aegean Sea. We could hear the waves pounding below.

"We like to work at the edge of the cliffs," Diana said. The wind tangled her dark hair about her face as she drew a line in the rusty soil with her toe. "Oh who am I kidding? We don't like it. I sure don't. But it beats the alternative."

Dyonne gave a wry grin as she looked out at the water,

but I didn't miss the way her hands lingered over her stomach. "The way things have been going, it's better for us to practice our magic over the open sea."

"Let me know if I can do anything to help," I said, wary and more than a little fascinated. They had grown up in a world I never knew existed. Magic portals? No problem. Levitation? All in a day's work. It still blew me away.

I was still getting used to the idea of a ghost who liked to play Scrabble.

Diana drew a gleaming aquamarine stone from her pocket. It was beautiful, radiant. I was heartened to see how the stone responded to Diana's touch.

It hadn't been half as energized when Amara and Talos tried to use it.

"Can I see it?" I asked.

"Sure, Lizzie."

It felt heavy and solid in my hand. And I didn't miss how it lost its radiance the minute it left Diana.

"Show me what you've got," I said, trying to lighten the mood as I returned the stone.

"Okay . . . well, remember, this is basic," Diana said, holding her Skye stone out in front of her. It sparkled in the morning sun. "Talos wants us to weave clouds."

"No kidding." I had to see this.

The sun hung low over the sea, spending sparkling waves across the water.

Diana spread her feet wide, like a volleyball player getting ready to defend. "It's kind of like weaving wards."

"Only clouds won't implode if we weave wrong," added Dyonne.

"Are you going to do a pattern?" I asked, trying to picture a giant loom in the sky.

"We'll start with an *X*," Dyonne said.

"Ready?" Diana asked.

Her sister nodded.

Diana and Dyonne braced themselves, holding their Skye stones in front of them like offerings to the gods.

They were the last of their kind, the two remaining women of the Helios clan. But they were not alone. I could see it in the way they stood, in the murmured words they used to call to their ancestors. It sounded like some form of ancient Greek, the low, thick syllables blending to form a harmony of strength and love for the family they were trying so desperately to protect.

I'd always understood why Dimitri worked so hard to save them. Now I knew why the clan itself had to go on. This place, these people could not disappear. We needed them and their kind, just like we needed the biker witches and other countless magical creatures who wove their love and strength across the world. Only together could we defeat the forces of darkness.

I squeezed my hands into fists and rooted for them. Not just because they could protect us, and not because we desperately needed to know what had happened last night. I wanted to see them succeed because of who they were. Since I'd become a demon slayer, I'd focused so much on the evil that I'd almost forgotten about the good. We had the right—no, the responsibility—to not only survive, but thrive, live, reach our potential.

Together, we could do it.

It was at that moment, when I truly believed in the possibility of total victory, that a blaze of light shone down from the heavens. Diana held her stone aloft and trailed a thin cloud across the sky. Dyonne wove a similar cloud to intercept Diana's. I held my breath and watched the two lines cross.

The clash blinded me. I turned away, pulling my sunglasses down, wrapping my hands around the sides. I saw orange beneath my closed lids and felt the raw heat of it on my back.

The door of the house slammed open. I squinted and saw Amara storm across the lawn, her feet bare.

"Even out the energy!" she hollered. "It's pulsing. Stop the pulsing." She ducked as a particularly bright surge slammed down from the sky. "No. Wait," she said, hands cupping her eyes, running again. "Cut it! Cut it! You're going to get zapped!"

The stones blazed and darkened in the sisters' outstretched hands.

"I got it!" Dyonne hollered, struggling to control the fire in her hands.

"No!" Amara dashed straight past me, standing in front of Dyonne and Diana with her back to the cliffs. "You're stuttering it," she said. "Push it out like a stream. Don't let it pulse. You can do this."

I found myself opening up, willing for them to push through, to own the power that was theirs already.

The sea rose and churned as Amara clenched her body tight, willing the sisters on.

Diana fought as the stone began to flicker rapidly in her hands. With a shriek, she collapsed to the ground.

"Di!" Amara rushed to her.

Dyonne's stone flickered and died. "Diana!" She dropped her stone.

"What's wrong with her?" Dyonne dropped to her knees at next to Diana. "What did it do to her?"

"Let's get her inside." Amara gathered Diana against her. I took the other side, and together we carried her home.

Talos frowned. "The magic was weak and uneven."

"Well, sorry," Diana muttered from under the ice packs piled on her forehead.

Dimitri thought for a moment, worried. "If they're not ready, they're not ready."

Diana cracked her eyes open.

"Um, hello? We're in the room," Dyonne said from her sister's bedside.

"We can do this," Diana said, her voice surprisingly strong given the massive headache she suffered. It had to hurt to open her eyes, much less talk.

"Tomorrow," I said, effectively ending the argument.

Darned if the sisters didn't take me at my word.

The next morning, we marched back out to the training grounds, with Dyonne and Diana in the lead.

"No weaving today," Dimitri announced. "Let's start with something simpler. Just create a cloud or two," he directed them. "Here. Over the cliffs."

I tried to hide my surprise.

Sure. Just create a few clouds. No big whoop.

But I wasn't about to question. This wasn't about me. We were here for Dyonne and Diana.

It had to be intimidating for them to stand in the same place where they'd failed so miserably, but Dimitri's sisters were nothing if not stubborn. I liked that.

Talos joined us as well. He lingered on the edges, apart from the group. Amara stood next to me. For the first time, I didn't mind having her around.

"Your dog is chasing bees, Lizzie," she said, her dark eyes focused on the water.

I glanced over to Pirate, dancing in circles behind us, leaping at the buzzing insects.

"Don't worry. He never catches them."

"I heard that!" Pirate said, before flipping over backward into the grass.

The exercise had begun well enough, with a few wispy clouds gathering over our small party. I resisted the urge to cheer. Dyonne and Diana stood deathly still, arms held out in front of them as they focused everything they had on drawing out the clouds.

"Harness it," Dimitri warned.

Amara stiffened next to me. "You're uneven again. Draw it out."

Diana's stone began to flicker.

Oh no. "Pirate?" I didn't need him exposed if anything went down.

My dog jumped into my arms as the small cloud above us darkened and rumbled.

"Oh Lizzie." Pirate pawed at my arms. "What's going on?"

"Uneven magic." I just hoped Diana didn't get zapped again. Dread swelled in my stomach as the lone cloud spit lightning.

It was too familiar. I searched the sky for green as the isolated storm grew in fury. It roiled the sea deep enough to send fish and other ocean creatures crashing into the rocks below.

"Watch out, turtle!" Pirate yelled.

If only the biker witches were here with us to hurl protection spells. "Yikes," I said. "And there's a marlin."

"No, it's not." Amara frowned, madly weaving a sea spell. Her arms darted above her head as her brows knit and she murmured something in a language I'd never heard.

When the waves calmed, I saw Amara was right.

A real-life mermaid flopped like a caught fish on one of the flat rocks below.

Amara gave one final incantation before dropping her arms to her sides.

The mermaid pulled her red hair out of her face, gave us the finger and dove back into the sea.

"Some thanks," I said.

Amara grinned. "Doesn't matter. I'm just doing my job."

"I'm sorry," Diana called, still trying to calm the winds battering the cliffs. She looked more desperate than she had at the start of the lesson. Tired too.

"Is it too soon?" I asked. Maybe they needed more rest.

Talos shook his head. "This is much easier than what they tried yesterday."

Diana's shoulders dropped.

"Lay off her," I said.

I knew how tough it was to push yourself to the limit, to have someone simply expect you to do something amazing. Yes, we were in trouble if the sisters didn't recover their magic, but this wasn't going to happen overnight.

"Maybe we do need to give them a break," Amara said.

"No," Talos replied, watching them struggle with their stones. "They *must* succeed." He stepped closer. "They are losing power. At this rate, the wards will not hold much longer."

Amara nodded. Then to me, she said, "Don't worry. I'll be here."

The worst thing was, Amara's presence comforted me. She was from this world. She really could help Diana and Dyonne. And for that, I was thankful.

While the days felt normal, at night I could feel the lingering evil. It pressed on the estate like a besieging army, soaking up the energy of the land as it readied the invasion. Dimitri and I searched the grounds twice more, trying to find the woman who had taken my magic. But ever since she'd touched me that night, I couldn't detect even a hint of her. We couldn't let her escape.

Dyonne and Diana worked as hard as they could, but after four straight days, things looked worse instead of better.

I wasn't sure what I could do to change it, but I had to try.

On the evening of the fourth day, I walked to the stables, knowing I'd find Diana there. She visited Zeus every night. He was a Clydesdale, black and completely wild. Well, at least it looked so to me.

Dimitri told me how in years past, Zeus and Diana would race across the estate, her hair trailing behind. She'd laugh and call to him and he'd gallop even harder, like a horse out of Hades. I wished I could have seen it. Ever since Diana had begun training, she had no strength left for anything more than a canter.

It didn't bode well.

At least tonight I'd be able to bring her some happiness. In the chaos of the past few days, I'd forgotten about the very special memento I'd brought for her.

I ducked into the long building, my hand scraping along the wood as I took in the earthy smells of hay and manure.

The evening light filtered softly throughout. A half dozen or so horses moved and made soft noises in their stalls. I could see Diana toward the end, stroking the nose of Zeus, her head bent as she spoke to him in cottony tones.

I almost hated to interrupt as I reached into my pocket and withdrew a small velvet bag.

"Lizzie," she said, nuzzling the horse's muzzle. "I'm glad you came. Would you like to meet Mr. Zeus?"

"Sure," I said, stopping a few feet away.

My adoptive mother had enough equestrian medals to drown an ox, but I hadn't inherited her way with horses.

"Come closer," she said. "He's very friendly."

I studied Zeus, considering it. Despite his size and power, Zeus had the prettiest eyelashes I'd seen on a horse.

"Are you a handsome fellow?" I reached out to touch Zeus's coal black muzzle. He jerked back and so did I.

Maybe I'd just stick to obnoxious Jack Russell terriers.

"Oh Zeus." Diana rubbed him along the snout as he turned his head into her and snuggled her like a cream puff. "He just likes to be dramatic."

Oh my. As if we didn't have enough drama queens. Biker witches, Harleys and now a crazy horse.

But that wasn't the reason I came out to see Diana.

"I have something of yours," I said, tipping the velvet bag. Out slipped an intricately woven hairpin. At its tip, a gold griffin snarled, its orange eyes flashing despite the dusky light in the stable.

Dimitri had given it to me shortly before we faced the

demon who had cursed Diana and Dyonne. But it had always been Diana's.

She gasped. "Lizzie! I thought I'd lost this."

"Dimitri had it," I said. "He gave it to me for safe-keeping."

"My mother had this made for me before she died. There's only one other, and that belongs to Dyonne. My mother said these jewels would remind us of our family and of everything we've worked so hard to achieve."

I watched her slip it into her hair. If possible, the griffin eyes sparked even brighter. "Is it magic?" I asked.

"No," she said, "but it is a most cherished gift."

"It's beautiful. Although I have to say, reminders of your clan and your heritage are all over this place, from the mosaics at the entrance to the family villa to the Helios crest carved into the stable door."

Diana gave a wry grin. "I know." She shook her head, her playfulness dissolving. "It makes it even harder to forget the fact that we're failing."

"It's only been a few days," I said, knowing at the same time that the sisters should have progressed further. They *should* have been gaining strength.

Diana rubbed Zeus, her eyes filling with tears. "I don't know what to do." She shook her head, "I don't know what's wrong."

"Practice," I said softly.

She closed her eyes, forcing the tears back. She brought a hand up to the coral necklace at her throat. "We shouldn't need this much practice. The magic is already in us. The stones just help us draw it out. I don't know what's wrong."

I didn't know what to say.

"Dimitri told me that he brought you to the altar at the Callidora."

"Where the women of your family made the final sacrifice."

"There are generations of power stuck in that altar, and we can't get it out. That's how I feel. I have all of this power in me and I just can't get it out. I don't know what I have to do to unlock it. And every minute I wait, the wards on this estate grow weaker."

I tried to hide my reaction.

"Yes," she said quietly. "I know about the wards. Talos tries to protect us, but I know what's at stake. That's why I let him sneak away with my Skye stone."

"You trust him?" I asked.

"He's sworn to protect this estate and everyone on it. Griffin pledges are unbreakable." She gave a small smile. "Just as I pledged to find my power again."

My heart ached for her. "I understand exactly how you feel." To sense greatness, to know it was within your grasp, and to be unable to make that final move to seize it, to make it your own.

"We'll do it, Diana. We'll get you there."

I didn't know exactly how—for her or for myself. But I knew we had to try.

The three of us hit the training grounds early, while Talos patrolled.

Diana drew a fresh line in the rocky path. "Talos wants us to try something simpler today," she said, regret flashing across her features.

"Oh yeah?" I said, in attempt to lighten the mood. I'd learned time and again how important it is to relax and let instinct take over.

"We're going to summon one cloud and that's it," Dyonne said, dejected as she surveyed a perfect sky.

"Ready?" Dyonne had her stone out. It was wider than Diana's, flatter.

Together, they began drawing patterns in the sky above us. At least I hoped that's what they were doing. I shaded my eyes with my hand and waited for the cloud.

It never came.

"This is none of my business"—I was still trying to figure out my own powers—"but what I do is locate my power like this spark of energy in my mind. I know exactly where it is. Then I aim my whole self on it while I try to do what I need to do."

Dyonne lowered her hands. "What? Like focusing your energy?"

"Exactly."

They spent the rest of the day holding their stones out in front of them, sweat beading their foreheads, desperate for a wisp of a cloud.

But still nothing came.

They worked so hard, and they supported each other. I wished I could do something, anything, to help them.

I tried to act like this was a minor setback, but I was really worried.

Diana and Dyonne should have been growing stronger since Dimitri had saved them. Something was very wrong. I understood their fears. It was killing me to watch them weaken, and I hadn't nursed them for months, seen their struggle from day one.

"I give up." Diana sunk down onto the red soil, the Skye stone tumbling from her hands. "Don't you see?" Tears filled her eyes. "This isn't going to happen."

"It has to happen." And not just because I could lose a part of myself if they failed. "This is what you were meant to do."

"We were meant to die, Lizzie," she said, her fingers digging into the earth.

"But you didn't." I crouched down next to her. "Look at me. This is your destiny. It's not easy and it's not pretty, but this is where you are supposed to be. You can't control the circumstances that brought you here, but you can decide to do your best. Right here. Right now."

Diana swallowed. "Okay."

I didn't know if she believed me or not. Heck, I didn't know what I was doing either. All I knew is that we could not fail.

Chapter Eleven

The earth rumbled as hot flares shot out from the direction of the villa.

I scrambled to my feet. "What the—?"

Diana's eyes widened. "It's the attack alarm. We have to go!"

"To the house!" Dyonne streaked past us and somehow managed to scoop up Pirate on the first try. His stubby legs flailed in midair, still running.

"Who's attacking?" I asked, searching all around as Diana and I ran for the house. I didn't see anything. Of course, that didn't mean something wasn't about to try and eat us alive. After being in the magical world for almost a month, I knew how these things worked.

And it worried me to no end that I'd lost the ability to sense the woman who'd stolen my magic.

I stubbed my toe on a rock as I looked to the sky. At least it was still blue. I almost hoped it was the imps again. It's not that I wanted to face down monsters hurling curses, but it was better than another green sky.

I steeled myself. If somebody felt confident enough to strike, I was willing to bet they had the upper hand.

Yeah, well too bad for them I was used to fighting on the fly.

Talos streaked across the sky from the direction of the

forest. Dimitri soared over the hills beyond the gardens. The griffins dove toward the main villa like giant eagles. As we rounded the corner of the house, I could see Amara out in front, waving her arms over her head. She bent and set off another round of flares. They burst from the mouths of the stone lions flanking the stairs to the porch.

"Quickly!" Amara dashed for us, her white dress plastered to her legs as she ran. "An attack is coming! Get in the house. Arm yourselves and stay down!"

"Already done," I said, one hand on my switch stars as I reached her. "What's coming?" I hadn't seen anything. My radar wasn't going off.

She shook her head, swallowing hard. "I don't know what's after us. But we're about to be invaded." Her eyes bugged out. "Chaos shall rain down!"

Okay, so having a psychic around could be handy—as well as scary.

"When?" Dyonne demanded as Pirate tried to bury himself in the crook of her arm.

"Soon!" Amara urged us toward the stone lions.

"No more fireworks!" Pirate pleaded. He was a brave dog, but everybody has a limit.

Amara took the porch stairs two at a time. The front entrance was stacked with bronze swords and battle-axes. "The wards in the house should protect you," she said, opening the door to the villa. "But grab a weapon anyway."

Good. Backup weapons. I liked how she thought.

"I'll fight," I said, handing Dyonne a sword as she passed.

"No," Amara snapped. "I have it covered." She unhooked her chunky gold necklace and shoved it at me before starting in on the thin gold belt at her waist.

She had to be kidding. "Why? Because you don't want a demon slayer on your side?" I hooked her necklace over the front doorknob. It was time to let go of petty differences and fight the true enemy.

Her eyes blazed at the challenge. "We don't know what's coming. I've fought for this house before." She tossed her gold belt off the porch. "I will always fight for it, even if it seems hopeless."

"Ever faced a demon?"

"Ever fought with a griffin?" She struggled as her side zipper caught on her barely there pink bra.

Oh please. "What does that have to do with anything?"

"We're fast," she said, as if I'd never seen a griffin attack. "We're everywhere when we fight and I'm not about to have you or any other inexperienced yahoo shoot one of us in the back."

"For Pete's sake, if chaos is going to rain down from the sky, you flying lions needed all the help you can get."

The side of her mouth quirked. "Flying lions?" That's when Amara the arrogant Greek actually smiled at me. "You don't know anything, Lizzie."

"I'm not the one stripping on the front porch."

She groaned as she pulled a bronze sword from her scabbard. "Here, use this. It's the lightest one I have."

"I'll stick with these," I said, patting the switch stars at my belt.

She watched as they began to respond to my touch, spinning and throwing off sparks.

"They're pink."

"So's your bra."

She barked out a laugh. "Yes, well let's hope I don't have to use it as a weapon."

Talos landed hard on the lawn like an immense cat. He folded his wings and crouched in attack mode, watching the road. Dyonne and Diana had retreated into the house. I felt bad for them. But at least they knew their magic, in its present state, would do them no good in a fight. And poor Pirate. At least he'd calm down now that Amara had stopped shooting off flares.

Where was Dimitri? I scanned the sky. It was as if he'd disappeared.

He'd better not be doing anything heroic.

Dimitri liked to strike out in his own. At best it was dangerous, and at worst—well, last month it had almost gotten him killed.

Amara's fingers turned white as she battled with her zipper. She lost her grip. "Gods! I hate women's fashion."

I was about to agree when I heard the most beautiful sound in the world—the symphonic roar of dozens upon dozens of Harley motorcycles.

"Brace yourselves!" Amara abandoned her zipper and went for her bronze sword. "It's the sound from my vision!"

"Grandma!"

"Wait, stop!" Amara grabbed for me as I dashed past her onto the lawn. Talos tried to block me, but I dodged him too.

What was it with these Dominos griffins?

I sprinted down the driveway, well aware the Red Skulls could be driving into an ambush, but I didn't get far. The biker witches rumbled straight for me, a wave of chrome and leather with Grandma in the lead.

They whooped and hollered, and a second before I became a human speed bump, they split and thundered past on both sides, popping wheelies, leaving choking dust in their wake.

Yeah, well we had an emergency here.

But even though I was frustrated, tired and dusty, I couldn't help giving them a big thumbs-up. Hell's bells, I was glad to see them. I needed something I could count on.

The Red Skulls slowed and came to a grinding stop on the road ahead of me, even more rough-and-tumble against the elegant white walls of the villa rising behind them. I could still feel the heat from their engines. A month ago, if you'd told me this motley gang of biker witches would be the one constant in my life, I'd have laughed. Hard.

They looked so out of place in their biker boots and do-rags, a small army of chrome on this country load lined with cypress trees and bathed in tradition. Right now, they were the most beautiful sight in the world. I received at least a dozen high fives and pats on the back as I made my way over to Grandma.

"You don't know how glad I am to see you," I hollered over the engines as she strangled me in a sideways hug. "We're in trouble." In fact, I wasn't sure where to start—with my problems or the fact that the wards on this place could go down any minute.

She slapped a hand glittering with silver rings over her chest. "Of course you're in trouble," she said, her gravelly voice full of humor.

This was no time for jokes. "Grandma, there's something after me."

She tilted up her dusty riding glasses. "No kidding." She held out her arm. "Like my new tattoo?" Red skin puffed at her wrist where she'd had her half brother Phil's name and date of death inscribed. Fairy wings flanked the Old English script.

"Grandma, listen to me."

"I just did. Something is trying to kill you. Join the club." She pulled off her black leather riding gloves. "We got motorcycles." She and the bikers around her let out belly laughs.

"Sure. Fine. I'm glad this is amusing to you. But I've got some dark-haired woman attacking me, stealing from me, supposedly going to kill me, and I don't even know what she is!"

Grandma sobered, but not before I caught a slight eye roll. "Okay, we'll powwow as soon as I get the gang settled." She stuffed her riding gloves into her back pocket. "Oh, and your trainer will be here tomorrow."

"Thank goodness." The sooner I learned how to use all of my powers, the better.

Grandma looked past me and raised an eyebrow. "Well don't he look madder than a boar in a peach orchard."

"What?" I turned to see Dimitri hiking toward us, with a griffin and a frantic Amara in hot pursuit. Dimitri must have shifted back at the house. He was barefoot and buttoning a pair of jeans as he went.

No wonder griffins preferred warm climates. They had a hard time keeping their clothes on. Normally, I wouldn't have minded.

"Don't move, Lizzie! We're coming." Amara kept a tight hold on her sword. "This is a disaster," she wailed.

I walked out to meet them, keeping a choke hold on my control. "This is not a disaster. This is *my* family."

Dimitri stood between the griffins and the bikers, fuming. "Everyone calm down," he ordered.

"They're here!" Pirate dashed past Dimitri, his paws barely touching the ground. "And they brought beef jerky!"

With the road blocked, the bikers began shutting down their rides.

Amara's perfect brows knit as she looked over my shoulder. "Those people are with you?"

"Yes," I said, as if everybody had biker witch relatives.

"Well, they look nice enough," she said, not fooling anybody.

But I had bigger problems than Amara. Half the Red Skulls had killed their engines, and it wasn't because Talos was being a big, bad griffin. The witches were doing it so they could start digging in their saddlebags for who knew what kind of magic spells.

Amara's brother could find himself floating home to Rhodes.

Ant Eater leaned back on her bike, her curly gray hair peeking out from underneath a do-rag covered in glittering red skulls. "Who's the chippie?"

Amara stared at the witches decked out in Harley gear, tank tops and American flags. "Where are you people from?"

A skinny witch in pink leather pants and a leopard-print shirt shrugged and pulled a cigarette out of her cleavage. She held it between two fingers. "We're from that part of the South where sushi's still called bait."

Amara stared as the witch patted her blonde bouffant hair and accepted a light from a Harley-riding fairy who looked a lot like Danny DeVito.

"You're more than welcome here," Dimitri said to the witches. His voice didn't even hold a trace of irony. He was either brave or crazy. "Come, we'll take you back to the house."

The Red Skulls idled up the drive as we walked with them. Pirate was on his back in Sidecar Bob's lap, feasting on Cheetos and beef jerky, undoing about a year's worth of Healthy Lite dog chow.

Grandma cursed under her breath as she shut down her bike on Dimitri's perfect lawn.

"I don't know Lizzie," she said to me under her breath. "I'm not saying we need to be living in high cotton, but I'm not so sure I want to stay here. With him." She nodded over at Dimitri, who was sending Talos out on another mission from the look of it.

Talos shook his large eagle head, but Dimitri was insisting.

I had to admit that these people, this estate, everything here was different from what I was used to as well. But still, we grow, we change.

"We can fit in here," I told Grandma. "Just try. For me."

"Maybe this'll help." She pulled a Smuckers jar from her saddlebag.

The jam inside was long gone, replaced with Grandma's brand of magic. This recycled jar held a swirling green mass and . . .

"Is that a squirrel tail?"

She held the jar up to the light, revealing yellow flecks in the goo. "Let's just say my ultimate Southern cocktail should liven things up a bit."

"No, Grandma," I warned, giving her the stink eye until she sighed and tucked the jar inside a black leather-fringed saddlebag. "I've done a pretty good job fitting in around here and you can too."

"I won't spell him," she said. "Yet," she added under her breath. "But I ain't staying in no namby-pamby villa."

"Yeah." Ant Eater slapped Grandma on the shoulder. "Any place where you can't ride a bike up the stairs—"

"Or have pickled-egg fights," Frieda added.

"Or even let the band practice," Sid the fairy said, glitter showering his shoulders.

"*You* have a band?" Leave it to the fairy to have musical ambitions. "Never mind." I had to figure out a way to keep them from tearing up the place. "Grandma . . ." I began.

Dimitri stepped between us. "It's okay, Lizzie." He reached down for Grandma, but then thought better of it. "It's not as if we have thirty-eight extra bedrooms anyway."

"Thirty-seven," Ant Eater said, making eyes at the fairy.

Oh please.

"We'll find you a spot," Dimitri said, ushering them into the house. "Now follow me if you want to eat."

That did it. The biker witches paraded into the villa with the couth of a gaggle of five-year-olds on a field trip. I almost wished Dimitri had thrown them a picnic outside. Ant Eater tested out the banister on the main staircase and I cringed. Those snarling griffins carved into the ends had withstood decades of Dimitri's family's trauma. But surviving Ant Eater would be another challenge entirely.

"Stay away," I told her, just as Frieda bumped a pink leather-clad hip against the potted fig by the doorway, sending it crashing to the floor.

Dimitri kissed me on the top of the head. "I love you," he whispered, his breath tickling my ear.

"Why?" I asked him. We'd only known each other for a few months. I had a longer relationship with my sneakers, and now my whacked-out family was about to destroy the home he'd fought so hard to preserve.

He was a sacrificing individual, loyal to a fault. So far, I'd tainted his royal blood, replaced his steadfast griffin fiancée, whose family could no doubt help him through this crisis better than I could, and now Battina the witch was sliding down the banister of the grand staircase.

"Stop! Watch the—!" Too late. My head pounded as the moment seemed to freeze in time. Battina decapitated an antique griffin hand-carved by none other than Sir Nikkos Kallinikos. "Oh my God." I buried my face in my hands. "Dimitri, I—"

"We'll fix it," he said, leading me and my nutso family deeper into his home. He deposited them in the dining room, where they feasted on MoonPies, Mountain Dew and pork rinds. Don't ask me where Dimitri found it all.

"I'm so sorry," I said as we watched Jan the Library Hag spit Mountain Dew out of her nose. "I was thinking of myself when I invited them here."

I'd been thinking of myself way too much lately. I needed protection. I needed training. This man had given those things to me and I still wanted more.

My fingers found the emerald at my neck. It had become so much a part of me that I'd barely noticed it unless I wanted its protection. I was taking Dimitri—and everything else he'd given me—for granted.

The worst thing was, I had no idea what to do about it.

Ant Eater's voice dragged me out of my thoughts. "Hey!" she called from the gardens. "I think I found a spot."

We piled outside to find her pointing to a stone building beyond the rose garden. I'd barely noticed it before, as it was covered in vines. The building was made of the white stone common on the estate, with bronzed accents that had turned green with age.

Dimitri cleared his throat. "That's the original house."

"It's nice," Grandma murmured.

"No one has lived there in years," Dimitri said, as the witches began milling around the building. "Half the rooms are underground, it has no kitchen and it's most likely infested with brownies."

"It sounds perfect!" Frieda squealed. She clapped her hands together as Grandma and Ant Eater started clearing vines away from the door.

"If you think this will work for you," Dimitri said, helping them, "I have the key inside. We've been using this to store our family weapons arsenal."

Ant Eater grinned. "This keeps getting better and better."

Sidecar Bob piloted his wheelchair past me, with Pirate on his lap. "Come on, this'll be like Sturgis in '83."

Pirate danced on his front paws. "I've never eaten Sturgis!"

"Do you really want to let them in there?" I asked, following Dimitri as he headed back to the house.

"They're family," he said, meaning tingeing his every word. "I have a responsibility."

"Responsibility my foot," I said as I watched him go.

He was about to have a garden full of holes.

I crossed my arms over my chest. Was that what I was to him as well? A responsibility?

Come to think of it, most of our relationship had been based on a certain tit for tat. He needed me to help his sisters, and I had. Now he owed it to me to find the dark-haired woman. Give some here, take some there.

But what about after that? Did we have anything else in common?

As if proving my point, a half dozen biker witches stomped through the rosebushes with Amara hot on their tail. I admired her dedication.

Somebody had to keep this estate in one piece.

"You're right," Ant Eater said to the three witches behind her. "There doesn't seem to be any reason for it."

Amara dug a rock from her sandal, her cheeks pink from exertion. "It's a sundial fountain, symbolizing the marriage of sun and sea." She pointed to a bronze, sixteen-pointed sun at the top of the fountain. "The sun of Vergina is for the virgin goddess Athena, pure until she mates for life. The trident," she said, dipping her fingers into the bowl at the base of the fountain, "is for the sea god Poseidon. He was one of the original caretakers of the oracle at Delphi, and hence, many sea griffins possess psychic abilities."

Amara might as well have been speaking Chinese.

Ant Eater shook her head. "It'll have to go."

That's when I noticed Amara's dress was still snagged on her pink bra. Her black hair frizzed around her face and she looked about as on edge as I felt.

Amara drew up to her full height. "This was an engagement gift from my family."

Ant Eater shrugged. "It's also in the way."

"Of what?" she pleaded.

"Demon slayer training," Ant Eater said proudly.

Oh no. We did not need to train in roses that had been here since Jason got together with the Argonauts.

"This is the perfect spot," Ant Eater said, yanking on the pergola. "What is this? Twelve feet?"

"You can't tear that down," I protested.

The witch looked at me like I was the crazy one. "Of course not. This is where you learn how to pass your levitation test."

She had to be kidding. "I'm not getting up on top of that."

"Well, not right now." Ant Eater shrugged.

"Look at this!" Grandma emerged from the stone house with a medieval battle-ax. She gave it a swing, taking out the tops of two rosebushes and nearly blowing Sidecar Bob's tire. "Isn't she a beaut?"

No. This was getting out of control. "You could chop an arm off with that thing!"

"Oh, more than that." Ant Eater grinned, her gold tooth glinting in the sun.

"And how did you get in?"

"Magic."

"You should have waited for the key. This is Dimitri's

home." This was his life. He'd risked everything to make a place for himself here.

I glanced back at the porch door. *Just where is Dimitri, anyway?* It couldn't take him that long to find the key. He was probably hiding the breakables, stowing the liquor and wondering what the heck he was thinking by bringing us here.

I stalked down the porch and through the rose garden, determined to save as much of the place as I could.

"Well geez, Lizzie. Don't you want to be trained?" Grandma asked.

"Yes," I said. Of course. I needed all of the control I could get right now. Still, I didn't think we needed to tear apart the estate. "We need to put this back in—oh Sheboygan." I ducked into the white stone house and found an arsenal.

A huge wooden rack of sabers, war hammers and swords lined one wall, with another entire wall for shields and armor. I sneezed. The place reeked of metal and dust.

Scale armor lay in heaps on the floor next to immense bronze breastplates and leg plates. No doubt they'd been meant for griffins. I also counted two catapults, a war scythe the size of an ox and even a battered iron cage. And that's only what I could see. There were hardly any windows in the place.

Ant Eater slapped me on the back. "Isn't it great? There's more downstairs."

"You can't train me here." We wouldn't make it a day without someone impaling themself, losing an eye or chopping their head off—hopefully not all three.

"Why not?" Grandma asked. "This place is secure." She gave it a once-over as if she were a decorator approaching a particularly challenging job. "It'll be even better once we set the booby traps. Plus, there's no question about it," she said, pointing a stubby finger at my chest. "You need training."

"I know that." I'd been trying to figure out what I was doing from the moment I became the Demon Slayer of Dalea. Talk about a surprise—locked in my bathroom, needing to get to my thirtieth-birthday party, having no idea *this* was in store.

And now, with part of myself gone, death threats breathing down my back and the wards on the estate weakening, well, let's just say I needed all the help I could get.

Focus on the problem at hand.

I rubbed a hand over my face. Because even if I trained to be the perfect slayer, I'd never be a griffin and never be what Dimitri needed to make his family whole.

"Rachmort will be here tomorrow," Grandma said. "He's already instructed two generations of our family."

I stood a bit taller. "He trained my mom?"

"Nope. Your Great-great-great-aunt Evie."

She was the greatest slayer of all. "And you just tracked him down now?"

Grandma looked quite pleased with herself. "Do you know how hard it is to get on his schedule?"

I had no idea. "There can't be that many slayers." The power ran in a very select, distressingly small number of families. Every third generation, these families would produce a pair of slayer twins.

Demon slayers were treasured, trained, given every advantage. Of course, my mother had used her knowledge and gifts to foist off her destiny on me before she dropped me at the adoption agency.

I was the accidental demon slayer. The clueless one. I'd never even known we existed until I stumbled into my powers—and what remained of my family. I'd never met another one of my kind.

"Listen to Rachmort," Grandma said, accepting a war hammer from Ant Eater. The thing was immense, with a sharp pick on one end and a blunt crushing plate on the other. "He's the best. And don't get on him for being late. Most families search for an instructor as soon as they learn they're going to have twins. That's what we did with your mom and your aunt, God rest her soul."

Well of course, but, "You have to admit I could have used a little help before now."

Grandma hefted the hammer and I took three steps back. "Zebediah Rachmort usually gets five years, nine months' notice. So I think it's pretty good that he dropped everything to see you in a few months. Anyways, he was in purgatory with the Department of Intramagical Matters' Lost Souls Outreach program. Took a while to track him down."

"Lost Souls Outreach?" I'd never heard of such a thing. "What does he do?"

"He's a necromancer." Grandma rested the weapon on her shoulder like a baseball bat. "He spends half the year in purgatory and the rest in Boca Raton."

I stared at her.

"You wouldn't believe how out of hand purgatory has gotten. There's no law. Demons walking around all glamored up, tricking people into hell. Rachmort finds people.

He helps them remember their goodness so they can rise up out of there."

I shook my head. "I had no idea."

Grandma shot me a conspiratorial grin. "Personally, I think he's also there to keep an ear to the ground. Rumor has it, there's something brewing in hell. Worse than usual."

"Lovely."

"He's the best, Lizzie."

"Good. Because there's something you need to know."

Grandma's eyes widened as I told her about the attack on me, and the green sky.

She planted her war hammer into the ground. "Pea green?"

I nodded.

"And you say it burned you?" She scrubbed a hand across her face.

"It stole a piece of me."

"And a green sky means something evil has been created."

I told her about the dark-haired woman—how I'd felt the hate rolling off of her, how she'd touched me and disappeared.

Grandma planted her hands on her hips, the jelly jars on her leather-studded belt clanking together as she looked to the sky. "I'm getting too old for this."

"Really?"

"No."

"Well, I've had enough. Between stolen magic, death prophecies and cursed imps—"

"Hold it!" she threw a hand up. "Cursed imps?"

She wasn't going to believe it. "They fly and throw these cursed arrows and—"

"I know what they do," she said, her voice going cold. "Those are Vald's."

Impossible.

"Vald is dead," I reminded her. I'd killed him myself.

"You kill all his little friends too?" she asked. "That demon liked to experiment. Cursed imps are his creation, part of his personal army."

"Why didn't Dimitri know about this?"

"Lover boy didn't have Vald chasing him for thirty years. My coven has seen enough to make the Odyssey look like a three-hour tour. No question about it, Lizzie. The demon might be dead, but that doesn't mean his followers aren't bent on revenge." She stopped cold. "Or perhaps they want a demon slayer of their own."

Holy Hades.

"I'm strong," I told her.

She looked me up and down, clearly worried. "You'll be even stronger after Rachmort trains you. Listen to him, Lizzie. You're in more danger than we ever imagined."

I chewed at my lip. If Vald's followers were behind this attack on me, then it stood to reason they wanted Dimitri's sisters too. We needed to know more. "We need to go into the cave of visions."

Grandma's eyes narrowed.

My previous experiences with a cave of visions involved a Dumpster and a covered wagon in a replica Wild West town. Neither had been pleasant. Then again, I knew the magic worked.

"I'm not tied to this," she warned.

"I know." I cringed.

"That means I can't go in there with you."

"I know." I avoided her gaze. I knew what she was thinking. The last time I'd gone to the cave of visions, I'd landed right in a demon's trap. It could easily happen again. "Maybe Rachmort can help me prepare."

"I don't like it."

"You?" She was the one who'd rushed into the cave of visions—right before it sent her to the second level of hell.

"Believe it or not, I learn from my mistakes."

"You know we have to do it."

She eyed me. "Then we do it my way. You give me and my witches the time we need to prepare the cave right."

"Agreed."

"In the meantime, you listen to Rachmort," Grandma ordered. "Learn," she said, as if ordering could make it so.

"Grandma . . ." I began. I knew the risk I was taking. Besides, I'd learned a lot since my showdown with the Vegas demons.

She looked past me, lost in thought. "We'll build it for you as soon as we get settled here."

"Where will it be?" I asked. Hopefully not in Dimitri's living room.

"Leave that to me."

I didn't press. "What's Rachmort like?" I asked.

"Tough," she said, with uncharacteristic brevity.

Never mind. I'd find out soon enough.

Besides, tough was good. I needed it. I'd craved it since I first gained my powers.

"You'll need your mother's training bar," Grandma said as we headed back out into the gardens.

"Anything else?" I asked, watching the witches roll a sundial past a shrieking Amara.

"Oh yeah," Grandma said, thumbs dug into her belt as she looked me up and down. "Every ounce of courage you've got."

Chapter Twelve

Two hours, eighteen new weapons and a decimated rose garden later, a hand touched me on the shoulder.

I nearly jumped a foot.

"Relax, Lizzie. It's me." Dimitri stood behind me, looking all studly in a black T-shirt and jeans, his black hair damp and curling at the ends. He was a six-foot-six reminder of everything that was good in the world.

"Where have you been?" I could tell there was something big on his mind.

"I've been making inquiries. We have an issue," he said, his gaze darting to Grandma, who was sitting on the ground in front of the stone house, mashing leaves with a mortar and pestle. "Do you have things handled on your end, Gertie?"

"Oh yeah," she said. "Can't you smell the turtle knees toasting?"

He looked at her like he didn't quite have an answer for that one. I knew the feeling. "Do whatever it takes," he said, and turned back to me. "Lizzie, I need a word."

"Good," I replied. It seemed he'd taken to heart our conversation at the ruins. If we were going to make it as a couple, we needed to be honest with each other, even when it wasn't happy and fun. "So tell me. What's going on?"

He took my hand. "Come with me. We need more privacy than we're going to get here."

Could he have been referring to Sidecar Bob, who was fashioning a barbecue pit out of the bottom half of a wine cask, or Frieda, who was mixing spells in the other half?

"You can go on into the house. Don't mind that," Grandma said, pointing to the pinkish haze around the stone armory. "A couple of the brownies got into Battina's instant-evaporation spells. They'll be okay once we put them back together."

"Thank you for the offer. I know how busy you are," Dimitri said. "But I have a place where Lizzie and I can talk in private."

We headed up the gray slate steps to the villa. "Don't apologize," he said when he saw my mouth open. "I understood the consequences when I invited them in. Frankly, after all that's happened, I'm glad for the extra support."

"We are talking about the Red Skulls," I said, recalling his less-than-cordial relationship with them in the past.

"I love you, and therefore I must love your clan. It is the griffin way."

I had a feeling I'd be counting on that a lot in the future.

The opening beats to Grandma's favorite Kiss song vibrated through the house. Before we could "Rock and Roll All Nite" with the biker witches, Dimitri took me to the old library off the foyer, a round high-walled room flooded with natural light. I hadn't noticed on my first visit that the ceiling of the room was made of glass. It was set in triangular pieces to resemble a sun.

Dimitri closed the heavy oak door behind us. It gave us a measure of privacy, even if it didn't completely block the bass beat on the other side of the wall.

"We've been surveying the grounds, and it seems the security situation is more dire than I imagined," he said. "If things don't change soon, I fear for all of our lives."

I nodded. I knew.

"Therefore . . ." A dark look crossed his face and I could see the muscles in his neck tighten. "Amara and I must leave immediately in order to consult with the Dominos clan on Rhodes."

That I didn't know. I fought to keep my voice even. "You're going?" We didn't know what was after us, and he was taking off . . .

"With Amara?"

He looked almost pained. "The Dominos council is assembling right now. It's the only way."

"No, it's not." We weren't backed into a corner. Not yet. "There are a lot of ways to approach this." My stomach churned. "We can all stay. We can fight."

"Or we can ask for the help we need," he said evenly.

"I don't believe it." Now was not the time to leave. "It seems like every time I need you, you go off to fight some battle and I have to pick up the pieces." I watched my words strike home and guilt dampened my pity party. I knew I wasn't being fair, but I was hurting. I didn't want to be alone here. I didn't want him leaving with her. This felt wrong.

He closed the distance between us. "We're in a precarious situation here. Diana and Dyonne aren't regaining their strength. They're weakening, Lizzie. The entire estate is in danger, and you along with it. It would be foolish not to employ every single one of our resources." He stood taller. "Including the Dominos clan on Rhodes."

I crossed my arms over my chest. "I know. I'm just not sure if I trust them." Since they'd been helping Dimitri's family, his estate had been invaded by imps, his line had almost died out and his sisters were losing power.

Dimitri wrapped an arm around me. "I know you've had your differences with Mara."

There he went with the *Mara* again.

"It's not her," I said. Ironically, I didn't question Amara's loyalty.

Amara had been with Dyonne and Diana since they recovered. She knew them and the estate, and she even had a gift for predicting what may come next. I'd seen firsthand how she'd tried to use her powers to help us.

"I just have a bad feeling about the entire situation."

Maybe I was too independent minded, but I didn't understand the idea of accepting protection from a griffin clan I'd never met.

"You can bet I'll be keeping an eye on Talos," I added.

Dimitri pulled me closer. "I believe Talos may be pursuing his own interests as well. So far, I haven't been able to determine what. But he is sworn to protect this house. I don't think he will fail us at that. Be cautious, but know Talos can and will assist you." He looked down at me. "I also talked to your grandmother. She and the Red Skulls know more about wards than any group I've ever met. They're going to put up some barriers for us."

"Thank you," I said. I was touched that he'd trust my family with his home and his sisters. "They're also building me a cave of visions," I said against his chest.

I could feel him darken. "I don't like it, Lizzie."

"Grandma said the cursed imps were made by Vald. I need to see who is controlling them now."

He was torn. I could see it on his face. "Be careful. And try to wait until I come back. It won't be long."

Yes, well I didn't know how long we had. "I'll try," I said, snuggling into his arms, inhaling his clean male scent.

Despite everything, it felt good to be here with him.

His breath tickled the hair on the top of my head. "At least we're talking about it this time. That's what you wanted, right?"

"I just wish none of this was happening."

"I know." He kissed me on the top of the head. "To tell you the truth, our journey to the Dominos clan is a last resort, like your cave of visions. But you're at risk, along with my sisters. I don't see any other way."

"I get it," I said. Logically, I understood why he felt he needed to do this. But logic didn't calm the churning in my stomach or the fear that gripped me at the thought of handling things here by myself. Even if I could avoid the cave of visions until he returned, there was no way I could control thirty-eight biker witches. Even now, I could hear them whooping and hollering outside on the front lawn. "Sorry in advance for your trashed estate."

With a hint of a grin, he said, "Just try to keep them out of my study. We don't want any of them to get slimed."

I was glad he could joke about it, but in all seriousness, my family could and would destroy his house. It was on me to keep them in line, like a busload of crazed toddlers.

He touched my shoulder. "I'm trying to let you in, Lizzie. In the past, I've wanted to do things on my own. I was alone. Now I want to include you."

And Amara. I didn't say it, but he knew what I was thinking.

"I'd ask you to come," he said, "but it would be unwise for you to leave the estate right now. You're needed here."

"I know." Not to mention the fact that the Dominos clan would probably be about as eager to meet me as Amara had been. They were the ones who had arranged for those two to be married.

"You have to go. With her. I don't like it"—that was the understatement of the year—"but I understand."

Now it was up to me to keep his estate in one piece when everything seemed to be coming down around my ears.

He kissed me long and deep. "I love you, Lizzie."

I felt him down to my toes. "I know," I said, scrunching my fingers against his black T-shirt, watching it fold up under them. "I wanted this to be our vacation, a time for us to get to know each other better."

"We'll have our time. Soon," he rumbled against my fingers.

I wished that were true, but I didn't know what to count on anymore. I had my whole life planned out before I became a demon slayer. Now I was grateful to make it through an afternoon.

But I could depend on Dimitri—strong, loyal Dimitri. If only I could spend a week with him without someone's life being on the line. Could we even be a normal couple? Where would a guy like him take me on a date?

What would it be like to simply talk?

I tilted my head up. "We've spent our entire time together running from one disaster to the next."

He nodded. "And now it's followed us."

"Do you realize we've never even been on a date?"

He thought about it. "What about the time I cooked dinner for you at the Hairy Hog biker bar?"

He'd turned hamburger patties and mac and cheese into a poor man's version of pastitsio. It had actually been delicious, eaten on a picnic blanket out back. But that wasn't a real date or any real time alone.

"Our life is what it is," he concluded. "It's not as if we don't know each other. It's not like I don't feel what I feel for you."

I couldn't argue there. The man had ignored his estate in order to battle demons with me in Las Vegas. He'd gone to hell and back with me. Now I come to find he'd compromised his relationship with the only clan powerful enough to help him save his family.

"You are my world," he said, drawing me into his arms. "But I have to go. The Dominos council is assembled and waiting for us."

"How long will you and Amara be gone?" I asked, his chest warm against my cheek.

"Not long—I hope."

Me too.

Dimitri lowered his mouth to mine for a toe-curling kiss. "I'll miss you," he whispered, nipping at my lower lip.

With a twinge of regret, I realized I hadn't appreciated

Dimitri enough lately. Everything he'd done since I met him had been to help me or someone else, yet it always seemed like somebody wanted more.

Well, not this time.

I'd let him go with Amara. I refused to be jealous. Instead, I'd spend the time training to be a better slayer. I'd help him save his home and I'd try to look at things from his perspective.

It was about time I put him first.

"Lizzie!" I heard a voice call from outside. There was a banging at the door.

Oh geez. It was starting already.

I opened it and was about flattened by a blast of rock music. "Heaven's on Fire" pounded through the house.

No kidding.

Frieda stood outside. "Lizzie, your dog is looking for you!"

"I have to go anyway," Dimitri said.

Yes, but did it have to be now?

He kissed me briefly once, twice. I shuddered at the thought of letting him go. I sank into him as he ran a thumb along my chin, tilting my head back for a kiss that left no doubt he'd be thinking of me, that night and every night.

Dimitri broke away slowly and, with a nod to Frieda, left the library.

I followed him out as Pirate dashed out the back hallway, skidded past the staircase and ran paws first into the back of my knee. "Ow!"

Pirate continued his assault on anything he could reach. "Lizzie! Come quick—it's alive!"

"What's alive?"

Pirate danced like he was on a hot plate. "My momma always said, 'You're a dog. You have instincts.' And I knew something was up with that egg. I just knew it."

This sounded like something I didn't need. "Egg?"

"Go," Dimitri said, his lips brushing mine one last time. "They need you here, and so do I."

"I love you," I said as he walked out the door.

Pirate yipped. "Now don't tell me you don't remember because you're the one who said to be gentle with it and I was gentle with it and it's a good thing because it's alive!"

Holy smokes. "Where?"

"Follow the bloodhound!" he said, dashing out into the foyer.

"You're not a bloodhound," I said, trying to keep up.

"I always thought I had some in me," he said, nose to the ground as he made quick work of the foyer, then bounded up the stairs two at a time and dashed down the second-floor hallway. To Pirate's credit, he did not stop for crumbs, biker witches or the flickering rays of colored light cast by the stained-glass sconces lining the hall.

"This way!" he said, leading me straight to the door of our guest room.

Oh no.

I opened the door to my room to find it blessedly intact, save for the sticks and grass littering the area in front of my bed. Then I noticed the smooth yellow rock inside my brand-new backup pair of silver Adidas cross-trainers.

"What did you do?" I asked, lifting the tennis shoe. I thought we were beyond destroying things.

"I tried to make a nest like a mama bird, but I figured your shoe would be warmer."

"Nest?" I repeated, my mind working on the problem. "For a rock."

My instincts had led me to a rock on a cliff face. Not an egg or a nest or whatever Pirate thought I'd found.

He'd lined my shoe heel with mud-caked grass and twigs and—

"What is that smell?" Like burned rubber and gasoline.

The rock shook and I nearly dropped the thing. Holy cow, it was alive.

"See?" Pirate scratched at my legs. "Bob taught me a new word, *wicked cool*, and I'll say it right now. That egg is wicked cool."

"Stand back," I said, depositing the shoe on the ceramic-tile floor between the bed and the dresser. I'd found this thing the night we'd gone out searching for threats. Just because my demon slayer radar had gone off didn't mean it was evil. In fact, I wasn't detecting any malice right now, but I wasn't going to take any chances.

I pulled out a switch star.

I'd had enough things try to kill me in the last month. It paid to be cautious. Of course, Pirate didn't listen. He danced in circles around my abused tennis shoe, the tags on his collar jingling.

Smoke curled from the egg where a white claw began peeking through. "It's not a beak," I said, taking an extra step back.

"It's a tooth!" Pirate said, beside himself with excitement. I hadn't seen him go this crazy since the time I'd baked him a dog-biscuit cake for his birthday.

Pirate was right. A full set of teeth poked out, followed by a slimy head, a scaly ridged back and a set of wet, folded wings. Pirate rushed for it, his nose inches from the thing's head. "It's a lizard!"

"I think it's a dragon," I said, more than a little shocked as it flopped out of my tennis shoe. I don't know why anything should have surprised me at that point.

It was the size of a hamster, with dirty white scales and black claws. Its teeth were sharp and uneven. I'd say they were crooked, if I knew anything about dragon dentistry. In fact, one particular snaggletooth stood out nearly sideways. The dragon gave a tiny roar, which I had to admit was kind of cute, before it turned those teeth on my already-abused sneaker.

"Go for the laces!" Pirate instructed. "Those are the tastiest."

I resheathed my switch star and planted my hands on my hips. "You said you never touched my shoes."

"Whoops," he said, not sorry at all, his eyes on the beast. "Can we keep it?"

"Of course not. I don't know what to do with a dragon." Not to mention the fact that we already had the biker witches tearing up Dimitri's estate. We didn't need to start adding mythical creatures.

"But I need a pet!" he said, like the four-year-old he was.

"You are a pet," I reminded him.

"Exactly," he said, as if I was just catching up. "So I know how to treat a pet." He made two full circles before plopping his rear down in front of the dragon. "First rule: no Healthy Lite dog chow."

The dragon lolled out a snakelike tongue and licked Pirate on the nose.

"No," I said. No pets. No tearing up the estate. And

while I was at it, no flying imps, no scheming griffins, no more attacks and no Amara.

If I could only have had half of what I wanted, I'd have been in pretty good shape. As it stood, there was a distinct possibility the world was indeed scheming against me.

"Get rid of the dragon," I told Pirate. If I could have controlled one corner of my life, that would have been it.

Pirate's ears flattened and his shoulders slumped. "Sure. Fine. All I wanted was a pet, but I don't need no pet."

"No, you don't."

"Never mind where the poor dragon is gonna go because I sure don't know and I don't think he's got any friends and—"

"Pirate," I interrupted. "Diana said something earlier about the ASPCC."

His ears perked up. "The ASSP-what?"

"The All-Species for the Prevention of Cruelty to Creatures. I'm sure they'll take good care of him." They certainly wouldn't insert him into the middle of the trouble we had going.

Pirate cocked his head. "But will they love him?"

"Pirate," I warned.

He left with the dragon. I felt bad about it. I did. But I had my hands full enough with whatever was threatening me and this estate. Not to mention the biker witches. They'd switched to Merle Haggard. And karaoke. If I leaned out the window just so, I could see the smoke from their fire. I said a quick prayer that they'd started it in a fire pit.

In the field out back, I watched Dimitri join Amara. At least she'd left her clothes on this time. Maybe she realized he wasn't interested in her lacy pink bra, or maybe she figured she'd get to him later.

Soon she'd have him on her home turf, with her perfect griffin clan—the family he'd chosen to join.

They shifted together, their bodies shuddering and expanding. Massive forearms ripped through Dimitri's black T-shirt as claws erupted from his hands. Lion's fur raced down his back as red, blue, purple and green feathers grew into tremendous wings.

When they finished, two beautiful griffins stood side by side.

Dimitri called to her in a language only they understood, and she responded, spreading her silver wings and launching herself into the night. Dimitri followed and I watched them, majestic and proud, until they faded into the gathering darkness together.

Chapter Thirteen

That night, I dreamed of Diana's Skye stone. She kept it on the dresser in a room draped with roses. It shone like a bright summer's day, even in the darkness.

It wasn't as brilliant when Talos held it. I wondered what would happen if I touched it. Even more, I craved it.

I reached for the stone and was shocked to find that it shimmered against my fingers. I took it, cradling it in my palm and luxuriating in the warmth and power it sent flooding up my arms.

This energy was mine.

I raced from the room, through the house and out to the back gardens. Two of the Red Skull witches had fallen asleep in wrought-iron porch chairs, their chins against their chests. I rushed past them, out to the far edge of the garden. I ducked around an ancient oak and down a narrow path, over a bridge and to a secluded spot where the knapweed and wild orchids buzzed heavily with insects. I buried the stone at the base of a wild pomegranate tree growing crooked against a rock.

Soon it would begin. Fire would rain down. The earth would split and I would be the only demon slayer—the most powerful one of them all.

The sun was barely over the horizon when a pounding at the door had me sitting straight up in bed. My head ached.

I hadn't slept well, which meant I'd probably been having bad dreams. This one hovered at the edge of my consciousness, barely out of reach until Pirate flipped over next to me, taking the covers with him. "Lizzie, there's someone at the door!" His paws dug into my hip as he made a mad dash off the bed.

"What's wrong?" I asked, shoving my way toward the bedside clock. Usually when someone woke me up at five thirty in the morning, our world had just gone to h-e-double hockey sticks.

I stumbled past the sleeping dragon, unlocked the door and found Talos on the other side, his black hair an unruly mess and his narrow face etched with concern.

"Diana's Skye stone is missing," he said, wasting no time on niceties. "Tell me you know something about it."

"No," I said, concerned and mildly annoyed as he glowered down at me. "What do *you* know about it?"

He'd taken it the night the sky had turned green. What was to say he hadn't stolen it a second time?

He had the nerve to look offended. "It wasn't me. I gave my word I wouldn't touch it again."

Oh, well wasn't that a comfort? "And your word is . . . ?"

"Everything to a griffin," he said. "I don't think you understand the severity of the situation. Diana needs the stone to focus her power and recover her magic."

Not to mention protect us all.

I didn't need the hand-puppet version. I knew what was at stake.

"I'll be ready in one minute." I left him in the hallway while I changed into black leather pants and my lucky purple bustier. I threw my hair back into a ponytail and slid on my black leather boots.

I'd been trying so hard to be on vacation. Now it almost felt good to get back into my work clothes, like I was no longer in denial. This getaway had been over before it began and I might as well admit it. I hitched my demon slayer utility belt around my waist and fastened the crystal buckle. No telling what we'd have to face today.

"Okay," I said, pleased at how Talos took a step backward when I opened the door. "Take me to Diana."

"I can't," he said, stiffly. "Diana and Dyonne have gone to their private retreat. We dare not interfere."

"Fine." They could handle it their way; we'd hit it from our end. "Come on," I said, slapping Talos on the shoulder and heading down the hall toward the stairs. "We'll enlist the witches."

He gave a slight gurgle. "Do you think that's wise?"

"Probably not," I answered truthfully. The Red Skulls tended to complicate things wherever they went, but I'd bet my last switch star they knew more about Skye magic than I did.

"Truly. You're a demon slayer! What of this internal locator system you have?" he asked as we hurried down the stairs

He said it as if I were a human metal detector. "It's more like a sixth sense for danger, and it only pings when something is about to attack me."

"Too bad," Talos answered. I resisted the urge to shove him down the last two steps. The griffin needed an edit button.

"Answer me this," I said, stopping at the bottom of the stairs. "What can someone else do with Diana's Skye stone? You told me yourself you couldn't use it for anything but to see where their magic had weakened."

"Yes," he said, like I was the slow contestant on *Jeopardy!* "But if our enemies can't use it to gain power, they can still use it to make Diana lose power. The end result is the same. I'm strong, but I can't defend this entire estate by myself."

He saw my shock and it only urged him on. "Make no mistake, we will die for this place. We pledged ourselves and we shall go down fighting."

"Frankly, I'd like to find another way," I said, heading for the back hall. I wasn't optimistic enough to think I'd survive this if Talos didn't.

"I agree," he said.

Too bad I still didn't trust him. I wasn't about to take his word that he couldn't do anything with a stolen Skye stone. If only Dimitri were here. He'd know whether Talos was telling the truth.

I thought about calling him and realized my Sprint calling plan didn't include Greece, much less ultrasecret griffin clan meetings. Maybe Diana or Dyonne would know how to reach their brother.

This was the second break-in since I'd arrived. We had a traitor among us, and I was willing to bet he'd just yanked me out of bed, pretending to help.

I pushed my way out the doors to the patio. The garden looked almost serene in the early-morning light. Birds chirped and hopped over the muddy hole where the sundial fountain had been. The witches had also cleared out a large swath of rosebushes that had blocked the stone house, and installed a barbecue pit made from half a wine barrel. Classy.

Maybe they'd know what to do with Talos. "Where were you last night?" I asked him as we approached the armory.

He walked with me through the remains of the rose garden as if he expected to step on dog poop. "Believe it or not," he said, with no small amount of disgust, "I spent the night with your biker witches."

"You've got to be kidding."

"I wish I were. A woman named Ant Eater shoved homemade whiskey under my nose. Being hospitable, I tried it." He winced at the memory. "The next thing I remember was a man named Bob rolling his wheelchair past my head this morning, asking if I'd like bacon."

"So they know what's going on?" I asked. Good.

"No, I'd returned to my room when Diana sounded the alarm. I came straight to you."

Lucky me.

Frieda threw back the wooden front door so hard it bounced against the wall. "Talos! How ya doing?" she waved. "Your head feeling any better?"

"No," Talos said.

She wore lime green leather pants and a zebra-print halter top. "Would you like a hangover spell?" she asked, chomping on gum. "We got plenty brewed up in the house."

"No," he repeated.

There was no time for Talos's headache anyway. "We need to talk to Grandma and Ant Eater. We have a situation."

Good thing the biker witches were used to things

going wrong. Grandma and Ant Eater rushed right out, along with the half dozen or so other witches who liked to eavesdrop. They munched on bacon while Talos and I explained the situation.

"Who did it?" Grandma demanded, tossing the last of her breakfast to Pirate. Sneaky dog. I thought I'd locked him in the room.

Ant Eater shook her head. "Talos was with us, Dimitri and Amara are gone, our witches are clean, the sisters are clean." She tapped a finger against her gold front tooth. "Nothing from the outside came in through the wards last night."

"How do you know?"

She gave me a look that could tan leather. "I know."

"Fine." I believed her. "So we don't know who took the stone or where it is now." It was completely unacceptable. We needed a plan.

Frieda patted her stack of blonde hair. "We could work up some magic traps, and unlike the time in Little Rock—"

The witches glared at her.

"What happened in Little Rock?" I asked.

Scarlet, the red-haired witch, winced. "Frieda got eaten."

Frieda shook her head, remembering. "Lost a perfectly good pair of hot-pink platform shoes, rhinestone buckles and all." She sighed wistfully. "But never you mind. This time, we'll make sure our magic is immune."

"You're forgetting about the wards around this place," Grandma said. "Traps would pull them down."

We were interrupted by a wide-eyed Diana rushing out onto the patio, followed closely by Dyonne.

"It's gone!" Diana announced, tears in her eyes. She sank into a wrought-iron patio chair. "I thought if we did some meditations, focused our remaining strength, we could sense where it is. But . . ." She gestured helplessly.

"This won't do," Talos said. "Diana, you must try to track your magic."

"I can't," she wailed. "One minute it was on my dresser and the next minute—poof!"

Grandma shook her head. "It can't just disappear."

"It did!" Diana insisted, clutching at her pink silk nightgown.

Grandma inspected Diana's pupils, then started looking under Diana's fingernails for who knew what.

In the meantime, I tried to think of something, anything, that would help us look. The Skye stone was no bigger than a billiard ball. I could see it disappearing to a safe place. It glowed with an inner magic from the moment Diana touched it during training. It shone even brighter in my dream. I remembered it now. It had been so real.

The facts clicked into place in my mind.

I had a logic teacher who always said you should never discount an answer simply because you didn't expect the data to lead you there. And boy, did I love logic.

"I'll be right back," I said, backing away from the group.

"Lizzie, are you on to something?" Grandma asked.

"Maybe—just give me a minute," I said, heading down the stone path and into the garden. "Alone," I added, before I had a herd of witches and griffins following me.

I didn't want to try to explain where I was going. I didn't even know if the hazy place in my mind existed in real life. Pirate's nails clicked on the slate path behind me as I made my way toward a spot at the very edge of the gardens. Subtle he was not.

"I'd rather do this alone, Pirate," I said, searching for the overgrown trail leading into the thick of the garden.

"Um-hum," he said, his nose tickling my heels. "I saw how you looked when you took off, like you're about to go get the mail without me."

I dug around one of the pink flowering bushes invading the walkway. Yeah, well getting the mail with Pirate took twenty minutes. He had to sniff every rock, tree and blade of grass within twenty feet of the curb.

"Stick close," I said. "This could be nothing or . . ." I didn't know what, but I wasn't about to ignore anything that could help me find Diana's stone.

"Um-hum." Pirate huffed, his hot breath tickling my leg. "You need a watchdog."

We made our way down the tangled path together. Pirate kept his nose to the ground while I searched the thick garden foliage for anything out of the ordinary.

"You know I asked Ant Eater about the ASPCC," Pirate said, leaping over a prickly branch like it was a track-and-field hurdle.

Sweat trickled down my back. "Pirate, buddy. We don't have time."

"She said dragons are wild animals and they don't take wild animals. So see? That dragon needs me."

This trail, overgrown as it was, seemed so familiar. Yet I knew I'd never been here before. "If dragons are wild,"

I said to my dog, trying to make sense of this place, "then you can let him go. He'll be fine."

We, on the other hand . . .

I stopped dead when I ducked around the branches of a prickly, flowering bush and spotted an ancient oak like the one I'd seen last night. To the right of it, I found a narrow path, almost invisible among the crush of bougainvillea bushes and overgrown olive trees.

"This is it!"

Pirate danced in place. "Oh, Lizzie. You think so?"

The branches scratched at my arms as I followed the besieged trail from my dream. Pirate dug his nose into the ground as he launched into full protective mode. His body stiffened and his stubby tail quivered. Lucky for me, he took his job as a guard dog seriously.

"You okay, buddy?" I asked as I swatted gnats away from my face.

"Are you kidding? I am on duty. Hole!" he hollered.

I looked down and saw a crater in the ground, deep enough to turn an ankle. "Nice watch-dogging."

Pirate puffed out his chest. "I know you need me."

I was about to reach down and pat him on the head when I saw a wooden bridge around the bend—exactly where I expected it to be. This was no longer a coincidence.

"Come on," I said, clearing the hole in a single leap. "Let's move."

We crossed the bridge and came to a secluded spot where the knapweed and wild orchids buzzed heavily with insects. The strangest sense of déjà vu overtook me, although I knew it wasn't just a feeling. I *had* been here before.

Straight ahead, at the base of a wild pomegranate tree growing crooked against a rock, I'd find Diana's stone.

I found a broken tree branch and started digging.

Pirate slipped in at my elbow. "Oh, no, *no*. Allow me."

His front paws went to work like a mini–trench digger, the volcanic soil flying out behind him. I knelt to the side, watching, until his paws hit pay dirt. "It's slippery!"

"It's the stone!" I lifted Pirate out of his hole with one hand and used the other to pull the brilliant blue Skye stone from its hiding place. Even caked in grime, it was majestic. I wiped it against my pants and it shone even brighter.

Amazing.

"Now how'd you know to look here?" Pirate asked with a tilt of his head.

"You're not the only one who's going to ask me that," I said grimly.

Right then, a chill slid up my back as I spotted the dark-haired woman watching us from the trees. "You!" I struggled to see her face through the leaves.

She turned and fled.

"Wait!" I shouted, charging after her.

She must have been some kind of Amazon, because she moved through the dense foliage like water. I, on the other hand, tripped in the tangled underbrush, banged against every trunk and tree branch and even managed to catch a spiderweb in the face.

"Hold up!" I called, yanking the gooey mess from my mouth. I hate spiders. "I just want to talk."

Which was a lie. I was pretty sure she'd stolen my magic, which meant she deserved a switch star up the butt.

I slowed and came to a stop in a puddle of goo. She was long gone.

Pirate charged ahead of me. "Whee! What are we looking for?"

"The woman. Can you follow her?"

My dog spun twice, his tongue lolling out. "What woman? I thought you saw a rabbit!"

"You chase rabbits. I chase people who want to kill us."

He shoved his nose into the underbrush. "Yep. We sure do have fun. Now what is that smell?"

"Evil," I said.

"More like dead bird with a hint of mouse. Mmm . . . odiferous."

"Odiferous?"

Pirate nodded. "Thirteen-point Scrabble word."

"Right," I said, wishing the ghost who taught Pirate Scrabble was handy right now. I couldn't believe the dark-haired woman could just disappear. Again.

It creeped me out to no end that she'd been watching me.

At least I had the stone.

We filled in the hole because, well, I like to leave things how I find them. Then we headed back for the house.

If I were in a soul-searching mood, which I was not, I would have realized I was avoiding going back. I let Pirate sniff his way to bliss on the trail ahead. We stopped to inspect the bridge and I kept an eye out for our dark-haired spy. We didn't see her again—not that day, at least.

Diana cried and the biker witches whooped and cheered when I returned the stone. Talos watched me with barely contained fury. I didn't blame him. I couldn't explain how I'd known the stone would be under a remote tree, or how I'd known where to dig.

A chill slid up my spine. I'd tapped into something evil. Or worse yet, it had sunk its claws into me.

I'd have given anything to talk to Dimitri, or simply to hug the man. But he was doing what needed to be done and so was I.

At least he had Amara there to support him. My stomach hollowed at the thought. I wished it could have been me.

But facts were facts. I couldn't begrudge him the space he needed to rebuild his family. After all, the Dominos clan and Amara seemed to be a better fit than me and the biker witches. Perhaps they'd return soon, flags flying. In the meantime, I'd do my best to fight our battle on the ground.

Grandma handed me a Pabst Blue Ribbon. Don't ask me where she found it on Santorini. Knowing the witches, they'd brought their own stash.

"That was weird," she said.

"Understatement of the year," I replied, holding the welcome cold of the can against my forehead, actually considering a swig. I'd never had beer before breakfast, but this whole thing was wigging me out.

"You going to be able to do your job?" she asked, taking a sip of her own can, more serious than I would have liked her to be.

"Of course," I said too quickly, lowering the can. An unholy being had stolen part of me. This time, it had helped us. But that's usually how evil got a foothold, by posing as something you could control.

I refused to be fooled. I'd keep my eyes and ears open—and my dreams closed.

"You gonna drink that?" Ant Eater asked. I hadn't even seen her walk up. She cocked her head at a puff of smoke beyond the stone house. "'Cause Rachmort just popped in. Literally."

"Good," I said, handing her the beer and heading for the educational equivalent of ground zero.

Maybe he'd have some answers. I was more than ready to meet my destiny.

Chapter Fourteen

The legendary demon slayer instructor Zebediah Rachmort, who was also a cursed-creatures consultant for the Department of Intramagical Matters' Lost Souls Outreach program, stood under an apple tree and dusted off his black top hat. He wore a burgundy waistcoat and brown pants with pinstripes. When he was satisfied with the state of his hat, which was still billowing modest clouds of white dust, he spun it once in his fingers before planting it squarely atop his head.

"Lizzie Brown," he said, greeting me with all the pleasure and familiarity of a long-lost friend.

The wrinkles around his eyes and the angle of his cheekbones gave him an air of jocular authority. His white hair reminded me of Einstein's, while his Victorian-era clothes, neatly clipped sideburns and large gold watch fob looked like something out of a Dickens novel.

It was impossible to tell how old he was. The man seemed almost timeless.

He gestured me over with no small amount of glee. On his middle finger, he wore a humongous gold and copper ring that looked more like a compass than a piece of jewelry.

"You're taller than your Great-aunt Evie," he said, leaning way too far into my personal space. "But you have her eyes."

A pungent odor, like ammonia and sulfur, rolled off him. Perhaps he'd been in purgatory too long. "Er . . ." I resisted the urge to step away. "You know my Great-great-great-aunt Evie died in 1883."

"She led a most extraordinary life." He straightened as he began to unscrew a large brass dial at the top of his cane. "I was there when Evie had to make a portal in the middle of the blizzard that nearly buried Tulsa. It was the only way to do it back then. You modern demon slayers don't know how lucky you have it."

He had no idea. "We need to talk," I said. Where to begin? "First off, there's this—"

"Patience," he instructed.

He had to be kidding.

"Trust me, demon slayer," he said, a bit too amused for my taste. "I've done this before."

Yes. Exactly how many years had old Rachmort been teaching?

I studied him from his gold-buckled spats to the garnet stud in his left ear. "You don't look like a necromancer."

Not that I'd ever seen one, but still—he looked positively cheery for one who manipulated death.

"Why does death have to be gloomy?" he asked.

Why indeed?

No matter. From day one, I'd said I needed instruction, and here he was.

Rachmort turned his cane over and tapped the open end to the ground. "Go on," he said. "Get some air." Three dark-skinned humanoids tumbled out onto the grass. No larger than my hand, they were bug-eyed and spindly, made up mostly of arms and legs.

"Um," I said as the creatures began shoving large fistfuls of grass into their mouths. They chewed noisily with mouths open as half of what they jammed in fell right back out. "Should you be letting those go here?" I asked. "Most countries have rules about foreign plants and animals."

"Ha!" Rachmort snorted with glee. "Oh, you're serious," he said, shooing them into the garden, where they chattered loudly and climbed the nearest tree.

"Yes," he said. "Well, these little fellows were most useful in purgatory. They've earned a break."

"What are they?" Not that I wasn't used to strange magical creatures by now, but I at least liked to know what we were setting loose on Dimitri's estate.

Rachmort polished his round gold spectacles on his burgundy waistcoat. "North American tree nymphs, and excellent trackers, I might add. Hmm . . ." He pulled a chambray hankie from his back pocket and wiped the sweat from his forehead. "The Lakotas first found the Canotila and named them, but believe me, plenty have found their way to the Mediterranean. If you ask me, they have a little too much fun with the dryads." He made tsking sounds to himself as he added a purple flip-down sunglasses attachment that seemed to appear from midair. "I forgot how sunny it is up here."

If I ever considered myself nonmagical (and I did), Zebediah Rachmort was my opposite.

"Well at least let us set up a room for you in the house," I said, leading him toward the back porch. He didn't need to be staying with the biker witches, if only to protect him from whatever drink had flattened Talos.

"Oh goodness, no need," Rachmort said, adding a bifocal attachment onto his overloaded spectacles. "I've been offered the owner's suite of rooms off the main tower."

I stopped. Dimitri's rooms?

"I've inspected them and they are more than appropriate. There I will be close enough, should you have questions."

Of course. Why not? It wasn't as though Dimitri was using them. I watched a Canotila scamper from one tree to the next.

Rachmort pulled his starched collar away from his neck. "I came straight from purgatory and have all the wrong clothes. It's a bit nippy there, you know." He yanked off his gold cufflinks and rolled up his crisp white sleeves. "Not to worry. My housekeeper is sending a few things."

"Sure," I said.

A part of me rebelled at the idea of anyone else being up in Dimitri's rooms. I hadn't even made it up there. He'd moved down to be closer to me. It brought home again just how much I'd disrupted his life without even trying.

Not that a room change was a big deal. It was more of an inconvenience. Still, it had been a quiet one. Dimitri had done it. I'd accepted it, the same way I had when he'd chosen to stay in Las Vegas for me when his family needed him here, or the way he'd given up his prospects of marrying a pure griffin in order to be with me.

Slow, cold realization crept over me. If the situation were reversed, I didn't know if I would have made the same choices.

Rachmort tilted his head. "What are you thinking, demon slayer?"

I hesitated, annoyed that everything I thought tended to show up on my face.

He removed his top hat. "The better I understand you, the more effective I will be in your education. While I sculpt your skills, I also work on what is up here," he said, tapping the mess of white hair on his head.

"It's nothing big," I lied. "I'm only thinking that perhaps Dimitri is too loyal." Sure, I needed him, and he'd needed me in the past. But that's not what it took to build a long-term relationship.

"Ah, that he has sacrificed his own future—his pure griffin blood, the fiancée who fits into his world and would help him recover his clan. That he has done this in order to secure your future."

"You have done your homework."

"It would be a disservice to you if I didn't."

"Good point." On that and on so many other levels. This estate was Dimitri's life. I had no doubt the Dominos clan would have been here in a heartbeat to defend it if it was going to be Amara's future home. And what if we did manage to save his home? What then? I couldn't live like a happy housewife in Greece—even if we were heading toward marriage, which we weren't. Not yet. I'd have to leave to do my duty, and Dimitri would either have to come along . . . or he wouldn't.

Did I even want to do that to him?

He was a sacrificing person, and for the first time I wasn't sure if I wanted him to sacrifice all this goodness and beauty and magic for me.

"Yes, yes. Such heavy thoughts," Rachmort murmured. "This is good, Lizzie."

"Good?" What universe was he from?

"You must stop confusing what is good with what is comfortable," Rachmort said. "True learning will come when you are willing to step outside of what you think you know about yourself, the people you love, your abilities. I'm not saying it won't hurt. It will. Embrace that."

He began walking with me toward the house, his hands behind his back, his walk not unlike that of one of my favorite professors in college. "It is my understanding that some of your best moments as a demon slayer have come when you were experiencing this discomfort you seem to want to avoid. Be reassured that I shall endeavor to make you as uncomfortable as possible." He grinned. "That's when you're going to step out of your old ways of thinking and start looking for new possibilities, new ways to do things." He glanced at the house. "Now go fetch your training bar."

"Of course," I said, even though I dreaded the thought of touching the bar again.

Understanding change was one thing. Facing the thing that had predicted my death was another.

"Wait," I said to Rachmort as he began polishing his pocket watch on his waistcoat. I explained what I'd dreamed last night and what I'd seen in the woods right before he arrived.

He frowned, tapping his finger on his angular chin. "It's an unusual situation. You suspected that already, didn't you?"

"Yes," I said, appreciating the fact that he hadn't reacted like the others. Rachmort didn't doubt me or give me any funny looks or tell me I was imagining things. He took me at face value. It was a refreshing change of pace.

"We may be able to use this connection." He looked at

me as if the weight of the universe hung on what he had to say next. "Do you trust me to teach you?"

"Of course," I said.

"Tell me why," he instructed, his expression earnest.

As if it weren't obvious. This guy was the magical equivalent of Harvard. Everyone said so. "Well for starters, you've trained one of the greatest demon slayers in my family. There's something to be said for references. You've been chairman of Demon Slayer Development for the last nine decades." I ticked them off on my fingers. "You've won the Department of Intramagical Matters' Gold Halo Award for twenty-eight years running."

I'd done my research.

He wrapped my hand in his, gently closing my fingers as he brought it down between us. "Those mean nothing. You should trust me because of this." He reached into his pocket and pulled out a gold cord, thin as a piece of twine.

He tilted his head and I offered him my right hand, just like that. I watched with an utter lack of understanding as he tied the ropy cord around my wrist.

"When you understand this"—he held my wrist—"you will have learned much."

"Okay, Yoda."

"Yoda?" he asked with the seriousness of a scholar. "I don't understand."

I felt my ears turn pink. "I'm sorry. It's a dumb pop-culture reference." One that was completely out of place, given what this man wanted to do for me. I'd been a teacher. Granted, my classroom had consisted of a motley bunch of three-year-olds, but I did know good teachers taught through experience instead of just lecturing endlessly. He was trying to help me learn about myself and my powers, and I was making light of his methods. Well not anymore.

Praise be, I'd learned something already.

I left Zebediah Rachmort talking with Grandma and went upstairs to get the training bar. Dread settled in my stomach as I opened the door to my room. I couldn't shake the feeling that the bar was nothing but trouble.

Pirate nearly leapt out of the armoire. "Lizzie! Whatcha doing?" he asked, eyes wide.

"I could ask you the same thing," I said as the door of the armoire swung back an inch or so.

"Oh, you know," he said, his white and brown body strangely motionless, except for his slightly shaking ears. "Just hanging out."

"You?" I said, moving for the armoire. Pirate never hung out in a room unless there were ghosts around to play Scrabble with. Sure enough, Pirate was up to something.

I opened the doors to the armoire and found the dragon. And it had grown.

It was as big as Pirate.

The snaggletoothed beast sat on top of my best—and only—pair of black heels, blinking at me with big orange eyes. Next to him lay the charred remains of my Adidas Supernova cross-trainers, the white and silver stripes now curled and black. The soles had melted and the singed laces were still smoking.

"Pirate, that was my last pair of comfortable shoes!" I exclaimed. The dragon had slopped birth goo and Lord knows what on my other ones.

"I'm sorry," Pirate insisted. "He sneezed."

"I told you we couldn't keep it." We had enough going on without my dog adding pets to the mix.

The dragon unfurled a pair of dingy white wings and fluttered out of the closet. He landed on his chin, popped up and toddled over to Pirate.

"He needs me," my dog protested. "He even likes Healthy Lite dog chow and look! I taught him a trick!" Pirate turned in a circle and sat. "Okay, Flappy—," he began.

"Flappy?"

"On account of his wings. Okay, Flappy," Pirate said in his most stern voice. "Roll over."

Flappy tottered back and forth on tiny dragon legs.

"That's it!" Pirate said. "Roll over!"

Flappy licked Pirate's paw.

"He did real good this morning," Pirate said, trying to nudge the dragon over with his nose.

"That's what they always say." I slipped my key into the locked compartment in the bottom of the armoire and retrieved the small wooden chest with the training bar inside.

"Don't get too attached," I warned. "Flappy is a wild animal. We're going to have to let him go, okay?"

Pirate let out a loud doggie whine.

I felt bad. I really did. But Pirate was a pet. He didn't need a pet. We were here to save the estate—and my life—not to foster wild animals. Besides, I could do without any more complications.

Or sandpapery dragon tongues licking my leg. My

heart softened for a moment before reality crashed down again.

"No. No pets and that's final."

When I went back outside, Zebediah Rachmort was doing a pretty good impression of Rip van Winkle under an oak tree. Before I could figure out how to wake him, he opened his eyes.

"Ah, very good," he said, eyeing the wooden box under my arm.

"Are you sure about that?" I asked. When he didn't make a move to stand, I sat across from him in the grass, placing the box between us.

"This is a tool. Nothing more," he said. "You must learn to stop assigning meaning to things."

Easy for him to say. "But I'm afraid—"

"Nothing is to be feared except evil," he said. "This bar is not evil."

Yes, well my encounter with the thing hadn't been pleasant. "You have to understand. I touched it already and it showed me a vision of my death."

I waited for him to be horrified. Instead, Rachmort shook his head. "This bar does not predict. It merely showed you a possibility. Now take it. Without fear."

That was tougher than he thought. I hesitated before touching the thick iron bands that supported the bottom of the chest and wrapped around the lid.

Now or never.

I touched each of the fingers on my right hand to each of the five switch-star adornments on the box. They warmed under my fingers and I fought the urge to leave Zebediah—and the box—out here on the lawn.

Instead, I pulled the lid back. A wisp of smoke seeped from the box. It snaked across the ground below. The tips of the grass crackled and browned. The lavender velvet at the bottom looked empty. I knew it wasn't.

Heart hammering, I reached down for the bar.

"Without fear," Rachmort reminded me.

Right. And snakes don't bite. Fire won't burn. And imps bake cookies.

I did my best to tamp down my dread. "I'm not afraid," I said, not convincing anybody.

"May I?" Rachmort asked. He ran a ringed hand lovingly over the box before sliding the invisible bar out of its holder. I watched as he placed it in his other hand, palm up.

Bit by bit, a cloudy glass bar took shape.

"Holy Moses," I gasped. "How did you do that?"

"I decided to do it," he said simply. "Now it's your turn."

"Now?" Part of me was still waiting for yet another horrible vision.

"Take it," he said, sliding it into my hands.

It felt smooth and cool. "Amazing," I said, shaking slightly and watching the cloudy glass shift. "How can I hold it now, without the visions?"

"This is a tool," he said. "Nothing more. I can only guess that when you first held it, you projected your fears onto the bar. As a consequence, it showed you what you should most fear."

I didn't understand. My vision had seemed so real. "So what I saw wasn't true?"

"No," he said, "it was true. And you should strengthen yourself against it. But your, er, method is only one way to use the bar."

He placed a hand on my shoulder. "Why don't you ask it to show you a triumph, Lizzie?"

That seemed kind of beside the point.

Wasn't I supposed to be looking for things that were wrong? Not that I wanted any more visions.

Darned it if there wasn't something downright persuasive in his wind-chapped cheeks.

"Okay," I said, holding the bar tight in both hands. I closed my eyes and focused on what it felt like to win a battle.

"Clear your mind," I heard him say.

"Yes." I let my body go and focused on using the bar like the tool it was. It felt heavier than it had been. Heat pooled in my hand and raced up my arm. I gripped the bar tighter, and a door opened in my mind.

The grass shifted as Rachmort planted himself next to me. "Let it in," he urged.

I swam through a murky current, the vision just out of reach. I concentrated hard on my defenses, willing each of them to drop until I saw myself. Only it wasn't me. It was a shadowy copy. I could feel the malice and the hate dripping from it. It flung a volley of switch stars directly at my chest.

The cold sting of impact swept the breath right out of me.

My eyes flew open. "Make it stop!"

Rachmort gripped my shoulders, "What did you see?"

"Me. Only it wasn't me, but it tried to kill me!"

He pulled back. "Interesting," he said, tugging at his chin.

"Is that all you can say? I was almost gutted by a blast of switch stars." I was gutted. I felt the impact.

"Are you sure you focused on a great triumph?" he asked.

"Yes," I said with more force than I meant. I couldn't help it. I felt tricked, betrayed. "Why does this flipping bar think I have to die?"

Rachmort didn't answer. He simply looked at me, stroking his chin.

Lovely.

I glanced down at the bar. It was invisible again. One step forward, two steps back. "Why can't I see it?"

Rachmort seemed deep in thought. "You see it as invisible," he said. "You saw it that way from the start and choose to see it that way now."

Part of me doubted it. So far, I hadn't gotten to choose much about my new life.

"Try," Rachmort said. "You're more in control of your destiny than you imagine."

I found that hard to believe. If I were in control of things, I'd have been lounging on the beach with Dimitri with no imps, biker witches or trouble in sight.

I focused on Zebediah, his intense expression almost willing me to succeed. Okay. I could do this. I focused the bar, asking it to show itself. To my surprise, it appeared solid in my hand. "Amazing."

"Yes," he mused, "I suppose it is. The world is a shocking place, more so if you are a new demon slayer. I can't tell you what to think of the bar or of your vision. That is for you to decide. But you will find that no matter how situations seem to unfold in strange and unpredictable ways, you have more control than you imagine. Whether it is with a pack of rampaging imps or a boyfriend," he said with a wink, "the same rules apply."

He made it seem so simple, and yet . . . I turned the bar over in my hands. "How do I look at things in new ways if I don't even know I'm looking at them wrong?"

"It is the struggle of a lifetime, one we must always mind. The biggest danger is when we think we know all there is to know."

"Great. So you're still learning too."

"Always," he said. "Now come with me." He walked me to the oak tree near the path I'd taken that morning. "I plan to learn a great deal from you as well."

I didn't know if he was just trying to make me feel good or if he really could learn from a demon slayer like me.

"There is a saying. When the old oak stops growing, you know it's dead."

I lifted my eyes to the crooked tree, with its thick trunk and maze of twisted braches.

"Now why don't you climb it?"

"Excuse me?"

"It seems you are to be tested soon, and there is much for you to learn. We will start with one of your more basic skills, levitation."

"But Ant Eater said we'd use the pergola," I said, not quite sure why I was protesting the location when what really bothered me was the idea of a leap off of a tall object. The last time I'd tried to levitate, I'd been forced to jump off a tall ladder onto a bed of rusty nails.

Rachmort barked out a laugh. "The pergola, Lizzie? You'd crack your head open on the porch."

Yes, that possibility had occurred to me too.

"You're much better off landing in the grass," he said, kicking away some of the acorns and sticks from under the tree.

I could see his point. "You expect me to crash, don't you?"

"Perhaps."

"What about your expert training?"

He winked. "That can't begin until you climb the tree."

Chapter Fifteen

I flumped onto the ground for the second time that day, pain shooting up my hips and shoulders and no closer to levitation than Pirate was to keeping his pet dragon.

Rachmort's face appeared above me. "That was an improvement." The man seemed genuinely excited.

"How so?" I asked, digging an acorn out of the small of my back.

"You didn't hesitate as much before you jumped. Quite admirable after the way you landed on that Frozen Underwear spell the last time."

I really wished the biker witches would clean up after themselves. "I thought I'd cleared out everything from under the tree," I said, digging a curved, razor-sharp badger tooth out from under my thigh. Praise be to thick leather pants. "The Red Skulls better stop leaving me gifts." I tossed the inch-and-a-half monstrosity into the woods behind me. "I don't care if they're good luck."

"You must block out these distractions," he said, as if he'd never met the Red Skulls and their particular brand of magic.

Rachmort hunkered on the balls of his feet above me. "Levitation is about looking to the outside. That is a demon slayer truth, no? Lose the fear of what will happen next. Will I land on my back? Will I land on my head? Just what is under the tree?"

Actually, I thought those were all fair questions.

Rachmort didn't let up for a second. "Focus on the forces around you that will lift you up," he urged. "Trust them."

"Sure," I said, wishing I believed it.

"You must have the courage to fail," he insisted.

Yes, well I certainly had that.

"Now come," he said, helping me stand. "We will try once more."

My sore fingers protested as once again I dug them against the rough bark of the oak tree and began the climb of doom. I didn't see how repeatedly landing on my back was going to teach me anything, any more than I understood why I couldn't seem to land on my feet on a ten-foot drop. It's as if the universe wanted me in as much pain as possible.

When I'd climbed onto the heavy branch overlooking the (hopefully cleared) levitation area, I took a deep breath. Yes, the sun-dappled grass looked soft from here. Without a doubt, I knew it wasn't. But that was beside the point. I wasn't supposed to be landing.

I needed to float.

And as desperately as I wanted to have that happen, a little voice in the back of my head said, *Ha*.

I'd had a hard time believing in what I couldn't see before I came into the magical world. Now? Well, I was about to flop onto my back again.

Rachmort stood below, hands in the pockets of his striped slacks. He gave me his full attention, as if the climb itself meant something.

I should believe. He sure did.

I stood for a moment as a warm breeze rustled the

leaves around me. It's not as if I hadn't seen plenty that surprised me in the last two months. Between enchanted hotel rooms, grumpy fairies and biker witches hurling Lose Your Key spells at obnoxious drunks at the bar, I'd had my fair share of weirdness.

In fact, I could hear the Red Skulls working on the wards. Hammering, shouts and occasional explosions sounded from the front lawn.

"Look to the outside, Lizzie." Rachmort stood with his hands on his hips, the double-decker gold spectacles on his head glinting in the afternoon sun. "Don't overthink it."

Easy for him to say. The only thing he had to worry about was not getting crushed by my falling body.

My back, my hips, pretty much everything ached from the last two impacts.

The tree branch dug into the soles of my feet. I wanted to close my eyes, but I couldn't. Not while standing ten feet up. Instead, I looked to the blue sky. My stomach knotted. I couldn't put this off forever.

Trust it. Trust yourself.

Believe it, I told myself as I jumped.

I dropped like a hot pan full of trouble. A second before the ground rushed up to smack me in the head, I was swooped up by a dive-bombing griffin with a pink dress tied to her back paw.

"Diana!" I grasped the coarse fur at her back and struggled to ride astride the wild flying griffin.

Ever confident in my grip, she surged higher, breaking out above the trees. Now this was the way to fly. The wind streaked against my face; my stomach lurched with each bob and dip. I was on the amusement-park ride of my life, but even more, I was immensely grateful not to be on my back again, staring up at the old oak tree.

After a gratuitous lap around the gardens (did I mention Diana likes to have fun?) we landed next to Rachmort, who didn't seem to be disturbed at all by the griffin's rescue.

Instead, he stood regarding his watch fob with great interest. "Morticharius keeps Twittering from Limbo. I think he's bored," he said, flipping the bronze instrument closed and returning it the pocket of his waistcoat.

Diana opened her beak and gave a piercing call, like an eagle.

"Hup, hup." He held his hands up. "No need to apologize. In fact, I believe you are exactly what our Lizzie needs. Feel free to join us. Although no snacking on the tree nymphs."

Diana let out a half bleat, half choke.

Rachmort tilted his head. "Yes, well you'd be surprised at what some griffins eat. Certain people too. Now," he said, rubbing his hands together, "let's get back to work, shall we?"

"Of course," I said, wishing I had a ladder.

Think of it as exercise. Some people paid money to climb rock walls. This tree was free. Well, save for the cuts and scrapes on my hands.

Worry about it later. Or not. I had plenty of bigger things to worry about.

A few painful minutes later, I stood on the high branch again, contemplating my fate. Only, this time Diana stretched like a large cat below. She drew out one large back paw, then the other, before she straightened and looked at me expectantly.

She was like a large hairy cushion. Suddenly, jumping didn't seem like a big risk after all.

I blew out a quick breath, thought about floating and stepped off.

It took me a second to realize Diana wasn't coming to my rescue. Instead, I was floating to the ground, as though the air itself had thickened enough for me to glide gently to the earth.

"Look at this!" I exclaimed, shocked at the density of the air under my feet. It was solid and yet I could move through it. I just had to tell it what to do.

"Over there," I said, trying to direct it and realizing I had to use my feet, as if it were some sort of spongy walking surface. Floating surface was more like it.

Jesus, Mary, Joseph and the mule. I was levitating!

And I didn't even screw up the landing. Instead, I touched my toes to the ground, then the balls of my feet, all the way down to my heels. I stood in front of a beaming Zebediah Rachmort triumphant, invigorated and more than a little winded. I think I'd forgotten to breathe for a few minutes there.

"Look at me!" I exclaimed.

"Yes, yes!" he said, clapping his hands on my shoulders, as proud as I was. "You didn't worry about falling and you did it!"

"Well sure." I looked over at Diana, who had unfurled her massive wings and let out a squawk of triumph.

It was a lot easier to levitate when I had a griffin around to break the fall.

Rachmort stared at me until he had my full attention. "What you needed was the courage to fail." His steely gaze bored into me like he was trying to force the knowledge into my head. "Embrace your fears. Only then can you move beyond them and find something new."

He had me levitate for another hour. It was the most fun I'd had since . . . Well, I didn't want to think about Dimitri when he was so far away, but let's just say most of my spine-tingling memories had to do with him.

I was feeling utterly triumphant as I levitated down on one foot and did a small pirouette. My parents hadn't sent me to twelve years of ballet class for nothing. "Do I get extra points for style?" I asked, giving a bow.

"There are no grades here," he reminded me.

Darn. I'd always liked report-card day.

"Now," he said, as if the best was yet to come, "you will walk and think."

"Walk?" I'd just learned to levitate.

"Yes, yes," he said. "And you will ponder that, among other things."

It didn't make sense. "I thought you were supposed to be teaching me."

"I am showing you how to create what you need for yourself," he said, in a classy version of Grandma's "learn by experience" philosophy.

Well, I was tired of learning by trial and error. "I need real classroom, or at least under-the-tree, experience. You need to tell me what to do."

"I just did," he said, "and you levitated." He walked me toward the front of the house, where the biker witches had set out giant tarps to make sun-dried snakeskins. Heaven knows how they'd found so many.

He ignored the witches turning the snakeskins with tongs, not to mention Heather-the-Hard-Hat Creely. The engineering witch was rigging up some sort of assembly line.

Rachmort cleared his throat. "Think of your preschool class, Lizzie. Did they learn better when you merely told them things or when you showed them and let them also make their own discoveries?"

Oh lordy. "Exactly what am I supposed to discover in the woods?"

He practically clapped his hands together in glee. "I don't know!"

How fun—for him.

The tangled path lay in front of me, the trees rising tall on either side. "Fine, but I really think we should be doing something."

"Oh yes—doing, running, leaping into the fray. Not unlike the Charge of the Light Brigade. I warned them about that too. Never confuse action with understanding," he said.

Action was all I knew, I realized, as I started off through the cypress forest alone. From the minute Grandma had shown up at my front door with a bag full of Smuckers-jar magic and a demon on her tail, I'd been on the run. I hadn't had the luxury to lounge around and wax philosophic, let alone understand anything.

Now that I did have the time, I wasn't quite sure what to do with it or how to find the answers I needed.

The banging of the witches soon gave way to the sounds of the forest.

I fiddled with the gold cord Rachmort had tied around my wrist. As if I was supposed to learn something from that.

My hand wandered down to my switch stars and I found myself counting them. Five. I always had five.

The loose earth and rocks crunched under my boots as I walked. I tried not to think of the biker witches tearing apart the front lawn or what Pirate and Flappy might be doing to the remains of my wardrobe. Instead, I focused on the swaying of the trees, the birds darting from branch to branch.

Before I knew it, I was almost at the ruins without having had any deep thoughts at all.

I looked up at the sky, which was a gorgeously deceptive shade of blue. As creepy as the swirling green sky had been, I almost wished it were back. Then I'd at least have a stark reminder of the evil that stalked me.

How could I be of any use to Dimitri when I had my own problems to solve? He needed to protect his family, rebuild his home. So far, I'd kept him from doing both of those things. If I knew anything about the Red Skulls, I'd be willing to bet their brand of magic had knocked the rebuilding effort back a few paces.

I only hoped the Dominos clan would see past his relationship with me and give us the help we needed. And as much as Amara could grate on me, I was glad she could go with him. If life were at all fair, he'd be with another griffin like her, someone who could help him rebuild.

Now I felt like throwing something.

In the name of target practice, I set my sights on a thick spruce with peeling bark and a knot about six feet off the ground. I aimed and fired, slicing the knot in half.

Nice.

I waited for the switch star to dislodge itself from the

wood and come hurtling back to me. If only everything in life acted like switch stars.

Humming to myself, I selected another target—this time, a skinnier tree about twenty feet deep into the woods. It would take a bit more skill, not to mention finesse, to aim through the crowded forest. I zeroed in on my target and let loose.

The switch star shot through the trees and into oblivion.

Hell's bells.

I wanted to work on that shot again. Only my switch star didn't come back right away. I held out my hand, waiting.

They always came back.

Unease settled over me as I peered into the small forest. I wasn't getting any demon slayer clanging in my head, but something was definitely wrong. I pulled out another star and headed into the woods.

I tramped through the underbrush until I came to the spot where the star should have hit. The tree remained unmolested, which I knew already. But where could the star have gone?

Focusing, I tried to call it back to me, like when I'd aimed it in the battle with the imps. Nothing.

I searched every tree, shrub and anthill for the next twenty yards and came up with nothing, nada, zip.

Wiping my drippy forehead with an equally sweaty arm, I contemplated my options. There was no way I could lose a switch star. It wasn't done.

For one thing, even stepping on a dormant switch star could really hurt someone—human or animal. I didn't want anyone slicing a foot or a hoof or a paw.

Then there was the fact that I truly did need all five stars. I'd never met any other demon slayers, but I was willing to bet nobody else charged into battle with weapons missing.

It was almost like someone had taken my switch star. But nobody else could touch it. Well, except for another demon slayer, or a handler like Dimitri.

Geez. What was I going to tell Dimitri?

Sorry about your estate and your life. Oh by the way, can you run to Wal-Mart and get me another switch star?

I dropped onto a half-rotted log. It had to be here, but it wasn't. "As if there's another demon slayer just walking around in the woods," I said to the pine tree in front of me.

Ignoring the gnats buzzing around my face, I tried to think of some deep thoughts so I at least had something to show for my afternoon. When that didn't work, I headed back to find Rachmort.

He bustled around under an old oak tree, tinkering with an odd assortment of machines. "Lizzie," he said, a wrench in his hand, as I approached, "have you been thinking?"

"You have no idea," I said. "What are those?"

"Ah. Inquisitive. I like that." He stood proudly in front of something that looked like a bicycle attached to a late-1800s-style camera box, complete with a three-legged wooden easel. "This machine here measures the amount of magic pressing down on any given point. Good for diagnosing trouble with protective wards, as I hear you've been having." He moved on to a gilded birdcage with all kinds of twirling spikes pointed out of it. "This is a hell-bent–creatures trap." He pointed to a scattering of pearly white threads at the bottom. "The unicorn hair attracts the buggers. Although I hope we don't need to use that. Do you know how hard it is to shave a unicorn?"

I shook my head. "I have my hands full here."

And this," he said, holding up a small, brass-handled trunk, "is my dinner."

"We can certainly feed you."

"No, no, no. I'm a creature of habit," he said, patting the box. "You must allow me my indulgences." He placed his dinner under the tree and retrieved what looked to be some kind of double-headed socket wrench. "Come." Rachmort took the wrench to the large bolts that held the bicycle to the photo box. "Tell me about your afternoon."

I crossed my arms over my chest. "I'm a total failure."

He stopped his tinkering. "Tell me your definition of *failure*."

"Everything I've done so far has been cobbled together," I said. "Back before I was a demon slayer, things made sense. I may not have liked it all, but my life worked, my family was predictable, my job didn't involve a mysterious dark-haired woman who may or may not be out to get me. I knew where I stood. I was good at things. I had lists and a calendar with a backup calendar and color-coded files, and I never even forgot anything, much less failed at anything."

He barely glanced up at me. "You are so afraid to disappoint. But when have you ever truly failed?"

"You'd be surprised." I couldn't even hold on to my own switch stars.

"You succeeded in rescuing your grandmother from the second layer of hell. You ended a centuries-old curse on the Kallinikos family. You performed an exorcism on a werewolf. You defeated an army of succubi." He counted on his fingers. "From what I've heard you're also the only one to set Max the demon hunter on his ear."

I grinned, and he did too.

"Truth be told, I would have liked to see that," he admitted.

I couldn't help but brighten. I *had* done quite a lot, especially when I'd been forced to head out on a wing and a prayer. "When you say it, it sounds so different. Most of the time, I don't feel like I accomplish much."

"Why does it matter how you feel?" he asked.

I opened my mouth, but I didn't have an answer. I'd never thought of it that way.

"It matters who you are. I left a pressing job in purgatory because you are important. You don't even understand yet how vital your work is going to be to this world and everyone in it."

I drew back. "What are you talking about?"

"You cannot achieve greatness by playing it safe. Nor does it come without sacrifice."

"I'm not great." Most days, I struggled just to be good. When it came to sacrifice, I wanted to wince.

You'd think after years of reining myself in, sacrifice would be easier. It wasn't. Then again, I was beginning to realize there were events—and people—more important than me.

What would I give up to keep Dimitri happy and safe?

Would I be willing to let down those who depended on me? Would I say enough is enough, when it comes to duty? Could I have actually given up on Las Vegas a few weeks ago when Dimitri wanted to go back to Greece?

With a heavy heart, I realized I didn't dare, not when

lives and souls were at stake. I may not be the best demon slayer who ever lived, but I could and would make a difference.

"The choice is always yours, of course," he mused. "But sometimes we must think of the greater good. Let go of our own petty wants and needs. You are being called to greatness, Lizzie. Whether you chose it or not, it is up to you to decide what to do with your gift."

"Do you even realize what you're saying?" I asked. I was not a kick-butt heroine. I didn't dash into the fray, daring the demons to come and get me. I didn't have witty comebacks for the people in my life. So far, I hadn't even learned how to cuss. I was just a preschool teacher doing the best she could with the vat of cosmic spaghetti fate had dumped over her head.

I sat down on the grass. "I think we're in trouble."

"Doubt is natural, Lizzie. It is a way to grow."

Problem was, I didn't like where my thoughts were leading. If I was supposed to be some amazing demon slayer, I didn't see it. And worse, I didn't know how the rest of my life was supposed to fit.

How could I keep expecting those who loved me to risk their lives for mine?

Why did they have to give up their wants and needs for me?

The Red Skulls had traveled halfway around the globe on a boat, just so they could be here when I trained. Dimitri had let me into his life and family, only to have his home and all the precious things he fought so hard for trashed, for me.

At least the Red Skulls were used to being on the run. Dimitri didn't want that. It was unfair and I knew it.

How could I love him and not put him first?

Rachmort was right. I did have to think. Because so far, I'd only been considering myself. I wanted Dimitri. I wanted him with me in Las Vegas, while his family needed him here. Now I wanted him to follow me around the world, fighting other people's battles, when I could tell he wanted to settle down here, on this estate, with the family he'd fought so hard to protect.

I drew a ragged breath as the truth stung me like acid.

He'd sacrificed so much for me. Maybe it was time I did the same for him.

If I was going to be a powerful demon slayer, someone who could protect innocent people from the scourge of hell, I had only one choice.

My heart squeezed. My life would destroy any hope he had of rebuilding his.

Perhaps it was time to let Dimitri go.

Chapter Sixteen

Now I really did want to be alone. I set off down the path where I'd lost my switch star. Maybe an answer would hit me somewhere along the trail. Maybe I could find a way to have a normal life, at least one with Dimitri.

Maybe I'd just keep walking.

The kicker was, I'd wanted this knowledge.

My right hand rested against the remaining switch stars on my belt. Fallen leaves crackled under my boots.

From the very beginning, when I'd first learned I was a demon slayer, I wanted to know what it meant. Information, to me, is king. It's the ultimate form of control. If you know what you're doing, you don't mess up.

Now it seemed like the more I learned about myself, and especially this journey I'd begun, the more I wished I'd left things alone.

I ducked around a low-hanging tree branch, its large thick leaves fanning in every direction.

I'd always been one to help other people. I liked taking care of the kids at Happy Hands. I liked being the planner among my small group of friends back home. I liked taking care of Pirate. But this insistence Rachmort had about me being the one to save them felt like too much. It was more responsibility than I could have ever imagined.

And as odd as it sounded, I wished someone would have at least asked.

I walked until I reached the clearing at the Callidora. The tips of my boots stopped on the packed-earth path right in front of a tangle of weeds pouring from the clearing.

Get a grip. It's only strewn rocks in a clearing.

If I'd been more of a demon slayer, or at least a kick-butt heroine, I'd have barged ahead, consequences be damned.

But I was too practical. And I didn't even like to think of the word *damned.*

She will be lost at the Callidora, the first time in joy, the second time in death.

I couldn't do it. You just don't risk that kind of prophecy. At least I don't.

I turned to head back, when I heard something rattling in the foliage on the other side. I crouched behind the nearest tree, my left shoulder against the rough bark, my right hand holding a switch star.

A moment later, Pirate burst out of the clearing ahead, followed by a significantly larger dragon. The beast flew behind Pirate on paper-thin wings. It had grown from the size of a small dog to Great Dane proportions and it wore the dancing-doggies-and-fire-hydrants adjustable collar and retractable leash Pirate had selected the last time we were at Petco.

Pirate dropped the end of the leash and jammed his nose into the air. "Hold up, Flappy. I smell trouble."

The dragon let out a squeak and crouched behind Pirate.

"Oh now that's ridiculous," I said, standing.

"Lizzie!" Pirate exclaimed dashing straight for me. "I thought I smelled you! At first I thought it was wishful thinking, but it is you!" he said, leaping over tufts of grass.

I saw the moment where surprise and joy gave way to the realization that I'd seen Flappy.

His ears lowered slightly and he lost a bit of steam. "Now I know what you're thinking," he said, as if doggie diplomatic skills were going to get him out of this one.

"I'm thinking you still have a dragon," I said, eyeing the fire-breathing ugly duckling as it fluttered clumsily after my dog.

"Now that *is* true," Pirate said, spinning twice before launching himself at my leg. "But look at him. He needs me!"

I scooped up my dog and we both watched the doe-eyed dragon flounder across the clearing. His mottled body was far too big for his head—and his wings. Flappy dipped up and down like a baby bird, with the leash trailing behind him. I felt the insane urge to go out there and retrieve him, which was (a) ridiculous and (b) impossible, since the dragon probably weighed as much as I did.

"Why the leash?" I asked, hitching Pirate under my arm. I could tell he'd been finding many things to eat other than his Healthy Lite dog chow.

"Flappy's a pet. And that is my best leash."

Yes, but this was a dragon. It was unnatural. "Don't you think it's a little cruel?"

Pirate looked up at me in that guileless way that only dogs can manage. "You put *me* on a leash."

"Good point," I conceded. Still, the dragon had barely made it through half of the clearing. If we were in the middle of an imp attack, the poor thing would be ashes on the ground. Which was another reason we couldn't keep the animal.

As if I'd wished it on us, I could feel something lurking nearby. The hairs on the back of my neck stood up.

"Pirate," I said.

"Ouch. That's too tight," he said, struggling against my grip.

We needed to get Flappy.

Frickin' dragon.

But I wasn't about to walk out into that clearing.

"Flappy!" I hissed, taking cover behind the tree with Pirate.

"He don't speak English," Pirate said struggling against my grip. "In fact, I can't talk to him at all. Which is weird. Let me go and I'll get him lickety split."

"Hush," I whispered.

I couldn't tell where the danger was coming from, only that it was growing stronger by the second. The baby dragon's eyes widened as he fluttered its wings harder. Pirate's entire body was stiff with the need to run out there and get his pet. I knew the feeling, which is why I held him tight.

The threat was coming from low on the ground. Behind us!

I swiveled around the tree until we faced the woods. "You two stay down," I said as Flappy finally made it to the safety of the trees. The pets had a reunion as I stood slowly. I never did like throwing from a crouched position.

It was like a dot in my mind.

You want me? Well come and get me.

I moved from tree to tree, stalking it. I refused to be afraid anymore.

Then it hit me—I really could control my powers if I wanted. I chose to hunt instead of be hunted, and now I was suddenly tracking my attacker. It was a heady feeling.

Don't get cocky.

Rachmort's gold cord caught against my utility belt and I ripped the thing off and left it on the ground. My heart sped up as I caught a glimpse of my stalker rushing through the trees. It was a dark-haired woman, like the one I'd seen when I found Diana's Skye stone.

I sensed her now.

She wasn't getting away this time.

I tracked her malice and her anger. I fed on her hate as I dogged her through the dense woods. Sweat trickled down my back as I crashed through the underbrush, my breath coming hard as we dodged and weaved.

She was mine.

Mine.

Maybe Dimitri was right. I could take control of my own destiny.

She wasn't just angry—she was jealous. The dot of light turned into a smothering cloud. Suddenly, her rage boiled all around me. Fear gripped my chest as I dove for cover behind a thick sweet-gum tree.

Overheated and shaking, I had the sickening thought that maybe this thing had drawn me away from Pirate and Flappy on purpose.

I gripped my switch star until my fingers turned white

in the handles. No. Sure as I'd been shown my own death, I knew she was after me.

At that moment, something flew toward my head as I threw myself to the ground. I don't know how or why I knew how to fall, only that I had to check to make sure I was still in one piece. Heart pounding, I rolled and ducked behind a fallen log, scanning the trees for my attacker.

Like a fog, the danger in the air lifted away. I was left digging one hand into rotting tree bark. The other still gripped the switch star. And when I stopped looking for the dark-haired woman in the trees and started to take it all in, I found the switch star that had gone missing earlier today.

It was buried in the tree where my head had been.

With a shudder, it dislodged itself and sailed back to me.

"But why do we have to stay with you?" Pirate asked as we charged through the woods as fast as Flappy's wings would go.

"Because I don't know what's out there." We needed to talk to Rachmort. Now.

Unfortunately, we stumbled on Frieda first.

She wobbled on red, white and blue platform sandals much better suited for the mall. "Hold up, Lizzie Brown. Where's the fire?" she asked, hands on her white leather pants.

"Someone just tried to chop my head off," I said, all in one breath.

Frieda shook her head, her red Vegas dice earrings

swaying against her neck. "Again?" she asked. "Well, seeing as you're in one piece, can I borrow your dragon for one teeny-tiny second?"

"Why?" I asked, not appreciating the holdup. Then again, the witches were reinforcing the wards, so I'd be a fool not to help if I could.

"Ingredient gathering," she said, chomping on her gum.

Oh great. This could take forever.

Frieda clucked at Flappy like he was some kind of pet. "Now, Flappy." She pointed to the high branches of a spindly tree. "You think you could get that broken-down bird's nest up there?"

The little dragon let out a puff of smoke and beamed with pride.

"We need feathered mud to thicken up the wards," she said as Flappy began his laborious ascent. "Don't want anything slipping in."

"Fine," I said, taking off. "You're in charge of the dragon."

"Breathe for a minute, Lizzie," she called after me. "You try to stir too many pots and you'll end up putting vinegar in the pudding and vanilla extract in the turnip greens."

I didn't even know what that meant.

"Later!" I hollered back to her. Like when someone wasn't trying to kill me.

Then again, that could be a long wait.

I found Zebediah Rachmort near the crooked oak, reviving a stomped-upon anthill. He crouched over the little black ants, murmuring and touching his knobby fingers to each one. They wriggled their legs and came back to life under the necromancer's touch.

I stopped short. "Holy hoodoo." I'd never seen anything like it.

He grinned and kept at his work. "Ants are simple. They don't have souls."

"Can you do that to people?" I asked.

"Unfortunately, no. People, dogs, dragons," he said, glancing out into the trees where I'd left Pirate and Flappy, "elevated life-forms have souls that travel to the beyond when they die. Necromancers who follow the path of the light would not revive a soulless shell."

"But you could," I said slowly, grasping the depth of his power.

"But I would *not*." He tapped at the ants.

When he'd revived the hill, I told him about the dark-haired woman in the woods.

"I could suddenly sense her in a way I couldn't before. I don't know if she chose it or if I did."

Please let it be me.

"Where's your gold cord?" he asked.

It took me a second to remember what he was talking about. "It was bothering me. I took it off in the woods. Why does it matter?"

Rachmort nodded. "It was a simple test. Will you follow my instructions or your own instincts?" He wrapped a hand around my wrist, where the golden tie used to be. "It looks like you let go and followed your gut—in more ways than one."

I hadn't thought of it that way. "I suppose you're right."

"Of course I'm right," he said. "You decided you didn't

need my gold cord. You decided seeing the dark-haired woman was more important than knowing you couldn't. Lesson learned."

The truth of it crept over me.

Well how about that?

Rachmort studied me carefully, cradling his chin in his hand. "On the downside, we know for sure you are connected somehow to this dark-haired woman, or else she never could have used one of your switch stars against you."

"She stole a part of me. But I don't always feel a tie," I said, my eyes dropping to his bronze ring. "I can't be sure I'll detect her again."

Rachmort hung on my every word and then some. "It stands to reason that you wouldn't always be able to feel yourself."

"But she's not me. She's evil." I'd felt her rage when she attacked.

He rubbed the side of his chin as he thought. "Hmm . . . Yes." I could see the ideas whirling in his head. "But it does seem she possesses a connection, perhaps even a small part of you. We must seek to understand this new threat."

Despite my agitation, I felt a twinge of relief. "Grandma and the Red Skulls are going to build a cave of visions."

"Perfect," he said, searching for the glasses that were propped on top of his head.

"I'm scared," I admitted.

"The cave of visions is top of the line," Rachmort said. "Unconventional. But it works much better than anything I've ever seen. I'll even go with you, if you'd like."

"I would," I said, grateful again for this man.

Rachmort folded his hands behind his back as walked. "Don't worry. You are strong. You are capable. We will learn what the dark-haired woman wants from you."

"And then what?" I asked.

"That's up to you, demon slayer."

Chapter Seventeen

The front lawn was not only covered with tarps, but Sidecar Bob was roasting turtle knees in an array of heirloom griffin armor. I cringed and hoped the pieces were darned near indestructible. In any case, the damage had been done. Bob had lined the priceless shields and breastplates with tinfoil to make crude roasting pans. He'd set them in fire pits all along the front drive.

He made his way up the line, stirring them with a new—and expensive-looking—brass kitchen spoon. A scraggly witch followed him, carrying a baby-shampoo bottle, now filled with muddy sludge. She muttered to herself, her gray dreadlocks covering her face as she measured out capfuls of the slop.

Of course that was nothing compared to the giant planks that Creely the engineering witch was pounding into the villa's front door. She was too busy hammering to even notice me as I came up behind her and tugged on her brown leather pants.

"Lizzie!" she called to me, her green-streaked hair swaying with every pound of the hammer into Dimitri's pristine home. "It doesn't look like much, but this sling is going to be a beaut."

"Sling? You can't pull back a sling into Dimitri's house!"

"Sure we can. I've already got two going in the back."

Exactly how much of his family's villa did she intend to destroy?

"This is simply the base structural support," Creely said, motioning with her hammer. "The strongest joints are on the support beams near the door. We'll be on the roof with the actual slings."

Peachy.

"Is this necessary?" I asked, not really wanting to know the answer.

"Always," she said, pulling nails out of her pocket and planting them on the side of her mouth.

I turned back from the witch pounding on Dimitri's house and almost fell off the side of the porch in shock. Two figures strolled up the lane.

Dimitri and Amara.

It wasn't that I didn't expect to see him come home. I did. But I sure has heck hadn't pictured them walking with their heads leaning together, discussing *something* of intense interest to them both.

Griffin business, no doubt.

Well what did I expect? He'd just spent several days with his own kind—a griffin clan like the one he'd been hoping to build. And now he couldn't. I was no griffin.

Amara laughed at something he said, her voice ringing over even the incessant racket of the Red Skulls until she saw me and the joy on her face died.

At least one person looked glad to see me. "Lizzie!" Dimitri rushed for me, taking the front porch steps two at a time. He wrapped me in a bear hug. "I missed you." He nuzzled my neck. "I wished I could have called, but the Dominos clan is old-fashioned."

"No phones," Amara said over his shoulder. She just

had to be a part of our homecoming. Then again, maybe she played a bigger role in his life than I'd ever realized, a shadow behind everything he did and said.

"Did it go well?" I asked, leaning into him, relishing the pleasure of having him close.

Dimitri hesitated. "We'll talk about it later."

"That bad?" I asked.

"No," Dimitri said.

"Yes," Amara corrected.

"Which is it?" I asked.

"We didn't need their help anyway."

"Yes, we did," Grandma said, walking up, hands on her hips. "What'd you do? Did you piss 'em off?"

As if she were the one to talk.

Dimitri sighed. "The Dominos clan feels it's too risky to send their people over here, not until we know what we're dealing with. It doesn't make sense that our Skye magic is fading. We don't understand who is attacking." For a moment, he looked lost. "I didn't even tell them about the green sky."

"Or the protective magic we lost?" I asked.

He hadn't. I read it on his face.

Amara's gaze slid over Dimitri. "They were much more willing to help when Dimitri was going to be a future member of the family, so to speak. There doesn't seem to be much point anymore," she said, her comment directed at me.

Oh great. So let's see. I'd taken his pure griffin heritage, his ability to lead a normal, non–demon slayer life, and now he couldn't protect his home because of me.

Of course one of Creely's biker witches picked that moment to start tossing boards off the roof.

"Duck!" I hollered, making a mad dash off the porch as Dimitri attempted to shield Amara with his body.

I stood in the front yard, shocked.

Yes, I could take care of myself.

Perhaps she leaned into him first.

Maybe he knew she was a helpless jerk.

But he still stood there with his arms around her—protecting *her*.

Something in me snapped. "This is wrong. All of it." The witches on the roof and all over the lawn and Rachmort saving ants, while Pirate hid a dragon in the house. And when it came down to it, he went with her. He protected *her*.

I needed him. Hell, I loved him. But it was obvious he didn't even know what he wanted—or needed—anymore.

I wasn't going to ruin his life, at least not if I had anything to say about it. Tears stung the back of my eyes.

As much as it crushed me, I was going to have to walk away and let him be a griffin. It was either that or I was going to destroy him.

"I can't do this." I tried to say it out loud. I tried to be bold, but it came out on a whisper.

"Lizzie." Dimitri walked over and cradled me to him, the same way he'd done with Amara. "Whatever you're thinking, stop it."

"No." I didn't want to discuss it, not when my emotions were this raw. "Later," I said, knowing he deserved an explanation and a private breakup.

It was going to be awful living here with him until his sisters were strong enough to defend the house and until we recovered that stolen piece of me, but this wasn't about comfort. This was about doing the right thing.

"I just need you to leave me alone right now," I said, ducking out of his embrace and heading for the house. "Please," I said at the door when he tried to follow me.

I didn't look back, except for one time. From the window at the beginning of the hallway, I saw Amara slip a hand over his shoulder.

That night, I ignored his knocks on the door. It wasn't easy, considering the ruckus Pirate and Flappy made each time Dimitri came by. The darned dragon took up most of my room. If he cooed at me one more time, I was going to scream. But between my close encounter at the Callidora today and then almost getting my head chopped off, my emotional cup runneth over.

I lay in bed, Pirate snuggled against my chest. The fur from the back of his neck prickled my cheek as I cried silent tears. It was better this way. Better to feel hollow inside than risk anyone I loved. Just because Dimitri was willing to sacrifice everything didn't mean I had to let him.

He deserved a better life than this.

When I had no more tears left, I dreamed of a pair of radiant Skye stones. They shimmered with a light all their own, glistening like unearthly jewels. I touched them, reveling in the spark of power that flowed into me. They were unique, priceless, and they had to be destroyed.

I tried to fight off the wave of malice as I gathered up the stones. The hate was so raw I could taste it like metal in my mouth.

Diana and Dyonne must be eliminated. The Helios house would *not* stand.

I felt trapped in a body that wasn't my own as I carried the stones deeper into my dark fortress and laid them on a wooden table with moon symbols carved into the surface. Then my hands closed around a sledgehammer and in one blow, I crushed the first stone. Shards of rock flew. I smashed the second stone.

I gathered the pieces and beat them until they were dust on the floor.

Chapter Eighteen

I awoke to the unsettling feeling of a hot and squishy dragon nostril under my hand. "Pirate," I mumbled, cracking my eye to find Flappy curled up in the crook of my body and Pirate nowhere to be seen.

Of course Pirate never went missing for long.

"Here I am!" He popped up at the end of the bed. "Flappy needed more covers. He gets cold at night."

"Probably cold-blooded," I said, rolling away from the dragon and rubbing the grit out of my eyes.

Pirate pawed the bedsheets. "That's not nice. What has Flappy ever done to you?"

"Hush," I said, not because I wasn't up to teaching my dog about the reality of owning a large lizard-type creature, but because I heard something ominous downstairs. A woman's voice spoke in strained tones, although I couldn't make out what she said.

Dawn had broken, so I doubted it was the biker witches. They'd been up late with the wards.

The agitated voice was met with deeper male protests. It sounded like bad news.

Pirate cocked his head. "Want me to see what it is?"

"No," I said. "You stay here and think of what to do with Flappy."

Pirate's ears drooped.

Yeah, well I wasn't the one disobeying orders and keeping dragons in the house.

I dressed quickly while Pirate tucked Flappy into my bed. Lucky for him and his pet—who was now curled up in my blankets—I had bigger things to worry about.

Buckling my switch stars, I headed out. My boots echoed down the ceramic-tile hallway. I wished they'd quiet down so I could hear the voices again. Lo and behold, my feet began to move silently.

I about tripped. Hello, new demon slayer power.

My feet moved as gracefully as a cat's, and as soundlessly. Not that I had ever been awkward, but stealthy was a completely different story.

I couldn't help grinning. As abilities went, it was a good one. I tried to make noise again and I did—my heels echoing down the stone stairway. I hit the silencer again and presto!

This was really nifty.

I allowed myself a brief little jig at the bottom of the stairs before I focused on what had brought me downstairs in the first place. By now I could tell it was Diana and Dyonne in the kitchen. Then Talos's voice popped up. And Amara's. Heavens. It was the griffin club. No wonder I hadn't been invited. Well if there was something important going on, I had a right to know.

"I'm telling you, I don't know how it happened," Diana wailed.

"You've compromised us all," Talos snapped. "To think I could have ever considered marrying you."

"Zip it, lover boy," Dyonne said.

I rounded the corner into a large Mediterranean-style kitchen. "What's going on?"

"Lizzie." Diana looked relieved to see me. Dyonne looked like she wanted to slap Talos. And Dimitri stood fuming in the middle of it all.

"We've made an unwelcome discovery," Dimitri said, crossing the room to drop a kiss onto the top of my head. His touch was brief and distracted. "Both of my sisters' Skye stones have been taken and crushed."

A rock dropped in my gut.

"Crushed?"

He nodded. "By someone who knew how to do it. They were placed on an ancient altar and smashed."

The same way they had been in my dream.

I was going to have a hard time explaining the next part. "Was this a wooden altar, with moon symbols carved over the surface?"

Every pair of eyes in the room locked onto me. I felt their shock and more than that, the growing sense of betrayal.

"How did you know?" Diana all but whispered.

I swallowed. Hard. "I dreamed about it."

Dyonne's eyes widened. "Who did it? In your dream. Did you see who destroyed us?"

"No." I tried to remember, but I couldn't. "And what do you mean destroy you? Your magic comes from inside."

Dyonne grunted. "We could barely use our magic with the stones as conductors. Now it's impossible."

"Is there any way you can fix the stones or make new ones?" The ruins were still there, along with their power. I knew Skye griffins weren't supposed to lose their magical tools, but it had to have happened sometime in the past two thousand years or so. They had to have some kind of a backup plan.

For the first time, Dyonne seemed defeated. Her eyes lowered.

"What if you held another ceremony?" I protested. "You have to at least try."

"We have no other griffins with power that can conduct our clan ritual," Dimitri said. "My mother helped create those stones. The magic is infused generation to generation. Yes, the power of the stone belongs to the person who calls it, but it is family magic."

"And without the family . . ." I said, trailing off, not wanting to follow the thought to its awful conclusion.

"We are the last in our line," Dimitri finished.

I had no idea what to say to him, to any of them. This spelled the death of their family and their clan. Everything Dimitri had worked for was destroyed. He'd fought so hard to save his sisters. He'd wanted more than anything to come here and protect his family, to preserve this place and this heritage for future generations.

In one night, with one act of evil, it was gone.

While the rest of the group stood in silent mourning and shock, my heart hammered in my chest.

Please let it be my connection to the evil one.

Oh great. Was I really wishing for an unholy bond? Frankly, it would have been better than the alternative.

What if I was the one who had destroyed the stones?

I couldn't discount anything. Not when this family was at stake.

I'd watched it happen in my nightmare. It couldn't have been just a coincidence. Not twice. There'd been no reason why I should have known where the stone had been hidden in the garden—but I had, right down to the pomegranate tree it had been buried under.

And now I could see the ancient altar in my mind, as clearly as I saw my own cut and bruised hands.

"I think I know who did it," I said, breaking the silence in the room.

Saying the next part was one of the hardest things I'd ever done. How do you tell the man you love, the family you've come to care about so deeply, that you may have destroyed them?

I took a deep breath and blew it out. "It could have been me."

My statement sucked the air out of the room for a moment before it came rushing back in.

Dimitri spoke first. "That is the most insane thing I've ever heard."

"You wouldn't," Diana gasped.

Talos took two steps for me, his features unreadable.

"Remember how I found the stone in the garden?" I asked, looking at Dimitri. He had to be my rock right now. I couldn't quite face the others. "I knew it was there because I dreamed of hiding it. I *saw* where it was," I said, trying to make them understand. "I was right."

Yes, it was disturbing and awful and unnatural, but it didn't stop it from being true.

Tears surged at the back of my eyes. "Last night, I dreamed of crushing the Skye stones. I don't know why. You have to understand I'd never want to hurt you."

Heavens, Dimitri looked at me with such love and trust. I had to retreat from him. How could he even see me that way after he knew the kind of thoughts I'd had?

Diana cried softly, her fingers tangled in her lap.

Dyonne studied me. I stood, waiting. She was going to

look at this logically. It was her nature. With a sad twist of her lips, she gave me her verdict. "Lizzie, a dream doesn't mean you did it."

She didn't understand. "I didn't consciously set out to hurt you. I'd never do that. But I do think I'm compromised."

"I think she's right," Talos said from the corner, his arms crossed over his chest. "Lizzie is the only one with any specific knowledge of what happened last night. The rest of us just found the pieces."

"Who discovered it?" I asked.

"Me," Dyonne said. "We'd both dreamed last night that our power had fled. I thought it was only a nightmare, until the stones were gone."

"You should have kept them more secure," Talos grumbled. "Once stolen is a mistake. Twice is pure lunacy."

Dimitri made a move for Talos until Dyonne caught him by the arm. "I'll fight my own battles, if you please." She turned to Talos. "We had to keep the stones near us. The doors were locked, as were the windows. Perhaps we should have slept in the family safe or risked a green slime ward every time we got up to pee, but frankly, we were more secure than anyone else in this house." She glanced at Dimitri.

"My wards were designed to keep out any malicious entities," Dimitri said.

"Exactly." I cringed. "They weren't designed to keep me out."

For a second, nobody moved.

It made even more sense now. Dimitri's wards wouldn't have held me back. I was the only one with memories of what happened to the stones and how they were crushed. *I'd wanted them destroyed.*

"There has to be another explanation," Dyonne protested. "You wouldn't do this."

I scrubbed my hand across my forehead, purposely avoiding Dimitri's gaze. "I'd like there to be another answer. I really would. But I also have to think about protecting you and this house." If I was a danger to the group, it would be foolhardy to pretend otherwise.

"There is another answer." Dimitri moved behind me.

"That would be?" I felt an unspoken chill in our little circle.

"We'll figure it out," he said, as if we'd taken a wrong turn off the highway.

Why did that not comfort me?

Hell's bells, I'd have left the estate if I thought it would do any good. Somehow I knew whoever—or *what*ever—had a hold on me would not be swayed by a change in location. Nor would it be moved by Dyonne's sheer unwillingness to accept the only rational explanation.

What had my adoptive dad always said? *You must eliminate the illogical until only the logical remains, and that is your answer, however improbable.* (Yes, he was a Sherlock Holmes freak.) In plain speak, it meant I had to look logic in the face and accept what it was telling me—no matter how impossible it seemed.

I took in the scene in front of me, from the sobbing Diana to the obstinate Dyonne. Talos glared at me. Interesting, since he should have been the least personally affected of all of us.

I turned back to Dimitri and was shocked at the intensity in his gaze.

"We will figure this out," he said, as if he was stating a fact.

I wanted to wrap myself in his arms and let him tell me again it would be okay. I wanted to believe it more than anything.

Instead, I held my ground as best as I could. "Okay," I said, sounding more certain than I felt, "what do we do next?"

Dimitri unlocked his part of the Skye stone and spent the better part of the day in a last-ditch attempt to weave whatever protective magic he could over the estate. I watched, feeling helpless, responsible and guilty at the same time. I should have been training to fight this. Only I knew it would be impossible today. The witches shooed me away. They wouldn't even let me see the work they'd done on the cave of visions and only accepted Rachmort's help with the wards. Perhaps it was my imagination, but I felt fewer explosions that day.

Diana and Dyonne spent their time out at the ruins with Talos, trying to piece the stones back together somehow. It didn't work. By the time night fell, we were all exhausted.

We gathered at the bottom of the grand staircase as Dimitri walked Diana and Dyonne upstairs. The sisters would be sharing a room tonight, with Dimitri's protective magic woven over them.

"I'll go sit with them," Amara said, following the sisters up the stairs, pausing to run a familiar hand over Dimitri's shoulder.

I wanted to slap her away, but I had no right. If he'd only stuck with her, his life would be so much better right now.

"No. I'll stand watch," I said, ready to overtake Amara. Diana and Dyonne wouldn't have been in this situation if it weren't for me. I needed to talk with them alone.

"Don't worry about it, Lizzie," Dimitri said, his eyes on Amara as she sauntered up the stairs.

"You can trust me," I said. It's not like anything had happened when I was awake.

"It's not that," he said, turning to me, ignoring Talos's smirk. "Amara is a griffin. She has ways of seeing magic that you don't."

My heart dropped into my shoes.

"Hey," he said, touching my chin. "It's not like that. I know you have talents. Many talents," he added, with that slightly devious, heated look I'd grown to love. "We have to pick our battles, and right now Amara is the best person to help guard the Skye magic. Well, her and you," he said, nodding to Talos.

"I don't see what guarding them is going to do if they've lost their magic," Talos grumbled.

Dimitri stiffened, and for a second I thought he was going to pin the other griffin to the wall. Instead, he answered in clipped tones. "You are sworn to protect this house. That includes the people in it. Now go."

They went.

I followed them from a distance and watched them enter the sisters' room. As the door clicked shut behind them, I felt a familiar loneliness. I'd always been somewhat of an outsider, even with the few friends I'd had back in Atlanta.

I could never bring myself to share enough, to let down my guard enough to be part of a group. And now, when I wanted so desperately to be a part of this family, I didn't know how.

Inside, I could hear voices murmuring, comforting, as Dimitri wove his love and protection over Dyonne and Diana. They truly were a family.

I leaned my head against the cool stone outside the door. Perhaps I couldn't help, but I couldn't bring myself to leave, either. I slid down the wall until my bottom touched the cold tile floor.

My throat tightened as the emptiness threatened to overtake me. I didn't fit in here, but I wanted it so much that I ached.

The door clicked open, and Amara slid out. Her eyes flitted over me before she turned her back and stalked toward her own room, her heels pounding like hammer blows.

A few moments later, Talos emerged. And just when I realized I'd better get my sorry self out of there, Dimitri followed.

My muscles froze and my blood stopped short in my veins. I must have looked like a complete fool. Panic spurred me to action as I scrambled to my feet. "I was just—"

What?

Lurking outside your door?

"I'm glad you're here, Lizzie," Dimitri said, attempting to help me up.

I was too fast for him. "Look, I need to apologize," I began, trying to decide just exactly what I should list first. For compromising his sisters and their magic, for putting all of us in mortal danger, for following him here in the first place.

For demanding his love when I had no right to have him?

Dimitri let his head drop to his chest.

"Dimitri, I—"

He raised his head, his eyes a blaze of green. "Walk with me."

My stomach clenched. "Okay." Now was as good of time as any to break up with the love of my life. Might as well do it when I knew beyond a doubt what an outsider I was.

We walked out into the cool night air past the tarps, where a few lone biker witches harvested snakeskins and grilled lava rocks—although I had yet to figure out how you could tell if a rock was well-done or rare. Evidently, it mattered quite a bit.

Fireflies clustered at the edges of the trees and I heard the hum of a generator back behind the house.

I opened my mouth to talk, and Dimitri butted in. "If you're about to apologize again, don't."

"For your information, I was going to comment on the batch of turtle knees you're about to walk over."

"Oh," he said, adjusting his stride around the pretzel jar full of black goop.

It was a lie. I was going to apologize again. What good is an obsessive personality if I couldn't beat myself up every once in a while?

"Listen, Lizzie. We learned something at the council."

"That you should have married Amara?"

"What?" he asked, genuinely surprised. He shook it off. "No. We learned you're the one who has to solve this."

Why was I not surprised? "Story of my life."

Things always fell to the demon slayer.

"Are they telling you that because you broke ties and are dating me?"

"No, they told me because it's the truth. You and I both know there's something more at work than griffin magic. They don't want to risk any more of their people and I understood. They even wanted to keep Amara back in Rhodes."

"But you persuaded her otherwise?"

"She chose to come back. And not just for her cat. She's loyal to a fault." He gave me a sheepish grin, reminding me of the words I'd used to describe him. "It's a griffin trait."

"Yes, an annoying one."

He seemed to think that was funny. Sometimes, I had a hard time understanding the man.

"Well you're out of luck if you're depending on me," I told him. "I'm not what you'd call on top of the situation."

"That's just the thing, Lizzie. You know so much more than you realize."

"If I had a nickel, or in today's economy, a dime—"

"I talked to Zebediah Rachmort," he said.

"Behind my back?"

"Yes." He didn't bother sugarcoating it. "He said you need to think more."

"He would say that."

"Lizzie . . ." He faced me, his hands on my shoulders. "I love you, but I'll tell you right now, you stink when it comes to understanding the facts."

"You've got to be kidding." Had he seen my grades as a kid?

He stared me down. "You were going to break up with me last night."

I opened my mouth, and shut it quickly. "Tonight too," I admitted, dreading his reaction. "Let me at least tell you why."

"No. I don't want to know why. It's merely a symptom of a bigger problem."

Oh lordy. We didn't need our problems to grow any more immense. "What now?"

"You're so busy looking at me and yourself and everybody else and judging what they should be. Well guess what? Things aren't ever going to work out how they *should*. You have to take people and events—me and you—you have to take things as they are instead of how you wish them to be."

"You're crazy," I said, even as the realization crept over me.

I did like to have things a certain way, but darn it, that had always worked for me in the past. I had a plan. I had backup. I knew what I needed to do.

Dimitri leaned close. "Pay attention and be thankful for the people in your life. Take us as we are."

Did he realize what he was asking?

There would always be things I wanted to change about myself, about our life.

For the last two months, I'd been so shocked at my new powers and my new world that I hardly had time to focus on Dimitri. I'd taken him and his love for granted in the worst possible way. If I wanted to look at the facts—and I couldn't resist—there was no way he should put up with me.

"Hey," he said, his lips brushing mine, sending curls

of warmth down my spine. "I love you for who you are."

I found myself trembling.

"Can you accept that?" he whispered against my lips.

"Yes," I said.

"Then you need to accept yourself as well."

He made it sound so easy, but the reality of it was a different matter. When we lost the fireflies and the warmth of each other's touch, when the world was stark and cold and I faced evil creatures I wouldn't wish upon my worst nightmare, would I remember the lessons I'd learned in the moonlight?

"Too bad this isn't part of Rachmort's training. The old man taught me how to levitate." Of course, learning how to truly believe in myself would be infinitely harder.

"It's not part of Rachmort's training," Dimitri said, determination rolling off him. "It's part of mine."

"Oh no."

"Oh yes. You need to learn how to lay bare your feelings, go with your instincts."

"And you're the man to show me how?" I asked, a shiver racing down my spine at the thought. The man didn't look ready to teach me. He looked ready to eat me alive.

A slow grin tickled his lips. "Your lesson begins now."

Chapter Nineteen

I thought he was going to kiss me. Right there, in front of the house, with a warm evening breeze caressing my cheek and the fireflies dancing around us. No such luck. Instead, he led me out to the woods beyond the front lawn.

A shudder rippled through me as we passed the path to the Callidora. "You know this is where I almost got a switch star to the head."

"We're at least a half mile east of that spot," he said in true Dimitri fashion, choosing to focus on geography instead of fear.

I snuck a glance at the blackness behind us as we skirted the narrow ribbon of land between the forest and the edge of the gardens. "I don't like being out here." My demon slayer danger radar wasn't going off, but still . . . "It feels like something or some*one* is watching us."

"I'm taking you somewhere private, Lizzie," he said, his voice sliding over me in the dark. "Trust me."

I did. Dimitri had been my first teacher. He'd been raised with supernatural abilities. I didn't always agree with his He-Man philosophy on changing the world. My most heroic moments tended to come when I was backed into a corner. But when we came right down to it, I wanted to believe in the world as he saw it. I wanted to think I could change the way things worked. That someday I'd know what to do and have the courage and the ability to take on the powers that be and create something new, something better.

Dimitri took my hand as we stepped around a leaning olive tree. "Try not to set foot in the garden," he warned.

I swatted a few dozen gnats away from my face. "I don't understand. Why are we sneaking around? You own the place, right?" I said it only half-jokingly because frankly, I'd had enough surprises lately. It paid to be prepared.

"Look up," he said.

Dental floss hung like shadowy tinsel from the trees.

"The Red Skulls have spotted pixies in the garden."

Yikes. Pixies acted as scouts for the imps. We knew they were planning something big. This just confirmed it.

"The Red Skulls will know if we break their barrier," Dimitri said. "I'd rather not have anyone else following us.

"Else?" I turned my head and saw Zebediah's spindly little tree nymphs on our tail.

So much for being alone.

Dimitri dug in the pocket of his jeans. He pulled out several coins and jangled them in his palm. "You want this?" he asked the nymphs.

They chattered and leapt up and down like howler monkeys. Dimitri tossed the euros into the garden and the nymphs scrambled after them. "It'll take them hours to hide them all," he said as we began walking again.

"As long as there's nothing more sinister following us."

"That's the trick these days," Dimitri murmured.

Yes, it was. I didn't want to run into any pixies or cursed imps or—while we were at it—the black-haired woman.

We reached the edge of a steep hill, which looked more like a mountain at that point. Vineyards lined the base of the hill. Above them, vibrant greenery tangled down the slopes and jutted from the rocks.

"You can't possibly think . . ." I trailed off as Dimitri began the precipitous climb.

"I'm taking you somewhere special," he said, navigating the hill with the grace of a mountain climber. "No one knows about this place except for members of my clan." He turned back to me, the moonlight playing off his wide back and solid arms. "It's the only truly private place on the island."

"Wow," I said, because, well, I couldn't think of anything else. The trust he placed in me amazed me every time.

After a glance backward to make sure we weren't being followed, I began my trek up the small mountain.

We quickly made it through the vineyard. Then the climb grew more treacherous. I focused on Dimitri's solid form ahead, struggling to keep my footing on plants that barely covered the limestone.

Not that I was used to hiking back home in Georgia, but when I did climb a hill, I could dig my toes into the thick soil. Here it was like an alien planet, a dusting of plants over rock. Sweat began to slick down my back and I fought to keep up.

"It's not much farther," he said, as if he could hear me huffing behind him. "My sisters usually fly, but I don't see the need."

Well, then he had thighs of steel. Who was I kidding? I'd seen them. They were glorious. I, on the other hand, was in fiery pain from the waist down. The backs of my legs burned and even my toes hurt from finding footholds in the rock.

I reached out in the dark for what I hoped was a well-entrenched bush and heaved myself farther.

We continued until we reached an overhang swathed in vines. It was invisible from a distance, even from the bottom of the hill. Below it was an eight-foot vertical drop covered in slippery vines.

"I can't climb that," I said, out of breath, bracing my sweaty palms on the cliff face while I struggled to maintain my balance on a ledge that was maybe, *maybe* wide enough for a mountain goat. Three lessons at the Atlanta Rocks! indoor climbing gym would only take me so far. I hadn't even gotten off the beginner wall.

"Relax." Dimitri lifted the curtain of vines to reveal an entrance to what appeared to be a large cave.

"Well look at that," I said. "Griffin sized."

He flashed a quick grin. "You doubted me?"

"Never," I said, taking the last few steps with renewed energy. I had to see this.

Dimitri reached inside the dark opening and pulled out a torch. He lit it with the Bic from his pocket and tossed the light inside.

"Hey," I said, surprised. We could have used that.

The torch on the floor cut through some of the shadows, revealing a flat ceiling and craggy walls.

"We don't want to attract attention." He wrapped a steadying arm around my waist. "Come," he said, helping me into the semidark cavern.

The vines dropped behind us.

"This is cozy," I said, as Dimitri moved to light the

torches along the far wall. They rested in simple bronze holders, green with age, set into the cut stone every four feet or so.

I inhaled the scent of fresh, raw earth along with the smoky tang of the wood from the torches. Past the halos of light, the darkness seemed to go on forever.

"Who did this?" I asked, my voice echoing in the cavern.

I could feel his heat as he stood next to me. The shadows from the torches fell hard on the angles of his face.

"This place has been here for as long as any of us can remember," he said. "It was most likely built by the first of my family, the original griffins who settled on this land."

I believed it. The history of this place had suffused itself into the walls, the floor. I felt it all around us.

"I want to show you something," he said, leading me toward an opening in the far wall that I hadn't even noticed until he waved his torch over it.

This chamber was smaller than the first, with ceilings so low I could almost touch them. As Dimitri moved throughout the room, lighting the wall torches, I noted the stark differences here. Thick Greek rugs in olive, slate and burgundy covered the floors. A black leather couch lounged among stacks of books. A hint of sandalwood and sweat touched the air. I could tell in an instant this was Dimitri's retreat.

That he had taken me here spoke volumes.

Dimitri tended to give first and explain later. I didn't always understand what he was doing, but I knew what he'd offered me tonight.

The question was—could I accept it?

Could I accept *us*?

It was a completely different battle for me. Sure, I'd braved possessed werewolves and soul-stealing succubi—and come out on top.

It took a completely new kind of courage to face him, myself, what I truly wanted out of life.

I wasn't sure if I was ready. I could have grown old waiting to gather the courage.

Didn't the man understand we had problems? He loved me despite my flaws. That was good, because I had a feeling he'd be seeing plenty tonight.

More than anything, I wanted to learn how to accept Dimitri and my life and the danger we faced. I was tired of worrying, of holding back. It was like I'd hidden a part of my soul from everyone, including myself. It took too much energy and cost me twenty tons of heartache.

The depths of my power—unleashed for the first time—could be incredible.

Dimitri touched my arm. "Lizzie?"

I blinked back to reality and the handsome griffin standing in front of me.

"You left me for a minute," he said.

"Yes," I said, breaking his gaze. It was too intimate. Instead, my eyes traveled to the far side of the room. Next to a scarred and blackened wall lay several dozen switch stars.

"What are you doing with those?" I gasped. "They could kill you."

"Not if they're not branded to a demon slayer." He walked over to them. "In this form, they can merely take years off my life."

That's right. He'd thrown switch stars back when

he trained me. "What do you mean they took years off your life?"

He stood tall, the torch light flickering off his chiseled features. "Switch stars get their power from energy. As a demon slayer, you are able to offer them an unlimited power source, separate from your life force. It's not the same for griffins."

The truth of it hit me hard. "You sacrificed years in order to train me?"

"Yes."

I tried to find anger behind his words, resentment even. But there was none. "Why?"

His eyes never left mine. "It was the only way."

The answer seemed too simple. He'd done it so I could prepare myself to rescue his sisters. It was all well and good, but I came from a world that taught me to take care of myself, a society where Good Samaritans were sued as often as they were thanked and loyalty was a quaint and proper notion that came up when people talked about the Greatest Generation.

"Are you ready?" he asked, moving toward the switch stars.

"Don't touch those!" I said, rushing for him, ready to toss myself between him and the life-stealing weapons.

"I won't," he said, stopping in front of them. "I don't believe in sacrifice without cause." His fingers brushed my cheek and my insides went gooey. "But I will ask you to step outside what you think you can do."

I nodded. I was ready.

He tucked a strand of hair behind my ear. "You've prepared. You've built a structure. Now it is time to let go. Trust that you're in the place you need to be."

"But that's the thing," I said, reaching for one of his stars instead of the five at my belt. It seared itself to me with a hot certainty that touched me to the bone. "I can't plan this one out." And there lay the crux of the problem. How did I know I was on track if I didn't know where I was going?

Dimitri towered over me. "You rely on instinct. But you need to stop seeing the world as you think it should be and start recognizing your allies and your enemies for what they are."

"I see my allies," I said, irritated.

"You think so?" he challenged. "You see the biker witches. They're easy. They're ready to charge the demons of hell with jelly-jar magic and an army of motorcycles. They'd do anything for you. There's no risk." He stopped me before I could push back. "And don't say Pirate. He's another easy one. That damned dog tried to follow you into the second layer of hell."

"True." If we hadn't leashed him, Pirate would have gone through the vortex with me.

He took a step forward until we were practically touching. "But you don't trust me," he said, his mouth inches from mine.

Oh please. I backed away. How dare he hash out our relationship at a time like this? "I thought this was about my training."

His eyes flared. "It's all tied up, believe me."

Okay. Well then maybe that was part of my problem. "I don't belong here and I certainly don't belong with you." I'd felt it on some level since I'd gotten here, and I'd only grown more sure as time went on.

Did I really need another lesson like the one I'd gotten

sitting outside his sisters' door tonight? Alone. Knowing I didn't belong and wanting it anyway.

It was torture and I refused to keep doing it to myself.

Dimitri opened his arms wide. "Come on, Lizzie. Tell me what you really think."

He was the most annoying, infuriating, single-minded oaf I'd ever met. "I have no clan." I didn't belong here. When it came right down to it, I didn't belong anywhere.

Didn't he understand? "I can't settle down. Not here. If I'm going to be a demon slayer—and I'm working hard to be a darned good one—I have to go where I'm needed." Yes, the Red Skulls may be easy to get, but they were also the types who would follow me anywhere. After thirty years on the run, they didn't know anything but the open road. Dimitri wanted a home and a wife. I couldn't give him that. Not right now, at least. Maybe not ever.

He reared back. "Have you ever bothered asking me what I want?"

"Isn't it obvious?" Dimitri valued family above all else. He'd been willing to go to hell and back for the chance at a normal life.

I'd finally met a guy who wasn't afraid to commit, and I couldn't have him.

His eyes blazed. "You don't know jack about what I want because we haven't taken the time to stop and talk about it."

"And *now* is the time?"

"Hell, yes." He gripped my arms. "Everything has to fit in a nice box with you, doesn't it?"

"It helps," I said, purposely flippant.

"That's not life." He broke away. "In fact," he said,

backing toward the scarred wall, "you have to be okay with losing me in order to truly love me."

"That's ridiculous." I'd almost lost enough people in my life without his making light of it.

"Is it?" He wrenched the nearest torch from its holder. This one had been used many times before. It burned low, almost to his hand.

"What are you doing? Put it away or it's going to burn you."

He held it at eye level as he stood against the wall. Shadows played over his wide shoulders and a fine sheen of sweat coated his chest. "Cut the flame."

"What?"

"Cut the flame before it burns me."

"Dimitri," I demanded. He'd gone too far. I could fire and I was 99.9 percent sure I'd hit it. But I wasn't about to play that game. "Stop it. I don't want to hurt you."

"Then don't," he replied.

Ridiculous. "Why are you doing this?"

"Other than the fact that I don't believe you'll hit me?" he ventured.

I braced a hand on my switch stars. "You always were the dreamer in the relationship."

"And you're the deflector," he accused. "Not anymore, Lizzie."

I stormed straight for him. "What are you trying to prove?" I shouted.

"That I'm here," he ground out, back to the wall. "I'm not leaving."

It was an impossible promise—completely out of place in the real world. People left. There was always a reason. I'd abandoned my friends and my coworkers in Atlanta to become a demon slayer. My adoptive family dropped me to an every-other-Sunday obligation as soon as they realized I'd never turn into the perfect country-club daughter. My biological mom had walked out on me when I was still in the hospital nursery. No matter how perfect you were or smart you were or organized—and believe me, I was trying to be all that and more—everyone left eventually.

So now, being the imperfect girlfriend who was about to lob a switch star at his head, I didn't see any reason why Dimitri would stay.

"Damn it," he spat. "Believe in yourself. Just this once—trust yourself."

The flame inched lower, toward the edge of his hand. He had to feel it. It had to burn. He ignored it, his entire attention focused on me.

"You have amazing powers, Lizzie, and you won't use them because you don't even think they're there for you. You don't trust them."

I watched the flames lick lower. "I don't understand," I protested, with more than a hint of desperation.

A rivulet of sweat trickled down from his hair. "Why didn't you levitate outside?"

"What?"

"You climbed the damned rocks, Lizzie. Didn't it even occur to you to use your power?"

No. The horror of it crept over me.

It hadn't.

What kind of a demon slayer was I?

"You don't trust your powers," Dimitri said, "just like

you don't think my love for you is something that bolsters you, that fills you up. You look at me—and your gifts—like a damned obligation. It's insulting."

I opened my mouth and closed it. "I'm sorry," I whispered.

"Don't you ever imply that my loving you is a mistake." His hand shook under the flame. "I don't make those kinds of mistakes. Now back up and throw the damned switch star."

Oh my word. The fire almost touched him. My palms sweated. I could feel the blood thundering through my veins. He trusted me. He loved me. Could I find it in myself to accept that?

I backed up to a place where I could—if I dared—make a good shot.

My fingers touched my belt and I unhitched a switch star. The blades churned as I held the glowing pink weapon out in front of me, watching the sparks of energy that flew from its blades. Then I hurled it at Dimitri's torch.

I watched it with a mix of pride and horror as my switch star cut the flame away.

Dimitri, the jerk, stood motionless as smoke curled around him, the jagged remainder of the torch cut right at the edge of his hand.

"How did that feel?"

I swallowed, my mouth dry. "Awful."

"Good. Then you won't make me do it again."

Dimitri tossed the ruined torch on the ground and closed the distance between us.

He swept me up in a kiss that stole my breath away. Electricity slapped through me, the charge of what I'd just done and what this man meant to me. I tipped my mouth up to his again and again as his arms closed around me. When I had him like this, so good, so right, it made everything else worth it.

"I don't deserve you," I whispered against his shoulder.

"You don't."

"Then why are you here?"

He tipped his head toward mine. "You know I'm willing to go to hell and back for the people I love."

The very idea sent my blood pressure up a notch. "That kind of loyalty can get you into trouble."

"It always does."

I looked at him for a long moment, this man who wanted me to do the impossible. He believed it.

Did I dare?

He ran his knuckles along my jaw. "If you don't believe in yourself, if you don't trust your magic, you can't use your magic," he said against my lips. "It doesn't mean the magic isn't there. You don't trust my love for you, so you dismiss it. But that doesn't mean my love isn't there.

"You can count on it." He caught me in another mind-searing kiss before he pulled away, the intensity in his expression nearly taking my breath away. "And it isn't going away, whether you feel you deserve it or not. Because it's not your choice."

I pulled him toward me as he shoved us both back against the scarred wall.

Tears clouded my eyes. "It's not you," I said, fighting to be strong. "I accept you. For heaven's sake, Dimitri, you've given up everything for me. That's the problem. It's me. I can't accept me and I can't accept that my life will do nothing but screw up yours."

"You can't tell me whether I should be with you. I'm not something you can control. Love isn't controlled, Lizzie."

"I just want to have some kind of handle on my life." I'd had so little of that lately.

"If you're going to give it up because it doesn't fit into your idea of the way things 'should' be, then you don't deserve it. But I'll give it to you anyway, because I love you."

I choked up and felt the tears, wet and awful on my cheeks. I hated to give this up, hated to lose my control.

But at that moment, I also realized I couldn't live without him—without *this*.

It was like when he'd given me the emerald. I had to accept it freely. I never thought of him giving it freely, but the truth of it slammed into me. It was about free choice and acceptance, two things I'd always craved but never truly had in my life to that point.

"I'm sorry," I managed.

He kissed away my tears, his lips touching my cheeks, my chin. "I don't want your apology," he said, his voice like velvet. "I just want you to trust in yourself and your worth." He pulled away. "My love exists, just like your powers. It's yours and you have to accept that."

"I do," I said, crying, laughing, wrapping my arms around him.

His hands slid down me, held me, drove us together as his mouth seared mine. I poured all my love, my fear, my sheer desire for him into that kiss.

He made a low sound in his chest, base and primitive, as he demanded everything. But that was Dimitri. He gave as much as he took.

And he loved me.

Not because I deserved it, but because it was simply so.

He was hot and slick as I stripped him, easing the black T-shirt over his head, my mouth finding the pulse at the base of his throat.

There was no teasing this time. No pretending we didn't know exactly where this was going.

We'd torn away our defenses, cast out our pretty notions. What we had left was base desire.

Naked and panting, he took me up against the wall.

He held his body tight, his neck steely tense. His breath came in sharp pants, his eyes glittering shards. I wrapped my legs around him as he drove into me again and again.

Tears streaked down my cheeks at the sheer pleasure of letting go. It was wild and raw and it didn't fit at all into my view of how things "should" be.

Afterward, as I slid bonelessly down the wall, my mind was more settled than it had ever been.

I ran a hand down his arm and he wound it around me, kissing me on the top of the head.

For as long as I could remember, my life had been a muddle of trying to cover all my bases. I was everything to everyone, with color-coded file folders to prove it.

But at that moment, I saw what it was like to let go and just *be*.

In that space, I unlocked a part of my power I'd always held back. I hadn't even known it existed. It was like it was waiting for me to acknowledge it and I never had.

I hadn't looked because I didn't trust it.

The enormity of it filled me, and I suddenly saw the

thread of myself that had gone missing. It was trapped on the estate, exactly as Amara said.

Only it had taken on a life of its own. The dark-haired woman I'd first spotted in the woods had grown stronger. She was gaining strength with every hour that passed, just as the sisters lost their power.

I gasped and sat up straight. I squeezed my eyes closed. Just like that, I could see it.

She was on the move. She had an entire army behind her, waiting just outside the wards.

I could feel Dimitri's eyes on me. "What is it?"

"It's the dark-haired woman." She ran through the trees, laughing, snapping branches, charging forward. She tilted her head and I choked when I saw her face for the first time.

She looked exactly like me.

Chapter Twenty

I shoved my palms into the rock, elbows shaking as the realization swept over me. "I know who's been sabotaging the estate."

Dimitri crouched in front of me. "Who?"

"Me."

He leaned forward. "Lizzie?"

"Well not me." Not exactly. "But a mirror of me." I could feel her, see her. She was growing stronger. "She's so evil. Whenever I'm in her head, I feel pure hate."

I leapt to my feet. "That's who I saw in my dreams stealing from Diana, crushing the Skye stones!" Holy Hades. "How could something so awful come from me?"

"It didn't," Dimitri insisted, standing beside me. "This came from me. I didn't safeguard your magic well enough. God, Lizzie. I'm so sorry."

I touched his cheek. "I know why you did it." It was for the same reason he did everything—to keep the people he loved safe.

Well he was going to have a doozy of a time with my double.

"This thing, this evil twin, knows what I know. If I have her thoughts and memories, she has to have mine. She's done terrible things. And she wants to do worse."

"She also has switch stars," Dimitri said, grim.

"What?"

"Five are missing from my supply. They were here last night."

I shivered. So she had found this place.

"But what does she want?" I searched through my memories of her. What was her ultimate goal? "I need to see her again."

I closed my eyes and fought to bring the image of her to the surface once more. I could feel her outside in the forest—slinking through the trees, her movements barely a whisper. She was stealthy, at one with the estate. And she was very, very angry. I felt her rage and her suffocating darkness as she rested a steady hand against the five switch stars at her belt.

H-e-double hockey sticks. I didn't even want to try to imagine what kind of destruction she could wield with a belt load of switch stars, not to mention the rest of my powers.

She'd already hurled a switch star at my head.

"Training's over," I said. "We need to find Rachmort."

He had to have some idea of what had happened to me. He'd been an instructor for hundreds of years.

"This way." Dimitri turned and roundhouse-kicked a hole into solid limestone wall behind us. I jumped back, my eyes watering from the dust of the impact.

"What the—?" I stared at him. He'd kicked a foot-wide opening in a rock face as thick as my arm. I could taste the broken stone.

"Don't worry," he said, his boot coming around and bashing an even wider opening in the rock. "The ceiling is strong here. There's no danger of a collapse."

Yeah, that's not where my mind had been going.

He spun and gave the Lizzie-sized opening a final slam, the muscles in his legs and thighs taut with the effort.

Not to mention his firm backside. "Now you're just showing off."

He grinned, breathing heavily. "It might have been quicker to go out the front, but this way"—he reached out and yanked away a few vines that had fallen over the hole—"you get to use your powers."

"Jesus, Mary, Joseph and the mule." I poked my head out of the opening. The cliff face fell straight down, at least twenty stories, into a dried-up stream filled with shards of volcanic rock and petrified tree trunks jutting out at odd and rather sharp-looking angles.

"Think of it as a test," he said behind me.

"One that could turn me into a demon slayer shish kebab. My favorite." I cocked my head back over my shoulder, ignoring the twinkle in his impossibly green eyes. Um-hum. Green. Not brown anymore. The man was feeling positively devious. "You know most boyfriends like to open car doors or make dinner . . . you know, do *nice* things."

He gave me a smoldering look. "I'm nice."

My heart sped up. "Oh really?"

"I'm giving you the chance to truly levitate."

"Or fall on my head." It was a good thing I couldn't see exactly what was down there.

"Trust yourself," he said, tracing a hand down my cheek. "The battle is about to begin. I can feel it."

I could too, like a promise in the air.

"I know you're ready," he said. "You need to feel it too."

"Or die trying."

But I knew he had my back. In this last test, before the ultimate showdown, I had a griffin to catch my fall. And that gave me the courage to make the final leap.

I shimmied out until I was sitting with my palms grating into the broken stone and my legs dangling over the rock cliff. I took a deep breath, lifted a booted foot over the abyss and pushed myself off into thin air.

As the wind rushed past and the ground surged up to meet me, I didn't think about falling. Instead, I focused on floating. I gave in to the weightless feeling, the surety that I could and would do this. I was a demon slayer in charge of my own destiny. The air caught me, and inch by inch, foot by foot, I lowered myself to the ground.

As my toes met the sharp rock, I couldn't help grinning. Ever since I'd gained my powers, I acted on instinct. Today felt like a choice.

My favorite griffin landed beyond the old stream in a tangle of wildflowers. He was a sight for the ages—his raw power and strength under a full moon. He immediately shifted again, his feathers retracting, his body remolding itself, but not before I spied his jeans and T-shirt tied to his back leg and the laces of his combat boots hooked around an immense lion's paw.

The rock crunched like broken glass under my boots as I made my way for softer ground.

"Taking cues from your sister?" I asked as he slid the jeans over his hips.

"Don't tell," he said, reaching for his shirt, "or I'll never hear the end of it."

We cut through the gardens and found Rachmort outside the stone armory, inspecting an enormous heap of bronze armor with an instrument that could best be described as superlong binoculars. The immense griffin breastplates, shields and gauntlets were stacked like an American Indian tepee with an engraved griffin helmet at the top.

Rachmort nudged a finger into the pile. "There," he said to a spiky-haired biker witch with a blowtorch.

Oh no. It was Hawk.

She liked to blow things up.

"No explosions!" I hollered, breaking into a run. We were too close to Dimitri's house and gardens and . . .

"Chill out, demon slayer." Hawk lowered a pair of silver welding glasses as she fired up a hot blue flame. "We're constructing, not destructing."

That was debatable, to say the least.

Hawk put the torch to the metal and went to work, sparks flying. That's when I saw the Greek sun of Vergina on Dimitri's family crest. Holy moley. It was the Helios clan armor.

Using a breastplate as a kettle was one thing—destroying it was quite another.

"What are you doing?" I yelled, too far away to stop them as generations of griffin armor went up in sparks.

"Final touches on the cave of visions," Grandma said, trotting up to me, her headlamp nearly blinding me. She held up a ripped piece of cardboard. On closer inspection, it was the side of a case of Southern Comfort. "See?" she said, pointing to a set of crude drawings. "We're building it like a tepee."

It looked more like a mess.

I groaned as Hawk began melting a priceless engraved neckpiece into a lump of mortar.

Dimitri placed an arm around me. "My ancestors infused those weapons with ancient griffin magic. They hold power that has only grown stronger in the generations since. Why wouldn't we want to use that now?"

"*We*? I was thinking more like *you*." I stared as Hawk began slicing a door through a battered shield with ancient Greek writing. It had to be at least a thousand years old.

Dimitri didn't flinch. "They're materials, Lizzie. Tools. We'd be crazy not to use them right now."

"Says the man who did not grow up in a house where we weren't even allowed to use the good hand towels." My adoptive mom would have had a fit if she'd seen this.

I forced my eyes away. I couldn't look. Besides, we had bigger problems.

Grandma and Frieda took over the task of making the hulk of metal leakproof, while Dimitri and I took Rachmort aside. We told him about the other demon slayer. The old necromancer's eyes widened as I explained how the evil one was connected to me.

"A doppelgänger," he whispered, almost to himself.

"What do we do about it?" I demanded.

"Finish sealing the cave," he ordered as he flung open a shield at the front of the pile of armor. It smacked up against a breastplate with an audible *bong*.

I stole a final glance at Dimitri. "You can do this," he told me.

"Of course," I replied. The only other time I'd attempted to commune with my destiny in the cave of visions, I'd been taken prisoner by a soul-stealing she-demon. This time had to be better, right?

Hawk slammed the door and started up the blowtorch on the other side.

"You're not sealing us in," I protested.

"Nah." I heard a muffled voice from the outside. "Just saw a crack."

Lovely. I breathed the metallic tinge of flame-broiled heirlooms and methane.

Moving away from the door, I tried not to focus on the sparks dropping onto the ground behind us. A few faint streams of the coming dawn filtered into the structure, but for the most part, we were in the dark.

"Come," Rachmort said, sitting down cross-legged in the center of the structure. "I fear an attack is imminent. I've emptied my evil-creatures trap twice today."

"Imps?"

"Pixies."

I settled myself on the ground across from him. I'd never actually seen a pixie, and that was fine by me.

He took my hands and gripped them tight. "Let us see exactly what is behind this other demon slayer."

"We can do that?" I asked.

In the near dark, Rachmort reminded me of a wizard, his eyes burning with excitement, his white hair wild about his face, his pockets glowing with heaven knows what. He drew me closer. "We can do so much more than you ever imagined."

I didn't doubt it. In the short time I'd known this man, he'd helped me focus my powers, taught me how to levitate and informed me I must be uncomfortable in my own skin before I could grow. I must have been growing out of my supernatural hide right about then.

An otherworldly breeze touched us as we focused our powers. I almost hated to ask, but . . .

"Where's the goat skull?" We always had Grandma's dead goat in the cave of visions.

"You do not need any necromantic touches with me," he murmured, eyes closed.

"Goldfish?" I asked.

"You are not alone, Lizzie. We will protect each other."

Good point. I squeezed my eyes shut and forced my worries about Dimitri's home, the destruction of the Skye stones and my own future out of my mind. Instead, I focused on the power of this place. I let it seep through me, work its way inside me, until I was filled with possibility.

That's when the temperature plunged. Goose bumps skittered down my arms. The frigid air chilled me as my breath quickened and every hair on my body stood on end.

Rachmort uttered a low sound. "Do you see her?"

"No," I said, my own breath warm against my face.

"Look harder," he murmured.

I focused everything I had on the woman from the woods, how the mere sight of her made my heart drop and my skin crawl. She was evil incarnate, and as the veil dropped in my mind, I saw her.

She wore a twisted smile, along with my purple prairie clover bustier and black leather pants. And she stood *in my room*. My eyes flew open "Pirate!"

"Concentrate!" Rachmort ordered.

Right. *Focus.* I slammed my eyes shut. "If she touches one hair on his knobby little head . . ."

"He's not in your room," Rachmort said.

He was right. I saw her rifling through my jewelry box,

opening my drawers. "She's looking for my training bar." Good thing I'd left it with Grandma.

"Look beyond what she's doing," Rachmort said, sounding very far away. "See into her. Let us observe what she is *thinking*."

Hard to do, when she'd found the wild hyacinth Dimitri had picked for me in the desert outside of Las Vegas. I remembered the walk we'd taken together. It was so special to me that I hadn't even allowed myself to enjoy the flower. Instead, I'd dried it in my closet for later. It had seemed so natural at the time to sacrifice my pleasure to save it for another day. The doppelgänger crushed the flower in her hand.

I wanted to reach out and slap her away, to gather the scattered blooms. Instead, I dropped all of my defenses and bored right into her head.

Rage burned inside me. I saw my fingers crush the purple blooms. I enjoyed destroying Dimitri's gift.

The damned interfering griffin.

"Who created you?" I demanded.

I felt a suffocating tightness around my neck, as if invisible fingers had wrapped themselves around my throat.

It doesn't matter who created me. I am here.

I own you.

A chill ran down my body. As awful as her words were, as terrible as she felt—I recognized her, like a lost sister or the twin I never had. I felt as if I should know her. I struggled to remember. The answer was just beyond my grasp.

She placed a hand on her switch stars and I felt the familiar hum.

I touched my hand to my own belt. "They made you with that part of me, didn't they?"

Just call me your better half. You've had a good run, Lizzie. Now it's my turn.

"What do you mean?" Even as I asked the question I saw the door to her memories in my mind. I shoved it open.

Her fury cascaded over me.

Yet in the violence of the storm, I learned exactly who had created this awful version of a demon slayer.

"Talos!" I leapt to my feet, ready to do battle. "Talos made her." He'd stolen my essence. He'd called upon the very demons of hell to raise her up. Then he'd tried to kill me before I ever knew. "Talos called the cursed imps down on us."

She shoved back at me, pushing me out of her mind.

"Why?" I demanded, scrabbling forward. Fighting back with everything I had.

"Lizzie!" Rachmort grabbed my arm.

I flung him aside.

Do. Not. Stop. Me. I let her energy pour over me, through me. I used it to hang on to her. I didn't come into this place to be safe. I came for answers.

"What in Hades does Talos have to do with this?"

The answers crashed over me like a tsunami. I saw Talos at the scarred wooden table, the same table he'd used to crush the Skye stones. He took that living piece of my demon slayer power and mixed it with . . . Skye magic. By griffins, he'd stolen the Skye magic from Diana and Dyonne.

His gifts—his coral necklaces—seeped out their energy. They weren't powerless. They weren't damaged. They were compromised.

He'd planned this from the start.

"He wanted them to die," I said slowly, seeing it through the mind of the doppelgänger. "His clan has been doing this for generations, working with the demon Vald. They were the opening, the source of the curse. They gave the griffins to Vald in exchange for a cut of the power."

They'd sold their souls to the devil.

Hell and damnation.

Vald. I'd killed Vald.

Dimitri had needed me to save his family from the demon, and I did. I ended the curse.

None of us could have thought, imagined, *dreamed* that the curse didn't stop with the demon.

I raised my head to where Rachmort braced himself against the wall, watching me.

"The Dominos clan did it!" I told him. "They're the enemy."

It unfolded like a sick play in my mind. The Dominos clan had wanted Dimitri's family from the beginning. They'd helped Vald exterminate every woman for generations. Griffin magic was too pure for the demon to take. *He'd needed help from other griffins.*

It all made sense.

In my haze, I stormed toward the necromancer. "When Dimitri's family grew weak and needed help, the Dominos clan stepped in. While Dimitri's clan hemorrhaged from the inside, the Dominos clan stole bits of magic here and there. Scraps. But enough to elevate them above all the others."

Rachmort approached me, eyes wide, like a villager who stumbles upon a lion. I could only imagine what I looked like. "What do they want now? This is very important, Lizzie. Try to see it."

"Okay." I pushed forward, hard and patient at the same time. I waited for it to unfold in my mind. When it did, I nearly fell sideways from the impact. "They want Dimitri. They want this estate. That's why he's supposed to marry Amara. They're going to fold him into their clan. Only she doesn't know it. She actually loves him." I saw the Dominos elders plotting it all from a long blue room that backed up to the ocean. "They're going to rob Diana and Dyonne of the last of their power. Soon. In battle. Then they're going to kill them."

Of course they'd sworn to protect the land.

They wanted it. And they'd kill the people who owned the land in order to get it.

I saw it as it unfolded in front of me. The death of Vald had brought unlimited power to the Dominos clan. They had his army of imps, his mad desire. They'd use it to capture all of the Skye magic. They would have the strength of two clans.

They'd be the most powerful griffins on the planet.

"When Dimitri's clan is wiped out, this whole place and its energy will belong to them. They'll have enough power to control every griffin in the world."

Rachmort stood deathly still. "Griffins are in place in almost every government on the planet."

"Excuse me?" I said, fighting the haze.

This was Dimitri's family we were talking about, not the rest of griffinkind. At the moment, I didn't care about any other griffins. I just needed my love, my griffin—and his family—to make it out of this alive.

"Griffins are loyal," Rachmort said. "Unless they are corrupted, as the Dominos clan was by Vald, griffins are noble and just creatures. They are drawn to service. Almost every good leader out there has at least some griffin blood."

That's when the awfulness of the situation sunk in. "Don't tell me Talos and the Dominos clan could control them."

The look on Rachmort's face made me go cold.

"They could collapse governments and entire economies. They could start wars between neighbors, genocide. Anything they wanted."

"Why?" I protested.

"Do we really want to wait and see?"

"We'd stop them," I said.

Somehow.

"Not if they had their own demon slayer."

"What? The one they made from me?" It was all falling into place with a sickening thud. "I can beat her."

"Look into her mind."

I closed my eyes again and focused. I saw her running across the lawn—straight for us.

"She's coming!"

Rachmort had to get out of here. She wanted blood, death, destruction.

She wanted me.

"She's going to kill me. Take the rest of me, body and soul. Then she's going to wipe out any trace I ever existed."

"Yes."

"What do you mean, yes?" I stared at him, her wants and desires flooding me. "She wants the life and souls of everyone here—you, Grandma, Pirate."

Rachmort's eyes blazed as he drew closer to me. "With every life, every soul, she grows more powerful."

"How do you know this?" I demanded.

He stopped inches from me. "It is the way of the dark demon slayers."

"I didn't even know we had dark ones!"

I could see the sweat on his forehead and the fear behind his fury. "We wiped them out while you were still in diapers. We lost a lot of good ones in the process." He stared me down. "Didn't you ever wonder why demon slayers are so rare? Why you've never met one like yourself? Hundreds of noble and powerful slayers died out in the Vast War. Hundreds of lines wiped out—forever. Now there's just you."

A chill swept down my spine. "Me?"

"You."

I didn't even want to say it. "I'm the last of the demon slayers?"

"Yes."

Sweet switch stars.

Rachmort's eyes never left mine. "You're the only one who can defeat her."

"But I'm defeating myself."

"Yes."

"My powers."

"She is more powerful. She has your strengths and she has the power of generations of Skye magic behind her."

"Lovely!"

Yes, I'd get right to killing the more powerful version

of myself—with my strengths, my instincts, my powers, and an added dash of ancient griffin magic. Because I was the only one who had a shot in the world.

"She's heading for the Callidora," Rachmort hissed, right before the wards began to explode.

Chapter Twenty-one

I burst out of the cave of visions and choked on the acrid smoke outside. Witches called to each other and dashed in an organized, frightening chaos. The earth shook and fire shot across the sky as the barriers took the impact of an all-out invasion.

Grandma ran straight for me, a leather bag of bottles clanking on her back. "They're attacking at the Callidora!" An explosion rattled the ground under us.

"Who?" I demanded, hot on Grandma's heels, as a wave of imps darkened the sky, black and menacing against the red of the setting sun.

Frieda and three other witches hauled a rusted cannon past us. "They're breaking through!" she yelled, pointing to a spot in the sky where imps had already begun to dive-bomb the Callidora.

The creatures had torn through the Skye magic. Some of them. Others died on the sharp edges of the invisible barrier, their oily black fur erupting into flames and breaking into pieces as they fell onto the battle below.

Grandma grabbed Scarlet by the shoulder. "Tell Creely and the artillery witches to concentrate all defenses on that hole. Then bring up the other cannon. I want full aerial support."

Rachmort bounded straight for me. "You ready, Lizzie?"

I struggled to stand my ground, caught in the stampede of witches and weapons. "Where's Dimitri?" I demanded, scanning the chaos.

Rachmort grunted as he accepted a long tube from Hawk. "Your boyfriend shifted," he said, lowering a pair of goggles with a brass weapons sight attached to the left lens. "He's already in the middle of it."

Dimitri didn't know about Talos!

I took Rachmort by the weapon. "We need to warn him."

Just then I saw my salvation. "Amara!"

She hauled three glass bowls and a jug of water and she didn't even slow down until I stepped in front of her. "Not now," she said, trying to push past me. "My brother is gone and so is Dimitri."

"Yeah?" I said, catching her at the wrist. "This is why."

I told her about her family's deception—and what her brother would do to the man she loved. Amara's haughty control cracked and her eyes widened.

"Impossible," she murmured, her mouth barely forming the words.

But I detected the shift in her. On some level, she knew.

An anti-imp charge detonated over our heads, shaking the ground with a deafening boom.

It was suicide to stay where we were—in the heat of the battle.

"Come." I dragged Amara closer to the cave of visions, willing Dimitri's ancient family magic to protect us.

"We don't have time for this," she protested, struggling to keep a firm grip on the water, the bowls and whatever magic she had bursting from the linen bag at her shoulder.

My shoulder smashed against a rumpled seam of the cave of visions where armor fused with armor, and at that moment I felt the presence of the Helios clan.

"I don't have time for this!" Amara's eyes fixed on a spot past my shoulder and stared in horror—at what, I could only imagine.

"Make time!" I forced her attention on me. "I saw your father and his council through the cave of visions. They're in a long blue room that backs up against the sea. They plotted this attack."

"No." She shook her head, her long black hair tangling around her shoulders, panic rising in her voice. "You can't know about that room. I'm not even supposed to know about that room."

Even as she spoke, I saw her making the connections in her mind. "They wanted . . . my father told me . . ." She stiffened, and for a moment I thought she was going to pitch sideways as the color drained from her face. "In the garden, I felt the traces lead back, but . . . I didn't know!" She brought her hands to her mouth. "All this time and I didn't know!"

"They were using you to get to this family. Talos used you too. But Dimitri doesn't know about your brother. You have to warn him. Now. Shift. Go to him. Save Dimitri from your family."

She nodded, tears in her eyes.

Amara stepped backward, not even seeing me anymore as she shifted. Her dress tore, the fine gold jewelry at her neck and wrists cracked and broke. Her body rippled as she bowed her head and grew into a massive silver griffin. She gave a pitiful roar as she beat her powerful wings and took flight toward the Callidora.

And I'd sent her there—to betray her brother and her family for a man she could never have.

Rachmort ducked out of the cave of visions and about gave me a heart attack. "You did good," he said, flicking his wrist and unfolding a long scope. He peered through it. "Damn."

A yellow fog trailed out of the cave of visions and the sulfur in the air intensified. "What were you doing in there?"

"Determining the strength and size of the enemy."

"And?"

He removed the scope from his eye. "We're screwed."

Gangly tree nymphs chattered and danced around the necromancer. "Go to the hills," he ordered the nymphs. "I can spot the rest without your help." He folded the scope and hefted his weapon over his shoulder like the potato shooters we used as kids. "Now we do battle. And remember, you didn't set this in motion any more than Amara did. Now that Dimitri knows what he's up against, he can take care of himself." Rachmort drew a spiral of magic from his hip pocket and shoved it down the barrel. "You can too. You know what they want."

Yes.

Me.

And from the look of it, Dimitri's entire family.

Grandma clapped my shoulder, her gray hair a tangled mess and fire in her eyes. "You ready to kick some ass?"

I slapped a hand against the five switch stars on my belt. "Bring it on."

Excitement and fear roared through me as we raced for the Callidora. I could barely feel my feet under me as I hurtled through the forest. Witches had stopped along the sides to fire their weapons and reload. Imps streaked over us with a single purpose. They wanted what was at the Callidora.

Thick trees closed in on us from all sides, but I knew, I felt, I *saw* the danger ahead.

My hellish double—this doppelgänger—waited.

Blue flames catapulted from the house behind me. They soared, their magic like a thousand hot needle points to my back as they roared for the ancient ruins, taking out the flanks of the invading army.

We were close, so close.

I felt my toes hover for a brief second at the edge of the Callidora.

She will be lost at the Callidora, the first time in joy, the second time in death.

She will be split in two.

Holy hell.

My ears rang with the firing of the cannons, the clash of weapons and the screams of the imps and the witches. My eyes watered from the overpowering smell of sulfur and singed bodies, and my demon slayer radar screamed with danger.

I closed my eyes as the fear swallowed me whole. The battle raged ahead. My battle. I had a horrible sense of foreboding that I would not make it out of this place alive.

Think, I said to myself as Rachmort's words came back to me.

It doesn't matter how you feel.

It matters who you are.

"I am the demon slayer!" I yelled as I burst through in a blaze of switch stars.

Dozens of imps charged, hurling cursed arrows from both the air and the ground. Every tree, bush and blade of grass they touched turned to dust.

They stormed the witches, who fought back with Molotov-cocktail spells in Jack Daniel's bottles. Frieda hurled a bottle at the imp closest to her as it reared back to attack. The bottle caught the imp in the throat and exploded into flames. His blackened body hissed and curled as it shrieked and fell to the ground.

"Don't touch it!" I screamed.

"Fuck, Lizzie. You wanna tell me something I don't know?" Her eyes widened as she looked past me. "Stryker!"

Three imps descended on the witch with graying dreadlocks. The witch dropped her empty weapons pack and drew a glowing orange knife out of her hip pocket.

It wouldn't be enough.

I hurled a switch star at the attackers, taking off the head of the nearest one. Its scaly black neck smoked as it fell backward, one out-flung arm almost catching a band of artillery witches. They scrambled as their rusted cannon fell to dust.

Frieda grabbed another bottle from the fringed bag on her back. My second star hit the other imp in the throat. Frieda's bottle flew wide as the battle shifted.

"Stryker!" Frieda screamed as the last imp dove onto the witch. Stryker brought up her knee and got it in the nuts before the touch turned her to dust.

The finality of it hit me in the gut as a blue-flamed

anti-imp charge slammed into the ground to my right. I leapt back, ears ringing, as it splattered me with hot magic.

Holy hell. I didn't see how we were going to make it out of here alive.

Through the smoke and the clashing bodies, I saw Diana and Dyonne surrounded by a company of witches, battling their way through the ruins at the Callidora to the altar where at least a dozen imps hissed and spewed curses. Grandma flung magical Molotov cocktails to Diana's right. I watched in horror as she firebombed the imp closest to Diana before she took out the creature going for her.

Another one came up from behind. She didn't see it. "Grandma!" I wasn't going to make it in time.

A rush of orange flame burst past me. The imp fell backward, drowning in fire, as I looked to the sky. Flappy the dragon had grown to the size of a Buick. Black smoke shot out his nostrils as he huffed in pleasure at his imp-frying abilities. And on his back rode Pirate.

Oh no.

"Get yourself and that dragon home!" I bellowed. "Right now!"

Pirate ignored me. "Fire in the hole!" he shouted as Flappy took out an imp swooping down out of the sky.

Holy Hades. Pirate had strapped himself to the dragon Harley dog–style.

We were right below the tear in the protective magic. The witches had at least two more cannons set up underneath and they were shooting at anything in the air.

"Home. Now!" I hollered. I knew that dragon was going to be trouble.

Flappy fired off a shot and seared something behind me, no doubt saving my worried butt.

"Whoo hoo!" Pirate whooped. "I am Rescue Dog!"

Flappy shot straight up into the air, ending the debate, as I watched Diana and Dyonne close in on the ruins. The witch ahead of Grandma fell. An imp hissed and drew back to attack.

She'd never make it.

I raced for them. An imp screeched behind me and I turned, burying a switch star into his chest, the impact blowing me backward, bombarding me with countless pinpricks of energy. The impact seized me like an electric charge. I sat for a moment, stunned, as the battle raged around me.

Frieda and Ant Eater had turned a cannon on a horde of imps. They couldn't kill them all. I couldn't even count them all. Two griffins battled at the edge of the forest. Dimitri! He had a huge bloody gash across his neck and another ripping across his side. Talos circled him, limping as he lunged, one wing completely torn away, his beak a crush of blood. I couldn't tell who was winning, only that Dimitri's feathers had gone slate gray.

Please, God. Don't let them take Dimitri.

I stood, ready to fire, when I realized my switch star hadn't come back. They always raced back. Switch stars were the ultimate supernatural boomerangs.

That's when I saw my double.

The doppelgänger wore my black leather pants, my lavender bustier. She'd pulled her dark hair back into a ponytail and she grinned like a maniac as she walked straight up to Scarlet.

"I got you covered, Lizzie," Scarlet called.

Only she spoke to my double. Holy Hades.

"Scarlet—no!"

Scarlet tossed the doppelgänger an anti-imp charge before firing one, taking out the creature making a beeline for Frieda and the artillery witches. Then Scarlet uttered a choked shout as she watched the demon slayer, who she thought was me, bury a switch star in her heart.

Tears burned the back of my eyes. I knew Scarlet. I'd liked her. And now she was dead on the ground because she'd trusted me. I hadn't seen this warped reflection of me until it had grown powerful enough to have my strength, my powers—my body.

I whipped out a switch star, waited for a clean shot and fired it at the doppelgänger's head.

She caught it.

Shock slammed in my throat as she held my switch star, the pink blades churning for her as they did only for me. The same way she'd fired my own weapon at me in the forest. She turned, a contemptuous smile curling the sides of her mouth.

My magic recognized her.

Bloody hell on earth.

I fired another star, and another, in quick succession. I aimed. I shot. I aimed again. I shot. It was the only thing I could do—what I was trained to do. She couldn't catch them all.

She did.

She laughed, cold and hard, as she held up my five switch stars.

Her icy arrogance struck me like a blow.

I felt a burning on my left side and leapt aside as a

curse flew past. The arrow buried itself into the ground near my ankle.

A hail of fire rained down behind me.

"Damn, Lizzie!" Pirate craned his neck to see my double while Flappy roasted my attacker. The blackened imp fell in a heap next to two startled biker witches.

My double turned her hollow eyes on my dog.

"Don't you even think about it." I strode right for her. "You want me?" I asked the doppelgänger, one final switch star— the one I'd taken from Dimitri—at the ready. "Call off your imps and we'll fight this out."

Slayer to slayer.

"Oh, this is precious. Give us some space," she called, and the imps fell back. I stared at her across the narrow space. I just hoped my dog listened half as well as her imps. Pirate didn't need to be anywhere near this.

She waited, smirking, for me to fire my last round.

My heart pounded in my chest and every nerve ending blazed. I curled my toes inside my black boots.

Calm down.

Every bit of my training had brought me to this point. I had to trust it—trust myself.

No matter what it took, I had to take down the doppelgänger.

My fingers, slick with sweat, curled around the handle of my final switch star. I couldn't fire it. She'd catch it. I couldn't get close enough to bury it in her chest without her impaling me.

But if I didn't kill her now, if she gained the power from this place, there would be no stopping her. This was my last chance.

Sacrifice yourself.

I'd never wanted to do it. I wanted to have a life—with Grandma and Dimitri and Pirate. I finally had a real family.

Now, here at the Callidora, I had to sacrifice what I loved in order to save it.

"Lizzie!" Amara broke through the imps. Our eyes met for a brief second and I saw through to her soul. She loved this family as much as I did. Maybe she would survive this. The thought of it warmed and chilled me at the same time.

Hell and damnation.

I fired.

At the same moment, my double let loose with her arsenal of switch stars. I consciously slowed time as they hurtled for my head, my neck, my chest. I'd had this power. I'd only used it once before, locked in my bathroom. But now I felt it. For the first time, I deliberately used it.

It wasn't enough.

The barrage of switch stars hurled toward me and anywhere I could even think of moving—or levitating. I could see the impact of each one, the twisting blades, and there was nowhere to go. No time to escape them all.

Amara shouted to my left. At least there would be someone left who could love Dimitri.

Maybe Diana and Dyonne would survive. Maybe the clan could go on.

I did my best.

In that split second before the end, my eyes locked

with Amara's. I saw her terror, felt her rage. This was a woman who had also been betrayed.

At least I'd seen this before, in my vision. It would be over soon.

I braced myself and waited for the crush.

Chapter Twenty-two

Amara dove forward with the speed of a griffin. Precise and deadly, she leapt into the hail of fire and took the switch stars meant for me.

"Amara!" I shouted, stunned as the blast shoved her backward onto me. Her blood smeared my chest as several of the switch stars broke through her body.

I grabbed the nearest one and fired it at the doppelgänger. She'd already thrown up her hands in victory.

Amara slid away from me as I watched the switch star tear a hole through the doppelgänger's chest.

The monstrosity howled and fell to the ground dead.

She will be lost at the Callidora.

It had been about the doppelgänger. I'd seen death through her eyes, not mine.

I gulped, tears threatening. I was saved, but *Amara.* I touched her lifeless shoulder.

And what about the others?

The battle raged on all sides. I raised my head to see Diana and Dyonne reach the altar with Grandma at their side. They were surrounded, outnumbered as the imps surged forward. Grandma was out of weapons. Instead she clasped both hands around her turquoise necklace and chanted.

"Digredior. Digredior. Digredior."

It slowed them, but it didn't stop them.

I scrambled for a switch star as Talos fell from the sky, crushing the mass of imps at the ruins. Diana and Dyonne clutched at the altar of their ancestors, pushing, focusing, fighting for their life and their powers.

Dimitri kicked away the body of Talos and landed next to his sisters. Grandma shot out defensive fire as he lowered his head and shifted.

I hurled a star, beheading an imp as two more took its place. The limestone altar glowed under the sisters' hands as they chanted, desperately trying to draw even a fraction of the generations of power from the rock.

"Dimitri!" I yelled over the crash of battle. "The jewelry! Get it off them!"

He broke the coral from their necks and dropped it, smoking, onto the ground.

Dimitri stood in front of his sisters, fending off the imps with a bronze sword while Grandma's magic deflected the cursed arrows.

But for how long?

I took out another imp, but we had no hope of defeating the mass that continued to rain down from the sky. The Dominos army was too fast, too powerful. And they wanted the sisters. I lost sight of Grandma and Dimitri as the blackened mass closed in.

Holy Hades. Just what good had it done to defeat the doppelgänger if I couldn't save what remained of my family?

Diana and Dyonne clung to the ancient altar, fighting like wild women as they held the remains of their legacy.

A wind blew the imps back, and they struggled for

their footing as raw cerulean power shot from the rocks. Their hair blew and the skies above us thundered as the magic poured from them.

Diana and Dyonne channeled it into the altar where the women of their line had been initiated into their Skye magic, and where those same women—before they succumbed to the curse—had given the last of their strength, their power and their love at the Callidora.

Their magic rose out of the very stones and into the twins. Until the altar itself shot out streams of light. With a rush of heat and hot white energy, the limestone slab transformed into lustrous blue Skye stone.

Diana raised her arm, pure energy flowing from her as she decimated the horde of imps.

They fell in writhing piles, taking out trees and at least one cannon. The witches scattered as the creatures fell, turning the grass, weeds and fallen bodies to dust.

Dyonne raised a hand to the sky, sealing the estate.

A great thunder clapped over head, followed by an eerie silence.

We stood for a moment in a haze of smoke, charred bodies of imps littering the battlefield. Witches chanted softly. At least one wept.

"Lizzie!" Dimitri knelt among the ruins of the Callidora, near the broken body of the doppelgänger Sweat coated his broad back and glinted off his olive skin. He turned to me, his hands covered in blood.

"Lizzie," he called out, his face twisted in anguish. Bloody wounds streaked his chest and sliced across his neck.

Talos lay in human form, dead at his feet.

"I'm here!" I said, choking on the relief of it. "I'm not hurt."

Dimitri broke out in a dead run for me. He swept me into his arms for a crushing kiss. "Thank the heavens, Lizzie," he murmured across my cheeks, into my hair. "I thought I'd lost you."

"It was Amara," I told him, easing away, showing him the place where her body lay.

She lay crumpled on the ground, fear etched on her face, so alone. I cradled her in my lap, easing her hair away from her face. My throat tightened as I closed her eyes.

"She died for me," I said, as Dimitri wrapped his arms around me and touched his forehead to my shoulder.

"She gave her life to restore what her family took away."

The shock of it surged through me—joy for those of us who had survived, horror for the ones who had not. And a great ache for the ones still unknown.

At that moment, Grandma let out a mighty war cry. She climbed the sacred ruins to the topmost portion of the wall and stood. "Eeeeeya!"

The witches answered with a chorus of shouts. A cannon rang out.

"Give me a minute," I said to Dimitri, trusting him, letting him watch over me while I touched the training bar in my pocket.

My heart raced as I prayed there would be enough life left in the psychic.

I dusted my fingers over the glassy surface of the training bar before gripping it tightly.

Like running through a tunnel, I rushed toward my vision, throwing the door open on Amara. She lay in my arms, her chest a mass of blood and her beautiful black hair plastered to her forehead.

"Thank you, Amara," I said, tears wetting my cheeks. "You did it. You set things right."

Her eyes opened, glassy and distant. She smiled faintly. "Tell Dimitri I did it for him."

"I will. You helped save his family, Amara."

"No . . ." She shook her head weakly. "His sisters did that." She patted her hand over my wrist. "I saved his soul."

And with that, she left me.

I looked out over the battlefield strewn with bodies, weapons and debris. We defeated them. We won.

But what did we have to sacrifice in order to gain that precious victory?

Chapter Twenty-three

When Amara's family didn't want her back, we buried her next to the pergola in the garden. The witches said incantations over her as we willed her body to the place she'd loved most in life. A place that in her vision, she knew she'd never leave.

Later, we gave Talos to the Aegean, the waters of his ancestors, although with less fanfare and no tears.

Diana, for her part, had inherited a cat. The fancy white Persian took an immediate liking to Flappy.

The Dominos clan refused to acknowledge what had gone on that day, insisting that they were longtime allies of the Helios and always would be.

I only hoped most of their imp army had been destroyed.

We didn't need another rendition of hell on earth to know that they would remain vigilant, ready for another chance to seize power.

In the meantime, we cleaned up as best we could, toasted the dead and vowed to conduct ourselves in a way that would honor the sacrifices they had made.

Some of us even remembered to smile again.

I carried an ice-cold Diet Coke out onto the patio under the slightly charred pergola and joined Dimitri at a wrought-iron table. Sidecar Bob grilled weenies to the tune of "Won't Get Fooled Again."

Darned straight.

The witches played lawn darts in the remains of the rose garden. Pirate and Flappy chased bees with the tree nymphs, and Zebediah Rachmort chuckled and made his way up the gray slate stairs.

Somewhere along the line, he'd found a pipe. "The hell-bent-creatures trap is empty and I have a negative-three reading on the protective wards."

"That's good," I said. "Right?"

I glanced at Dimitri, who merely grinned.

"It'll keep out the Dominos clan," Rachmort grunted, taking the seat across from me.

Dimitri let Ant Eater pour him something brown and foamy. "We'll have to keep an eye on the Dominos clan," he said. "I don't think they'll look at this as a failure, only a setback. And they're more powerful than they were before."

"But we beat them once," Ant Eater added, urging the glass closer to Dimitri.

"You're seriously going to drink that?" I asked, thinking of the way she'd laid Talos out flat.

Dimitri brought it to his lips and took a long swig. "Best root beer I ever had."

Ant Eater broke out into a wide smile. "Damned straight."

"At least we know our enemy now," I said, as Frieda and Creely launched homemade bottle rockets out over the garden.

"We also have the strength of our ancestors." Dimitri said.

"And you have us." Diana bonked him in the head with the feathered end of a lawn dart.

"It's no fair when you two play," Ant Eater said to Diana and to Dyonne, behind her. "They control the wind," she said to us, with more awe than anger in her voice.

"I swear we don't do it during the game," Dyonne protested. "Much," she added under her breath.

I shook my head, enjoying the sun on my cheeks. "Just don't let Grandma keep score." The witches used creative math. Between the Red Skulls and Dimitri's sisters, it should be a high-scoring game.

"Yeah, I heard that," Grandma said, a shish kebab in one hand and a mess of darts in the other. She looked out over the lawn. "I'm telling you, Lizzie, that has to be the ugliest dragon I've ever seen."

"Are you still going to set him loose?" Rachmort asked.

"Just because he has a snaggletooth?" Grandma protested.

"It's not because he's ugly," I protested. "We don't have time or space for another pet. I told Pirate—we absolutely, positively, can *not* get another one."

Grandma shifted her lawn darts to a spot under her arm. "I hate to tell you this, Lizzie, but it looks like you've already got one."

"I know," I said, reaching for Dimitri's root beer.

"The dragon would have died on that cliff if you hadn't taken in the egg," Dimitri said. "That's why your demon slayer radar went off. He needed you."

"It was bad enough when I had a floating dog. Now I have a flying one," I said, watching Pirate climb up onto Flappy's back and give the ears-up signal.

"*That's* how Talos broke into Dimitri's office," Grandma said.

"Yes," I said. "He used water magic to float over the slime." And Pirate, as always, managed to find the left-overs. Talos had broken in once for my magic, but failed to retrieve the shard of Skye stone in Dimitri's safe. The imps would have handled the job, if we hadn't interrupted them.

Grandma scratched her chin with the end of a lawn dart. "I thought only the cheater sisters could use stones."

Dimitri shook his head. "Talos had stolen enough of their magic that he was willing to give it a try. It might actually have worked."

"If Lizzie hadn't whupped the cursed imps," Grandma added.

There she went, bragging. It felt strange and good at the same time. I changed the subject so I wouldn't have to think about it.

"So it's true," I said to Rachmort, studying the swirling brown liquid in the root-beer mug. "I'm the last of the demon slayers?"

The thought frightened me more than I cared to admit.

Rachmort nodded. "It is your destiny—the one you were born to fulfill."

I hated to admit this, but . . . "In case you didn't know, I was a mistake."

I was never meant to be a demon slayer. My mother foisted her powers off on me. I was an accident.

Rachmort bestowed me with an indulgent turn of the mouth. "Not a mistake. In your case, destiny rearranged itself. We will consider it a gift."

He leaned to the side and pulled a scrap of parchment

from his back pocket. Yellowed and crumpled, the paper had seen better days.

"I came to train you, yes, but also because of this. There is trouble brewing in Hades, young Lizzie."

"Oh no." I looked out over the gardens, the villa, this place that I could call home, if only for a little while.

"Yes, yes," Rachmort said, following my gaze. "Enjoy your peace while it lasts, for"—he shook out the paper and lowered his rounded spectacles—

She will be called, again and again,
Until the final victory.
For the accidental demon slayer
Will be the greatest slayer of them all.

My jaw loosened and my eyes shot to Dimitri. Curse the man. He was smiling.

"I knew it," he said, with no small amount of pride.

"What?" I stammered. "I thought you said to ignore prophecy. I can create my own future."

"True," he replied, "but I can't think of a more worthy future for you."

I shook my head. *The greatest demon slayer?* I had so much more to learn. Besides . . .

"You belong here," I told Dimitri.

His fingers closed around mine, warm and strong. "You belong here too. For a time. And when we are called, we will go."

"All of us?" I asked, looking out over the witches and their lawn darts, Pirate and his dragon and, of course, the man I loved above all else, Dimitri.

"Yes, Lizzie," he replied. "All of us."

Because this was my family.

And maybe I didn't deserve it, but I knew better than to let any one of them go.